"May I help you? I'

The girls stared at him,

"Are you selling something?"

The dark-haired girl shook her head.

"Did you find a lost dog?"

She shook her head again and held the dog tighter against her chest.

"Well, I'm running out of questions, so you'd better tell me what you want."

There was no response—just wide-eyed silence.

"I have to get back to work," he said, and stepped back to close the door.

"I'm Jilly Walker," the dark-haired girl blurted out.

Tripp paused. Was this Camila Walker's kid? Yeah, she had the same gorgeous hair, skin and eyes. That would mean…

"I make straight A's and I'm going to be a doctor. I'm a good kid, everyone says so, and your family missed a lot by not knowing me. You missed even more by not knowing my mama. That's all I have to say."

She took a step backward and ran into her friend, who seemed to have turned to stone. The two of them locked hands and ran toward their bikes, then quickly rode away.

Dear Reader,

If you've read *The Christmas Cradle*, you might remember Tripp Daniels, a rodeo cowboy estranged from his family. *The Cowboy's Return* is his story. After thirteen years, he returns home to face his past and a woman he can't forget.

Camila Walker is used to rumors and gossip. Those tidbits of malicious hearsay have affected her life, her relationships and the way she feels about herself. She is a survivor, though, and she's built a good life for her daughter.

Tripp is still drawn to the beautiful Camila, but he's determined to find out if her daughter is his dead brother's child. Through the lies and the secrets, they can't deny the attraction building between them. But will they be able to overcome the past?

Come along and get involved in the rumors and gossip. Just don't believe everything you hear.

Hope you enjoy Camila and Tripp's story.

Warmly,

Linda Warren

P.S. It's always a pleasure to hear from readers. You can e-mail me at Lw1508@aol.com or write me at P.O. Box 5182, Bryan, TX 77805 or visit my Web site at lindawarren.net or superauthors.com. Your letters will be answered.

The
Cowboy's
Return

Linda Warren

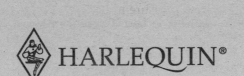

HARLEQUIN®

TORONTO • NEW YORK • LONDON
AMSTERDAM • PARIS • SYDNEY • HAMBURG
STOCKHOLM • ATHENS • TOKYO • MILAN • MADRID
PRAGUE • WARSAW • BUDAPEST • AUCKLAND

ISBN 0-373-75106-0

THE COWBOY'S RETURN

Copyright © 2006 by Linda Warren.

This edition published by arrangement with Harlequin Books S.A.

® and TM are trademarks of the publisher. Trademarks indicated with ® are registered in the United States Patent and Trademark Office, the Canadian Trade Marks Office and in other countries.

www.eHarlequin.com

Printed in U.S.A.

Mrs. Ida Baker (Big Mama)—To our amazing grandmother
When I first married my husband, his grandmother
would give us lye soap. Young and immature, I wasn't
sure what to do with it. But as always, years bring wisdom,
and I began to see this wonderful lady's ability to create
necessities out of the simplest things and admired
her indomitable spirit and immeasurable love.
We still miss you.

ACKNOWLEDGMENTS

Lola Dee Vavra—thanks for lovingly sharing
your knowledge of quilting.

Becky Hess of Eden Naturals for graciously explaining her
soap-making techniques. Thanks.

Any errors are strictly mine.

Chapter One

"We're gonna be in so much trouble."

Eleven-year-old Jilly Walker ignored her friend, Kerri, and pedaled her bicycle that much faster against the cool February breeze. She had to do this, even if it meant she'd be grounded for life. In two weeks she'd turn twelve and her mama had said that she could do something special for the big day. Special meant one thing to Jilly…meeting her father's family.

And this was the only day she could sneak away to make it happen.

The Danielses lived on a large ranch about a mile outside of Bramble, Texas, population 994 and counting. Everyone kept track of the births. The city council planned a big celebration for number one thousand, but Jilly wasn't thinking about that today. The bike's wheels slid on the gravel as she stopped outside the Danielses' entrance to the Lady Luck Ranch.

Patrick Daniels, her father, had died before her parents could get married. The Danielses shunned her mother, Camila, saying the baby she'd been carrying wasn't a part of their family. Jilly didn't understand how they could have said that, but she respected her mother's wishes and stayed away from the Danielses'.

Until today.

Over the years, she'd seen Leona and Griffin, her grandparents, in their chauffeur-driven car. She'd never had enough nerve to speak to them—she didn't know if she had enough today, either.

Kerri stopped beside her, gasping for breath. "Are we going home now?"

Jilly stared at the broken boards on the fence and the weeds growing wild around them. She didn't expect the entrance to be so unkempt. The stone pillars with the Lady Luck brand were impressive, though.

"Jilly?"

"No," she answered and pedaled across the cattle guard to the big house. Her hands trembled on the handlebars, but she wouldn't let her nervousness stop her—she was going to introduce herself to the Danielses. The bike bounced over potholes, jarring her insides, and finally she rolled to a stop in the circular drive. A round brick pond with a broken waterfall stood in the center of the overgrown yard. Stagnant water caked with mildew stank like Mr. Wiley's pig farm.

At the odor, she wrinkled her nose and jumped off her bike. She adjusted the kickstand and scooped Button, her Chihuahua, out of the basket on the handlebars. Button shivered and Jilly tucked the dog inside her navy windbreaker, stroking the dog's ears.

"It's okay. We won't be here long."

Kerri hopped off her bike and joined her. They looked up at the white stone two-story colonial house with the weatherworn and peeling brown trim. Shutters hung like broken arms, dust and spiderwebs coated the windows, and weeds had taken over the flower beds.

"This place is like totally spooky," Kerri said.

"Yeah," Jilly murmured. She hadn't expected this, either. The Danielses were supposed to be rich.

"Let's go," Kerri said. "I don't think anyone lives here."

"Yes, they do," Jilly insisted, clutching Button. "The Temple paper said *he* came home to the family ranch."

"I don't understand why you have to see Tripp Daniels anyway."

Sometimes she didn't, either, but from the moment she'd seen his picture in the paper, a handsome man on a bucking horse, she'd wondered if her father had really looked like that. Tripp was a national champion bareback rider and calf roper, and the paper had mentioned all the awards he'd won. The town of Bramble was very proud of him. Her mama had said that the Daniels brothers favored and she wanted to see the man who so closely resembled her father.

Kerri caught her arm. "C'mon."

She focused on her blond, blue-eyed friend. Jilly had dark hair and eyes and they both had long ponytails. They were letting their hair grow, to see whose would grow the fastest and the longest. So far Jilly was winning.

They'd been friends forever and lived two blocks apart. Kerri's parents were divorced and Kerri saw her father every other weekend and two weeks in the summer. Jilly wanted just a tiny bit of that—a bit of a father. She marched to the front door before she could change her mind. The bell didn't work so she tapped the tarnished brass knocker.

"We're gonna be in so much trouble," Kerri said from behind her.

"You can go home if you want," Jilly told her.

"Why do you have to do this?"

"I don't know. I just do." She tapped louder.

WEDGED BENEATH the kitchen sink, Tripp Daniels tightened the new drainpipe he'd just installed. He'd heard the knock and thought Morris would get it, then the knock came again.

"Morris!" he shouted.

Nothing.

He'd had a helluva time getting his long frame under the sink and he didn't want to quit until he'd finished the job. Another loud knock. Dammit. He uncurled himself and saw Morris sitting at the kitchen table knitting, the needles clicking, the yarn in his lap. Tripp shook his head in aggravation.

"Morris!" he shouted again.

The older man jumped. "Yes, sir." He pushed to his feet, blinking.

"There's someone at the door."

"Really?" He laid his knitting down and scratched his bald head. "I didn't hear a thing." He didn't move, just kept standing there.

"Morris, would you get the door, please? I'm rather busy at the moment."

"Oh." Morris gazed at him with a blank look. "Did you say something, sir?"

"The door, Morris."

"Yes, yes." He shuffled away in the direction of the front door. By the time he reached it, he'd probably forget what he was there for. Morris had worked as a butler and a housekeeper for the Daniels family ever since Tripp could remember. At seventy-two, he was hard of hearing and forgetful, but he was the only person to care for his parents.

A stab of guilt pierced him. It had been almost thirteen years since he'd seen them. After his brother's death, his father had told him to leave and never come back. They blamed him for what had happened. Tripp, too, blamed himself. He'd thrown himself into the rodeo scene, but he checked on his parents constantly through Morris.

His father had fallen and broken his hip six months ago. Tripp had gotten a call from Morris, who'd said Tripp needed to come home. He'd spent thirteen years avoiding the past, avoiding thoughts of Patrick, but he couldn't avoid the fact that his parents now needed him. He wasn't sure if he'd be welcome but he'd come anyway.

The moment they'd seen him, they'd begun to cry and he'd hugged them. The arguments and the pain over Patrick's death faded away. He'd realized then he should have returned long ago.

Nothing had prepared him for the dilapidated sight of the ranch and the house. Everything was in disrepair and run-down and his parents had gotten old. His mother's sight was so bad that she couldn't see the dust and cobwebs. His father had sunk so far into depression that he didn't care about anything.

How could he let this happen to his family? Guilt hammered away at Tripp, but all he could do was be here for them now and restore the place to its original splendor. That would take money, and he'd soon found there wasn't any. The oil wells had dried up and his father now leased the land for ranching. With that small income, along with their social security, they were barely getting by. Tripp had a little money and he'd spend every dime to make his parents comfortable.

Morris ambled back to his chair. "There's two young fillies to see you, sir."

He raised an eyebrow. He wasn't expecting anyone. "How young are we talking here, Morris?" He spoke loudly so Morris could hear.

"Schoolgirls," Morris replied with a twinkle in his eye.

Tripp frowned. "Do they have the right house?"

"No. They're not riding a horse." Morris picked up his knitting.

Tripp didn't respond. There was no need. He and Morris were seldom on the same page. Shoving to his feet, he laid his wrench on the counter. He grabbed a rag, wiped his hands and hurried to the door.

Two young girls stood there, one dark, the other blond. The dark-haired girl held a small dog inside her jacket. Neither spoke.

"May I help you? I'm Tripp Daniels." He ran a hand through his tousled hair.

They stared at him, mouths open.

"Are you selling something?"

The dark-haired girl shook her head.

The dog grunted and shivered. "Did you find a lost dog?" She shook her head again and held the dog tighter against her chest.

"Well, I'm running out of questions so you'd better tell me what you want."

There was no response—just wide-eyed silence.

"I have to get back to work," he said and stepped back to close the door.

"I'm Jilly Walker," the dark-haired girl blurted out.

Tripp paused. Was this Camila Walker's kid? Yeah, she had the same gorgeous hair, skin and eyes. That would mean...

"I make straight A's and I'm going to be a doctor."

"Very impressive."

"I'm a good kid, everyone says so, and your family missed a lot by not knowing me. You missed even more by not knowing my mama. That's all I have to say." She took a step backward and ran into her friend, who seemed to have turned to stone. The two of them locked hands and ran toward their bikes, then quickly rode away.

TRIPP GAZED AFTER THEM. *Camila's daughter.* The rumor mill in Bramble said Camila didn't know who the father was. There were some who named Patrick as the father, but the Danielses didn't believe that for a minute. Camila, a tramp like her mother, had slept around—that's what his father had said and his mother had agreed. Tripp had had reason to believe them. But now...

"Tripp, where are you?"

"I'm here, Mom," he called. He closed the door and found

his mother in the den. Leona Daniels had once been tall, regal and sophisticated. Now Tripp hardly recognized the stooped lady wearing thick wire-rimmed glasses. Her white hair was cut in a short style and she looked much older than her sixty-five years. Patrick's untimely death had devastated his parents, and him, too. It had been years since that awful car crash and still the family hadn't recovered.

"What do you need, Mom?" he asked and gently clutched her elbow.

"Oh, Tripp, there you are." She stroked the hand on her arm. "I was looking for Morris and I can't find him. I think he's hiding from me."

Tripp smiled slightly. Morris probably was hiding. Tripp sometimes wondered about the man's hearing problems. He could hear certain things, like the TV, just fine, but his parents' constant orders, he could shut out completely.

"Why do you need Morris?" He guided her toward the sofa.

"I was wanting a cup of tea."

"You have a seat and I'll fix it."

"Okay, dear. You're such a sweet boy." She slowly sat down.

A sweet boy. He was thirty-eight years old and he didn't think his mother realized it. His parents' frailty tore at his heart.

"Where's Dad?"

"In the bedroom watching sports. Sports, sports, sports, that's all he watches. It gets on my nerves."

"There's a TV in here. Why don't you watch a movie?"

"It's all sex and violence and not fit to watch. I can't see it anyway. No. I'll just sit for a while."

Leona had once been an energetic woman involved in all sorts of activities with the town, but now she barely went out and Tripp knew she was bored to death. *Death.* An eerie feeling came over him. His parents were marking time, waiting to die.

Filling the kettle, he thought how wonderful it would be if

Camila's daughter *was* Patrick's. Life would return to this house again.

What did she say her name was? Jilly. Yes, Jilly with the flashing brown eyes, just like Camila's. *Camila.* Her dark Latin beauty flashed through his mind. Something about her sensuous, sad eyes always got to him even though he knew she was his brother's girlfriend. He set the kettle on the stove with more force than necessary. Maybe he should have a heart-to-heart with Camila.

The mere thought caused his pulse to accelerate.

He could break a wild horse. Rope a calf in a split second. But speaking with Camila about her child's paternity could prove a bit harder for a man whose main goal in life was never to see, speak or think about Camila again.

"Tripp," Leona called.

"Coming, Mom." He poured water into a cup. This might be one of those times he'd have to bite the bullet for the sake of his parents.

And that meant talking with Camila Walker.

CAMILA GLANCED AT THE CLOCK. It was after five so Jilly should be finished. She and Kerri were working on a school project at Kerri's house and Camila thought she'd call and see if Jilly wanted a ride home. They could put her bike in back of the Suburban. This was the best part of her day—the time she spent with her daughter.

She stuck her needle in the pincushion, rubbed the tight muscles in her neck and looked around. The sign on the door read Common Threads and below that was printed Camila's Quilts, Soaps and Gifts. Every time she saw that sign, her chest swelled with pride. She owned her own business and was doing very well—better than she'd ever planned. She sold handmade quilts and homemade soaps on the Internet and people came from all around to buy them in the shop. Specialty shops in Houston, Dallas, Austin, College Station and Temple also stocked her soaps.

She'd bought the store from Millie, who owned the adjoining bakery and coffee shop. Millie used to have a craft shop and Camila had worked for her as a teenager, trying to make a living for her and Jilly. At that time, Mrs. Ida Baker had made the soap that Millie sold, but the arthritis in her hands had become so bad she couldn't do it anymore. People had come in regularly asking for it, so Camila had asked Mrs. Baker to teach her. And she had. Camila now used her own recipe, perfected over the last few years. She never dreamed it would sell so well—even younger people used it, young girls wanting something different.

Her grandmother, Alta, was born in Puerto Rico and sewed for people. She'd taught Camila how to quilt. When Camila, a young single mother, had been searching for ways to make money, she'd brought a quilt she'd made to the store. It had sold immediately. She couldn't seem to make them fast enough. Hand-stitched quilts were a dying art and people came to Bramble looking for antiques and rare goods. From then on, her store had been busy and profitable.

Four years ago, she'd purchased the space next door and expanded. She now had an up-to-date kitchen for making soap and large tables for working space. She'd hired a couple of schoolgirls to help in the store and, of course, Millie was always in the coffee shop. The double doors that joined the two businesses were always open. Millie made homemade *kolaches,* cinnamon rolls and bread, and her place was a hive of activity in the mornings, with people stopping in to get a roll and coffee on the way to work.

Dear Millie. What would she have done without her? Camila had been seventeen when she'd gotten pregnant. Being so young and raising a child alone had been frightening, but she'd wanted her baby. Back then, with Millie's help, she'd made all the right choices for her daughter. Jilly was the bright spot in Camila's life. She *was* her whole life. Everything she did, she did for Jilly.

Her mother, Benita, appeared on her doorstep from time to time when she was in between men and needing a place to stay. Even though they were so different, they were still mother and daughter. And Camila never forgot that fact.

Benita was known as the town slut, a tramp. Different people used different words, but even as a child Camila had known what they'd meant. Her mother worked in a bar and drank heavily, and when she did, she danced the Latin dances, and men loved to watch her. Benita had full breasts and long slim legs, and she didn't mind showing them off. As Benita's reputation had grown in the town, so had Camila's embarrassment. It hadn't taken her long to realize that everyone thought she was the same as her mother.

Everyone, except Patrick.

One night had changed her whole life. After Patrick's death, she'd discovered she was pregnant and she hadn't known what she was going to do. Her grandmother had raised her and had passed away six months before. Camila couldn't stay in Bramble and face the rumors.

She hadn't seen her mother in three months. Benita was married to husband number four and Camila knew she'd get no support from her so she'd packed her things and sat at the bus stop waiting for the next bus—not caring where it was going. In tears, she felt desperate and afraid. Patrick was dead and no one else cared about her. She barely had a hundred dollars in her purse and she had no idea how long that would last.

Millie found her sitting on the bench in the July heat with tears streaming down her face. She told her everything and Millie took her back to her house and they talked into the early hours of the morning. Camila confided her fears about raising a child alone.

Millie was her lifeline. She gave her a job and helped her adjust to being a young mother. Millie took care of Jilly so Camila could attend Temple Junior College. When Benita finally surfaced, she didn't like that Camila depended on Millie, but Benita didn't stay around long enough to voice many complaints.

Camila took business, marketing and computer courses, learning all she could. It was impossible to make a living working for minimum wage and she had to have some sort of skills to build a decent life for herself and Jilly. From there, her business savvy just evolved.

Within a few months of putting up a Web site on the Internet, she'd known it was going to be a success. Camila's specialty was baby quilts, which were very popular with doting parents and grandparents.

Her most popular style was the photo quilt. She transferred family photos to fabric and people liked that personal touch. The white eyelet was the most popular for newborns. She kept trying to think of new ideas.

Six years ago, she'd saved enough money to buy herself and Jilly a home. The Pattersons had been moving to Temple to be near their daughter and they'd put their place up for sale. When Camila had gone inside, she'd fallen in love with the country style of the three-bedroom brick house.

Benita now owned Alta's house, where Camila had lived as a child, but she'd wanted a place of her own. Her moving had angered Benita, but Camila had stuck to her decision. She wanted independence. She'd worked hard for that and she wasn't changing her mind.

Alta's house was two blocks away and Camila still took care of it so her mother could have a place to stay when she breezed into town.

Camila walked into the coffee shop. A domino game was in full swing. Bubba Carter, Slim Gorshack, Joe Bob Horton and Billy Clyde Yesak were semiretired ranchers and businessmen—widowers and bachelors who came in every afternoon to visit, drink coffee and play dominoes. They were also good friends; people who had not judged her according to the rumors they'd heard. They accepted her for the woman they knew her to be.

Last year they had encouraged her to run for a seat on the city council and she had. She'd won without a problem, which had been a big surprise to her. Then again, she had spent a lot of years building a good reputation for her daughter. Most of the town now saw her as a good citizen and an asset to the town, and she was glad. She never wanted Jilly to be ashamed of her.

She stretched her aching shoulders. "Do you mind locking up?" she asked Millie. "I'd like to spend some time with Jilly."

"No, sweetie, you go ahead." Millie poured a round of coffee for the men. "I'm giving these old coots thirty more minutes then I'm kicking them out."

Joe Bob held a hand over his heart. "Aw. You've wounded my manly pride."

"Yeah, right," Millie laughed, then she turned to Camila. "Got the party all planned?"

"Yes," Camila answered, her tiredness easing at thoughts of her daughter. "I told Jilly she could do something special for her twelfth birthday and I'm sure she wants to have a slumber party. She's going to be really surprised that I've planned a party here for all her friends. Thought we could push back the tables and they could dance."

"Do I get an invite?" Slim winked.

Camila patted his gray head. Slim was the youngest of the group. His wife had died of cancer about five years ago and he was lonely. "You're always invited. Now I'd better call and see if my daughter's ready to go home."

Picking up the phone, she dialed Kerri's mother. "Hi, Betty Sue, I was just checking to see if Jilly wants a ride home."

There was a long pause on the line.

"Betty Sue, are you there?"

"Yes, I'm just a little shocked."

"Why?"

"The girls are supposed to be working at your house."

Camila was at a loss for words, but she recovered quickly. "What are those girls up to?"

"I don't know, but it makes me nervous."

"Me, too," Camila admitted. "It's not like Jilly to lie to me." She'd never had a problem with her daughter. She made sure she was involved in her life and that she knew where Jilly was and what she was doing at all times. But something had slipped by her. Jilly wasn't where she was supposed to be today. She'd really be worried if this weren't Bramble, where everyone knew each other.

"I'm going home, Betty Sue. I'll call you when I get there. Maybe they just wanted to be alone. They're almost twelve, but Jilly assures me she's grown."

"I don't like them lying to us."

"I don't, either, and I will definitely get to the bottom of this."

Hanging up, she grabbed her purse and headed for her Suburban parked in the rear of the shop. Within five minutes, she was driving into her garage.

The house was quiet and the lights weren't on. Jilly wasn't there. She ran to her daughter's room. Button wasn't there, either. That meant Jilly had come home after school and gotten her, but where did they go?

She ran back to the kitchen and before panic could take root, she glanced out the kitchen window and saw Jilly ride into the garage on her bicycle. Camila took a deep breath, trying not to get angry. Jilly had thought that she'd be home before Camila and Camila would never have known she hadn't been at Kerri's today.

Camila busied herself at the sink and turned to Jilly with a smile, like always, as she entered with Button in her arms.

"Hi, baby," Camila said and kissed Jilly's warm cheek. Her daughter's face was red and she looked flustered. Camila held the back of her hand to Jilly's forehead. "Do you have a fever?"

"No, no, I'm fine," Jilly replied nervously. Button jumped from her arms and scurried for her bed in Jilly's room.

"What's wrong with Button?"

"I took her for a bike ride and I guess she didn't like the wind." Jilly avoided eye contact and Camila knew she was lying. Whenever Jilly had done something wrong, she couldn't look at her mother.

Jilly grabbed some bottled water out of the refrigerator and drank thirstily.

"Did you and Kerri finish your project?"

"What?" Jilly looked at her with rounded eyes.

"The solar system you were working on, did you finish it?"

"Ah…ah…I…" Her bottom lip trembled. "I'm sorry… Mama…I'm sorry."

Camila guided her to a chair at the table, then she sat beside her. "What are you sorry about?"

"I did something and…" She leveled a teary glance at Camila. "You know I wasn't at Kerri's, don't you?"

Camila nodded, glad her daughter wasn't going to lie further, and wondering why she'd had to in the first place. They were always able to talk about anything. But evidently there was something bothering Jilly that Camila didn't know about. "I called to see if you wanted a ride home."

Jilly winced. "Were you mad cause I wasn't there?"

"No, just worried. Why did you lie to me?"

Jilly twisted her hands. "You're going to be mad now."

"Why?"

"Because I did something and I should have told you first."

"Why didn't you?"

"I knew you wouldn't let me do it."

"I see," Camila murmured, getting a bad feeling in her stomach. "What did you do?"

"Remember you said I could do something special for my birthday?"

"Yes."

"When I saw Mr. Daniels's picture in the paper, I wondered if my daddy looked like him and the more I thought about it, the more I wanted to see…to see what my daddy's brother looked like in person."

"Jilly, you didn't."

"Yes. I went to see Mr. Daniels."

That bad feeling exploded into tiny pinpricks all over Camila's body, leaving her nauseous and weak, but she had to concentrate on her daughter and not a past that she'd managed to put behind her. Yet sometimes that past had the power to make her feel frightened and alone, as she had when she was seventeen.

She gathered herself. "You should have told me what you were thinking."

"I didn't want to upset you," Jilly mumbled.

"It upsets me more when you lie to me."

"I'm sorry."

Camila scooted closer and caught Jilly's hands. "If you wanted to see your father's family, I wouldn't have said no. But they've made no attempt over the years and my only concern is you getting hurt."

"I wish I hadn't gone," Jilly mumbled again.

The pinpricks turned to a cold chill, but she had to know what her daughter meant, "What happened?"

"Kerri and I rode over there on our bikes and the place is really run down and kind of spooky."

"I heard the Danielses are having a difficult time."

"It's like nobody lives there and I was so scared, but I knocked anyway and Morris answered the door. I had to ask three times if I could speak with Mr. Daniels before he heard me. Then he came and his hair was a mess and he didn't look too friendly."

Camila's stomach clenched. She'd seen Tripp's picture in the paper, too, and she was hoping he wouldn't be staying long in Bramble.

"I couldn't say anything for a long time, my tongue wouldn't work. He was going to close the door so I blurted out my name and told him I made straight A's and I was going to be a doctor and his family missed a lot by not knowing me...and you."

"Oh, Jilly." Camila wrapped her arms around her. She thought she knew her daughter, but she'd never dreamed she harbored these feelings. "Why didn't you tell me you were thinking about your father?"

"'Cause it makes you sad."

"There's nothing you can't talk to me about...even if it makes me sad. Don't you know that?"

Jilly's mouth trembled into a smile. "Yeah, and I won't go back."

Camila cupped Jilly's face. "It's okay to be curious about your father's family, but next time, please talk it over with me first. I don't like you riding that far on your bicycle."

"Okay." Jilly looped her arms around Camila's waist and squeezed.

"Mama?"

"Hmm?"

"Do my grandparents live there?"

Camila swallowed. "Yes, they do."

"But it's so dirty and unkempt. Do you think they're okay?"

This was her Jilly, always worried about everyone. There wasn't an old person in Bramble who didn't know Jilly. She ran errands and helped anyone who needed it. Jilly had a big heart and Camila cringed inside at the thought of anyone ever hurting her.

"Yes, they're fine. Nurse Tisdale checks on them three times a week." The nurse came in the shop occasionally and talked of the disrepair at the Lady Luck.

"I guess I'm like grounded for life," Jilly muttered against Camila.

"Pretty much."

Jilly drew away, her eyes worried. "But, Mama, I have to take out Mrs. Shynosky's trash and pick up Mrs. Haskell's groceries when she needs something and take Miss Unie food or she'll just eat cat food."

Camila tucked wisps of stray hair behind Jilly's ear. "Do you know how special you are?"

Jilly grinned. "Then I can still help out?"

"Yes, but no TV or listening to music for a week."

"Ah, piece of cake." She kissed her mother. "I love you and I'm sorry I lied."

"Just don't do it again."

"I won't. I'd better check on Button." She disappeared down the hall.

Camila buried her face in her hands. *Oh, Jilly. What have you done?* She'd thought she'd put the past behind her, closed that door forever. But now it was wide open and Camila didn't know if she had the strength to go through it, to face a past that was painful, to face her daughter if she found out the truth. But she would make sure that never happened.

She'd guard the truth with her life.

Chapter Two

Jilly's visit plagued Tripp and triggered thoughts of Camila. He'd often wondered how her life had turned out. Evidently she hadn't married, since Jilly's last name was Walker.

He worked until he was exhausted and still couldn't shake them from his mind. So he worked that much harder. He fixed the tractor and lawn mower and cut the weeds around the house and mowed the grass. He hired the Garcia brothers to repair the entrance and the fence, then he went looking for Earl Boggs, who leased the land.

The Boggs family owned the little town of Bramble. Otis Boggs had died several years ago and his widow, Thelma Bramble, was the matriarch of the family. Earl, Bert and Melvin were her sons. Bert ran the bank, Melvin the feed and hardware store, and Earl took care of the Boggs ranch. Tripp went there to talk to him, but he was told that Earl was in town.

He drove to town and still couldn't locate Earl. Frustrated, he went back to Lady Luck, not wanting to leave his parents too long. They were napping, as was Morris, so Tripp let them rest.

He called his friend and partner, Brodie Hayes. The two of them owned a Hereford cattle ranch near Mesquite, Texas, and Tripp had to let him know he wasn't returning as soon as he'd planned.

"So you're not coming back for a while?" Brodie asked.

"I can't leave my parents just yet and the place is so run down."

"Take all the time you need. I can run this place with my eyes closed."

"Yeah, right."

Brodie laughed. They'd been the best of friends since their rodeo days. The two of them and Colter Kincaid, another friend and rodeo rider, lived not far from each other. Colter had married the love of his life and now had two children.

"How's Colter and the family?"

"Wonderful. Every time I'm over there it makes me think about getting married. Then I come home and take a cold shower and it brings me to my senses."

"I guess we're going to be two old bachelors."

"Yep."

There was silence for a moment.

"Something bothering you?" Brodie asked.

He told Brodie about Jilly's visit.

"So you think this could be your brother's daughter?"

"I'm not sure, but I can't stop thinking how good it would be for my parents if she was."

"Then find out."

That would be easy for Brodie. He was a charmer, a talker.

"Hell, Tripp, you're not a shy sixteen-year-old. Just ask the woman, or do you think she doesn't know who the father is?"

"Not sure about that either, but I'll definitely speak to her. Talk to you in a couple of days."

Tripp stared at the phone. He'd never told Brodie or anyone about his feelings for Camila. Feelings? He scoffed at the word and forced himself to call it what it was—good old-fashioned lust. Every time he'd looked at her, he hadn't been able to think straight, and she'd been a teenager and… That was in the past—a past he'd just as soon forget. He knew what he had to do for his family. He left a note for Morris and drove back to town.

CAMILA LOCKED UP for the day and saw Eunice Gimble across the street, pushing her shopping cart of plastic bags filled with aluminum cans. Unie was the can lady of Bramble. She was close to ninety and picked up cans from the street, diner, beer joints and roadsides, any place she could find them.

Camila went over to her. A dirty black coat covered with cat hair hung on her thin body and she wore a multicolored wool scarf tied around her head. "Hi, Unie," Camila said.

Unie whirled around, a frown on her wrinkled face. "Oh, Camila, it's you. Thought you were someone trying to steal my cans."

Unie's mind wasn't right. Sometimes she made sense and sometimes she didn't, but she always talked about people being after her cans or her money. She lived in a run down house with weeds grown to the windowsills, and everyone knew she didn't have any money.

Camila didn't understand why the people of Bramble didn't try to help her. She and Jilly were the only ones concerned about Unie. They mowed her grass when Unie would let them. Unie didn't take kindly to charity. They still took her food and checked on her, but Unie needed more attention than that. People of Bramble tended to leave her alone, except those who made fun of her.

"Would you like a ride home? I can put your cart in the back of my Suburban." Camila always felt sorry for this old lady who was all alone and lived in her own little world.

"Nope. Not through for the day."

A purr rippled from the plastic bags and Lu Lu, Unie's black-and-white cat and constant companion, raised her head from the bags.

Unie stroked Lu Lu for a second then pushed her cart farther down the street, pausing to look in a trash can.

Camila shook her head and headed for her car and home. Jilly was in her room, doing her homework. As part of her punishment, she wasn't allowed to visit with her girlfriends after school.

Camila had been on pins and needles waiting for Tripp to make an appearance, but so far he hadn't. Maybe he was going to forget about Jilly's visit. Looking in the fridge, she tried to decide what they'd have for supper.

The doorbell rang and she went to answer it. Her breath stalled in her throat.

Tripp Daniels stood there with his hat in his hand. His chiseled features were bronzed by the sun and his blond streaked hair curled into the collar of a blue-and-white pin-striped shirt. Wrangler jeans molded his long legs and cowboy boots made his legs seem that much longer. A silver buckle gleamed on a tooled leather belt. His eyes were as striking and blue as a Texas sky, and he looked more handsome than she ever remembered. She hated herself for recognizing that.

And she hated that stir of excitement in her stomach.

"Tripp." His name slipped out before she could stop it. She didn't want them to be on a first-name basis.

"Camila." He nodded. "Could I speak with you for a second?" He had a deep Texas drawl that as a silly teenager had evoked visions in her head of satin sheets, champagne, roses and soft music. Sadly, it still did.

"That's not necessary." She shook the image away, her hand gripping the doorknob to still the nervous flutter in her stomach. "Jilly told me what she did and I promise she won't bother your family again."

"She wasn't bothering us," he said, twisting his hat. "Could I come in, please?"

No. No. No.

"We don't have anything to say to each other."

He glanced at the street, then back at her, almost as if he was resigning himself to the fact he wasn't getting past her doorway. "That's where you're wrong. I think we have a lot to talk about. If you want to have this conversation out here, well, I guess we can."

She glared at him for forcing the issue, but stepped aside, knowing she might as well get this over with. "You've got five minutes, Mr. Daniels."

He lifted an eyebrow at that. "Tripp, please."

She'd always thought that was a strange name to give a child. But it had been his mother's maiden name. Leona was the last of the Tripps and she wanted the name carried on.

They walked into the living room and Camila quickly moved the baby eyelet quilt in the quilting hoop from the sofa. She'd planned on finishing it tonight. As she turned, she bumped into him. She hadn't realized he was so close behind her. His body was hard and firm, and his tangy aftershave jolted her senses, reminding her of that night. She jerked away. She didn't mean to, but she couldn't be that close to him and not remember.

Was there a look of sympathy in his eyes? That was the last thing she wanted from Tripp Daniels. He eased onto the sofa and she perched on the edge of a chair and waited. She knew what was coming.

Suddenly the living room seemed small, way too small. He looked out of place on her beige sofa and colorful throw pillows. She had trouble breathing and she didn't know why, but something about having a Daniels in her home was unnerving.

He placed his hat beside himself and clasped his hands together. "I was surprised to see your daughter the other day."

Your daughter. No mention of Patrick. Her jaw clenched tight.

"I told you that won't happen again." She kept her back straight, her hands folded in her lap.

"Obviously she believes we've slighted her."

"As I said—"

He cut in. "Jilly looks a lot like you."

Camila stiffened even more. "Yes."

His gaze locked with hers. "This might be out of line, but I'd like to know if she's Patrick's?"

She sprang to her feet. "If you have to ask that question, then I don't want you in my house. Please leave."

As if she hadn't spoken, he said, "I've been away for a long time and I was surprised to find my parents in such bad shape."

She didn't know what to say to that, so she said the first thing that came to mind. "Then maybe you shouldn't have stayed away so long."

He inhaled deeply. "If Jilly is Patrick's, she could be what they need to give them a will to live. I'm asking a yes or no question."

She bristled even more. "Jilly is not a dose of medicine. She's a loving young girl and I will not have her hurt. Your parents have not shown the slightest interest in her."

"I said that badly. I apologize."

Camila marched to the door. "Mr. Daniels, Jilly is my daughter and no concern of yours or your family."

He didn't budge. "I'd like to have a DNA test done."

She whirled around. "What?"

"Patrick could be the father. I want to know for sure." His blue eyes turned to the color of steel.

Could be. Could be. Her blood pressure soared.

"Never. Now get out of my house."

Tripp slowly stood, knowing he'd stepped over the line of good manners, but something about being this close to Camila made him act and do things out of character. When Patrick had brought her out to the ranch, he hadn't been able to take his eyes off her. People had called her trash, but he'd seen an unbelievably beautiful young woman with dark eyes and hair who moved with a sensuousness he'd never seen before.

Looking at her now, he saw the same thing, but a mature version. The years had been kind to Camila. A clip held her long hair away from the clean lines of her face and her olive skin was touchable perfection. In jeans and a T-shirt, her body was more riveting than a starlet in a skimpy three-thousand-dollar gown. But the eyes were always what got him—dark as the night, as deep as the ocean and as mysterious as the Marfa lights, yet there was a hidden pain in them that she couldn't disguise.

Thirteen years and she still made his heart race, and his body... He cleared his mind, searching for the right words to apologize again.

Jilly walked into the room. "Mama..." Her voice trailed away when she saw him. "Oh, it's you."

"Hi, Jilly."

Jilly glanced at her mother then back at Tripp. "Hi."

"Mr. Daniels was just leaving," Camila said.

Tripp turned back to the sofa and retrieved his hat. "I just wanted to make sure I didn't frighten you the other day." The excuse sounded lame to his own ears, but he found he couldn't say anything that would hurt this young girl. He'd have to sort this out with Camila, but at the moment, her dark eyes were about to sear him into a pile of ashes.

Jilly reached down and picked up her dog, who was making soft noises at her feet. "No. I'm fine."

Tripp nodded. "Good."

He headed for the door.

"Mr. Daniels?" Jilly asked.

He looked back. "Yes."

"Are Mr. and Mrs. Daniels okay?"

Tripp was taken aback for a second. "Their health's not very good but they're okay."

"Do they need anything?"

This time he didn't know what to say. He'd never met anyone like Jilly before, except… For a moment he was shaken by the thought.

"Because I run errands for a lot of people," Jilly informed him. "And if they need anything, I can pedal it out there. It doesn't take long."

Don't do this, Jilly. Baby, don't do this. Camila's heart broke at the entreaty in her daughter's voice. Jilly wanted to help the Danielses. It was very evident Jilly wanted to know her father's family and Camila had to let it happen. But she would fiercely guard her daughter's feelings.

"I'll remember that," Tripp said and placed his hat on his head. At the door, he spoke to Camila. "I'm sorry if my visit has disturbed you. I didn't mean to do that."

"Goodbye." She closed the door, unable to deal with anything else right now but her daughter.

"I'm sorry, Mama," Jilly said as Camila walked into the living room.

Camila sat on the sofa, bracing herself to tell Jilly about Patrick. She looked at her daughter. "Never be afraid to talk to me."

"I'm not, Mama."

"But you're curious about your father and his family, so let's talk about it." She patted the spot beside her.

"Okay." Jilly nestled into Camila's side and Camila wrapped an arm around her. Button curled into a ball on her lap.

"Did my daddy look like Mr. Daniels?"

"Some." Camila ran her fingers through Jilly's dark tresses. "They have the same blond hair and blue eyes, but Tripp was the handsome older brother. Girls noticed him and he was popular. Patrick, on the other hand, was very shy and always felt overshadowed by his big brother. They lived on a ranch, but Patrick was never interested in horses or cows.

He always had his head in a book and when he got his first computer, well, he found his joy. He was going to be a computer engineer."

"But he got killed?"

"Yes." Camila's hand stopped. She could still feel that pain of long ago when she'd been told of Patrick's death.

"And you and he were in love?"

She chose her words carefully. "Patrick and I were very good friends. We had been since kindergarten. Patrick was my protector. When kids said bad things about me or Benita, he'd always take up for me. He had a very big heart and I loved him for that." She hadn't been in love with Patrick, though— that's what had caused the problem. She'd cared for him a great deal and had been so grateful for his support. But Patrick had wanted more.

"Why do the Danielses think you're so bad?"

Her hand curled into a fist and she dreaded this part, but she wasn't going to lie to Jilly.

Before she could find the words, Jilly asked, "Is it because Benita's been married so many times?"

"That's part of it."

"Is it because she worked in a bar and danced when men asked her to?"

"Partly."

"But that's not fair. Benita's a fun person and she's always happy. She's not a bad woman."

Camila tucked hair behind Jilly's ear. "That's because you love her. Other people don't see her that way." She swallowed. "And some don't see me that way either."

Jilly raised her head. "Why, Mama? You didn't sleep with other guys. I know you didn't."

She kissed the tip of Jilly's nose. "Thank you for your faith in me. You get that soft heart from Patrick. He was the same way."

"So why don't they believe that Patrick is my father?"

How did she explain this to her? "Remember last year when that new girl was transferred to your class from Temple?"

"Yes. Stephanie."

"Her father was in prison for murder and her mother was on drugs and I didn't want you playing with her. I didn't know anything about her. I just knew the type of family she came from, and the nose ring didn't help. Of course, I realized how unfair that was to Stephanie and she came to the house several times. She'd had a hard life and needed a lot of under-standing."

"She now lives in Kansas with her grandmother. I got a card from her at Christmas."

"Yes. Stephanie is doing better now that she's out of that en-vironment." She stroked Jilly's hair. "That's how people thought of me when I was her age. Benita worked in a bar and her dating habits were well known. People thought I was the same. So when I got pregnant, everyone said I probably didn't know who the father was. Like mother, like daughter." Those rumors still had the power to hurt, but she tried not to let it show.

"But you did, didn't you?"

"Yes." Patrick had been her only lover, and they'd only been together once.

"Everyone in Bramble loves you now, Mama, because they know you as the nice person you are." Jilly sat up. "How could they think anything else? You don't even date. All you do is work and take care of me. You're probably a saint."

"You need very little taking care of—just a watchful eye and some guidance."

Jilly curled into her. "I love you, Mama," she murmured sleepily.

"I love you, too." She reached for the Southern belle quilt on the back of the sofa and pulled it over Jilly. She'd wake her in a moment. For now she just wanted to hold her baby.

From an early age, Camila had realized Jilly was special. She cared about people and they responded to her. Jilly was the reason the people in Bramble now accepted Camila, the main reason they saw her in a different way—as a mother, businesswoman and friend. But there were those like the Boggses who looked down their noses at her. They were the influential people in Bramble who judged and condemned her for having a child out of wedlock.

That didn't matter to Camila. She'd matured and gotten beyond that—somewhat. At times it still hurt, like today.

She'd told Jilly the basics of the story. No one knew the real story but her…and Patrick. Young and insecure about herself, her life, she'd clung to her friendship with him. In school, he was known as the nerd and she was the tramp's daughter. They were kindred spirits who found comfort in each other.

Patrick's feelings changed in high school. He started to hold her hand and she'd told him to stop. But he wouldn't. He seemed to want everyone to believe they were a couple. She wanted just the opposite.

Years of being embarrassed by her mother's reputation caused Camila to avoid all contact with boys. It didn't keep boys from seeking her out, though, wanting her to go for a ride to the lake or to Lover's Point, the usual necking spots. They only wanted one thing—sex. They assumed she was easy and she never accepted any of their invitations.

Patrick was different. Until the one event that was the beginning of her nightmare. The Daniels were giving Patrick a big graduation party at the ranch. Camila didn't get an invitation in the mail like the other kids, but Patrick asked her to come.

The moment she arrived, she knew the Danielses didn't want her there. She wanted to leave, but Patrick insisted that she stay. Through the course of the night, Patrick became a different person, eager to please his classmates and to show them he had a hot number—Camila.

Patrick was drinking, which she'd never seen him do. He put something in her Coke. She didn't know he'd done that until she started to feel relaxed and at ease. Patrick said he wanted her to have a good time. When the kids started to dance around the pool, she and Patrick joined in. Out of the corner of her eye, she saw Tripp watching them.

Every girl in Bramble had a crush on Tripp and she was no exception. He never paid her any attention, but that night she wanted to dance with him. Later, feeling woozy from the drink, she thought she was going to faint. Then there Tripp was holding her and every foolish dream she'd ever harbored about him suddenly came true. She swayed in his arms to the beat of the music. Patrick had accused Tripp of flirting with her and they'd had a big argument.

Jilly stirred, but she didn't wake up. Camila's arms tightened around her daughter. She'd worked hard so Jilly would have a better life and the Danielses were not going to destroy that. Tripp could demand all he wanted, but there would be no DNA test.

Not now. Not ever.

TRIPP DROVE HOME CURSING himself for being so thickheaded. What did he expect Camila to say? But he sure as hell wanted to know the truth. He'd give it a rest for now because he wasn't getting anywhere barging into her house and demanding answers.

He'd never been sure about Patrick's relationship with Camila. They'd never gone on a date that he was aware of. His parents hadn't wanted him being friends with her and Patrick had always adhered to their wishes. That's why Tripp had been surprised when she'd shown up at Patrick's graduation party.

His parents were furious, but Patrick said that he'd invited *all* his friends. Tripp could see that she was nervous. None of the other kids spoke to her and he felt sorry for her. Patrick hung onto her as if she were his special gift.

As the evening wore on, Tripp realized something wasn't quite right. There was a lot of drinking going on and small white packets being passed around. Camila became mellower, laughing and dancing. All the guys were watching her and Patrick, and nudging each other. When Patrick went to change the music on the stereo, she stood alone, swaying, and Tripp grabbed her before she hit the concrete.

She pressed her body against his and began to move to the music. He was stunned that she was coming on to him in front of everyone. Before he could push her away, Patrick came roaring back shouting words Tripp had never heard him use before. Over the years, he cursed himself more times than he could remember for coming to Camila's aid.

She and Patrick disappeared, and he couldn't get the scent and feel of her out of his system. At two in the morning, he saw her coming out of Patrick's room. She was buttoning her blouse and she looked like hell. At that moment, he knew all the rumors he'd heard were true.

And he was disappointed.

He went in to talk to Patrick to see what was going on. Patrick was hyped up and nervous, which wasn't like his brother at all, and he knew Patrick was drunk or on something. Tripp told him to sleep it off and Patrick said things like Tripp was jealous and Tripp couldn't have her now. Camila was his.

Tripp helped his brother into bed, hoping that was the last of the insane talk. The next morning, Patrick came out to the barn upset because Tripp had mentioned to his parents that he thought there were drugs at the party. He told Patrick he needed to stop and think about what he was doing and that he didn't need the drugs. Patrick became subdued, saying that was easy for Tripp to say because the girls loved him. Then all of a sudden he became angry, saying Camila was his and Tripp couldn't have her. Tripp tried to tell him he didn't even know Camila and Patrick wasn't making sense. That made

Patrick angrier. He ran out of the barn before Tripp could stop him. He climbed into the Corvette his parents had given him as a graduation present and yelled that he wasn't coming back.

And he didn't.

He died two hours later.

One of the ranch hands told his father about the argument and Griffin wanted to know what was going on with Tripp and "that tramp." Tripp told him the truth and Griffin didn't believe him, just as Griffin didn't believe a word about the drugs. And Patrick had already told his father that Tripp had come on to Camila at the party. His father accused Tripp of the unforgivable, hurting his brother when Tripp could have had any woman he wanted.

Tripp was well aware that Patrick envied him, but he'd always thought they'd had a good relationship. The kids at school called him a nerd, a geek, and Patrick just wanted to be popular. He'd asked Tripp a dozen times about how to fit in. His baby brother had been a sweet kid and a lot of the nice kids had liked him, but Patrick had never seen how people had admired his soft-hearted, caring personality.

Like Jilly's.

Tripp crossed the cattle guard to Lady Luck. After his brother's death, he hadn't thought he'd ever return here. When the sheriff had come with the news of Patrick's accident, it was a day Tripp would never forget. His life, his whole world had changed.

As had his parents.

They blamed Tripp for upsetting Patrick. He'd been told to leave and never come back. Later, Tripp had realized they'd spoken out of grief and he'd called home, but his parents wouldn't talk to him. Even while he'd buried himself in the rodeo circuit, a day hadn't gone by that he hadn't thought of Patrick. Of his parents.

Guilt was his constant companion.

He'd cursed himself many times for that night, for the way he'd handled it. He'd cursed Camila, too.

Now, he had a chance to ease some of that guilt. He had to find out if Jilly was Patrick's, and he knew where to start— by asking the people in Bramble.

Chapter Three

After Tripp's visit, Camila managed to calm her shaky nerves. She fought hard against the memories of that night. She only prayed Tripp stayed out of their lives.

They ate supper and Jilly went to her room to finish her homework. Camila called Betty Sue and talked about the girls' punishment. They agreed keeping them apart for a week would suffice.

As Camila finished cleaning the kitchen, Millie stopped by. She'd gone to Brenham to visit her sister who was in a nursing home.

Millie took one look at Camila's face and asked, "What's wrong, kid?"

Camila folded a dish towel. "That's the same thing you asked me when you found me at the bus stop all those years ago."

Millie dropped into a chair. "Yeah. One of the luckiest days of my life. I found the most beautiful young woman—inside and out. I'm so proud of you. You and Jilly have brightened my life. I'd be a sour old widow woman by now if not for the two of you."

"Thank you." Camila blinked away a tear. "It was a lucky day for me, too. I'm not sure what would've happened to me if you hadn't taken me in hand."

"Pleeeaase." Millie rolled her eyes. "Don't you know by now that you're a survivor?"

She did. But those insecurities from her childhood sometimes weighed heavily upon her, especially when people questioned her child's paternity.

"How's your sister?" Camila asked, not wanting to think about Tripp anymore.

"Pretty good. I enjoyed visiting with her and I stayed at my niece's catching up." Millie looked around. "Where's Jilly?"

"In her room." She told her what Jilly had done and about Tripp's visit.

Millie's blue eyes blazed with fury. "He has some nerve coming here." Millie had red hair, or used to—these days it came out of a bottle. She wasn't letting anyone see her gray. But the quick temper was real. Everyone in Bramble knew better than to get on her wrong side. "I hope you told him to go to hell."

"No. But he got the message." Camila sucked in a breath. "He wants to know if Patrick is Jilly's father."

"It's a little late for that."

"I should forget about it, but Jilly made the first move. After I talked with her, I could see she's curious about the Danielses. She's curious about her father. What am I going—"

"Nothing," Millie told her. "That's what you're going to do. Absolutely nothing. Because if Tripp hurts Jilly or you, he'll have me and the whole town to contend with."

"Not the whole town."

"The Boggses don't count."

Camila managed a small smile, but it soon faded. "I feel as if I've failed as a mother. I didn't know Jilly had these feelings about her father. I thought we were able to talk about anything."

"She's turning into a teenager and you're not going to know everything she's thinking and feeling. So stop beating yourself up."

"I guess."

Millie watched her. "So why didn't you tell Tripp that Patrick is Jilly's father? All it would have taken was one little word."

Camila tucked a stray tendril behind her ear. "I guess it was the way he asked—kind of like I might not know and could Patrick be a possible candidate."

Millie's eyes softened. "Sweetie, everyone in this town knows Patrick is the father. It's not a secret or a mystery to anyone but the Danielses and a few hypocrites who don't deserve a second thought."

Millie was talking about the Boggses. They controlled the town. Melvin Boggs was president of the school board and his brother Earl was also on the board. Their brother Bert was mayor and superintendent of schools. Camila had gone to school with Wallis Boggs and Vance Boggs, sons of Earl and Bert. They told lies about her and their parents had believed them—even to this day.

Of all the Boggses, she liked Melvin the best. He was always nice to her and he had two daughters who were older and had moved away from Bramble. His twin sons, Max and Mason, were a year younger than Camila and she had very little contact with them. Maybe that's why she got along with him.

Betty Sue had married Max. Camila and Betty Sue had known each other in school, but hadn't been close either. When Max had left his wife for another woman and had moved to Temple, Texas, Camila became Betty Sue's friend. Betty Sue had told her that she'd never believed any of the rumors the boys had spread around—she knew they were just angry that Camila had rebuffed them.

Camila placed the dish towel on the counter. "One night out of my life and I can't seem to get past it or the repercussions."

"That's what happens when you're in love with two brothers."

Camila whirled around. "Don't say that—especially out loud."

"It's not a sin to care for one brother and love another."

"Please, Millie. I don't want to talk about this—ever."

"Okay." Millie got to her feet. "You were a teenager with hormones raging out of control. That's life, all women go through it, but it doesn't make you a tramp. Please understand that."

Camila didn't answer. She couldn't. After that night at the Danielses', she'd believed that about herself—she was like Benita, tempting men. She was to blame for everything that had happened. She was to blame for Patrick acting the way he had.

Tripp coming back had opened up those old wounds. She was struggling to understand them and to understand herself.

"I'm going home to soak in a hot bath," Millie said, heading for the door. "Oh." She stopped. "Almost forgot what I came over here for. I went by the bakery to check on things and Benita called."

"Did she say what she wanted?"

"No, sweetie. The less I say to that woman the better off I am."

Millie blamed Benita for not being there when Camila had needed her. Benita blamed Millie for sticking her nose where it didn't belong.

"Did she leave a message?"

"No."

"I suppose she'll call back." Despite all the turmoil in their relationship, Camila still worried about her mother.

"Or maybe she'll just disappear for good," Millie muttered under her breath as she went out the door.

Camila sighed, but she couldn't stop worrying. Maybe Benita was back in town, at Alta's house. She grabbed her purse and called to Jilly, "I'm going to check Benita's house. I'll be right back."

"Why can't I go?"

"You're grounded."

"Awww," her daughter replied.

"Finish the essay you have to write."

Within minutes, she drove into her grandmother's driveway. Alta had lived in the older section of Bramble in a white frame house that her husband, Charles, had built a few years after they had married. Camila had stayed in the house until she'd bought her own.

She entered with her key. For a moment, she soaked up the dark and quiet house. Clearly Benita was not here. Suddenly memories of arguments between her and her mother beat at her. Benita couldn't understand why Camila didn't want to live here, but then her mother didn't really know her. Camila turned and went back to the comfort and warmth of her own home. She had more urgent matters to worry about.

Like Tripp Daniels.

TRIPP FIXED THE DOORBELL then spent the day cleaning house. He hated it, but the place was a mess so he didn't have much choice. By mid-afternoon he had all the plumbing problems fixed, the laundry done and his parents' room cleaned. They complained the whole time that he was bothering them and for him to run along and do something else. He yelled so much at Morris that his throat was sore but the old man still didn't hear half of what he'd said. But he'd helped and Tripp couldn't decide if that was a plus or a minus.

He took a break and drank a cup of coffee, wondering if he ever was going to get this place back into shape. He needed to call Brodie again, but decided to wait. After his estrangement from his family, his rodeo friends had become his family. But there had always been a part of him that yearned for home. Again he realized he should have come back years ago to sort through the pain of Patrick's death.

Most of the night he'd thought about Camila and Jilly. Was Jilly Patrick's? If she was, why wouldn't Camila admit it?

In the den, his mom was listening to music and his dad was

watching a basketball game. They were in different parts of the room and both had the volume turned up high. Tripp shook his head and went in search of Morris. He found him on the patio, feet propped up, puffing on one of his father's cigars, the smoke spiraling above his head.

Tripp opened one of the French doors and stepped out. Morris crushed the cigar in an ashtray and swung to his feet. "Mr. Tripp," he said in a guilty voice.

Tripp didn't care that he was smoking cigars. He only cared that Morris looked out for his parents.

"I'm going into town. Please keep an eye on Mom and Dad."

"Always do."

"Don't worry about supper, I'll bring something from the Bramble Rose."

Morris looked around. "There's no roses. It's too early. It's just February."

Tripp stepped closer. "I'll bring something for supper," he said louder.

"Oh. Gotcha."

Tripp headed for his truck wondering how his parents had survived all these years without someone to guide them. After one week, he was totally exhausted. He'd check if there was someone in town who could provide some help. They all clearly needed it.

He drove into Bramble, which was barely a stop in the road. It consisted of main street that had businesses on both sides, mostly antique and gift shops, and a dollar store. There was a bank, a diner, two gas stations, a small grocery store, a feed store, and a hardware store and lumberyard. They also had a Dairy Queen.

Railroad tracks ran along the west side. On the east side was the residential area with the schools and city offices. Some people had lived here all their lives, only going farther to Temple or Austin when needed.

He stopped at the diner. A sign across the street read Common Threads—Camila's Quilts, Soaps and Gifts. Could it be? There was only one Camila that he knew of in Bramble. Without a second thought, he strolled toward the shop. As he went in, the bell tinkled over the door. A natural pleasing fragrance, like a flower garden, greeted him.

The walls were a pale lavender and shelves were filled with baskets of soaps in decorative boxes and some sort of see-through fabric. Folded quilts decorated racks and there was a special area for baby quilts. A couple of women oohed and aahed over one, clutching a box in their hands. The lavender box had a *C* written on it in calligraphy.

He removed his hat and spoke. The women eyed him with a strange look. He walked to the counter where a young girl was putting a quilt in a box; which was adorned with a fancy needle and thread logo.

"Can I help you?" the girl asked.

"I'm looking for Camila Walker."

"She's in the back."

"Thanks, I'll—"

"You can't go—" The girl stopped as another woman interrupted with asked a question.

Tripp went through the door to a large back room. Two quilting frames with quilts in them hung from the ceiling. One wall held spools of thread of every color. At the back were rows of fabric and a large table the size of a king-size bed, obviously a working area. A sewing machine was in a corner.

He didn't see Camila. There was another door and he opened it. A pungent smell almost sent him reeling back, but then he saw her. Camila, in rubber gloves and apron, was stretching plastic wrap over large molds of soap.

She glanced up, startled, her dark eyes like lasers ready to cut him in half. "What are you doing here?"

"I wanted to apologize for my rudeness last night."

"I don't allow people back here," she said in a sharp tone.

He should leave, but he couldn't. He was curious. Intrigued. "Are you making soap?"

"Yes." She continued to work with quick, sure movements, covering all the molds, then she placed boards on top and covered the whole thing with blankets.

"What are you doing?"

"The soap has to be kept warm while it sets for twenty-four hours. I then clean and wrap it, but it has to cure for three to four weeks before I sell it."

He twitched his nose in distaste. "What's that smell?"

Her eyes softened for a second. "It's the lye. This batch is almond scent and olive oil."

"Very impressive operation you have here."

She turned to face him, her dark eyes back in laser mode. "You said what you wanted to, now please leave."

Tripp nodded, knowing it was time to back off. Camila wasn't too friendly and he couldn't blame her—not after suggesting the DNA test. That was way out of line. Even a blundering cowboy knew that.

He headed across the street to the diner, straddling a stool at the counter. With plastic red gingham tablecloths and chrome-and-plastic tables and chairs, the place was a typical diner, like he'd seen all over the country. A jukebox stood in a corner and country music played in the background.

Melvin and Bert Boggs sat at a table and Tripp nodded in their direction.

"Hey, handsome, what'll you have?" Rose, a woman close to seventy, but nonetheless spry and energetic for her age wore an apron over jeans and a T-shirt. Her blondish-gray hair coiled at the back of her head had a pencil stuck in it. She'd owned the diner as long as he could remember and still looked the same.

"Coffee, and do you have any suggestions for supper for my parents?"

"Mmm." Rose poured a cup of coffee. "They're not doing too good?"

"They're just getting older."

"Aren't we all, hon." She placed the coffee in front of him with a napkin. "But you're looking mighty fine. Where you been all these years?"

"All over. Settled around Mesquite."

"That's too far away, hon."

"Yeah." He took a swallow of coffee and thought he'd steer the conversation back to the matter at hand. "So do you have anything I can take home?"

"Grif loves my meat loaf and it's on the menu today with all the trimmings, even homemade corn bread. How does that sound?"

"Great, I'll take three orders for my parents and Morris but I'll take a chicken-fried steak. No one can beat your steak, Rose."

"Now, hon. You're gonna make me blush." She turned toward the kitchen and Tripp thought her blushing days were probably over.

He glanced out the window and saw Camila loading packages into a Suburban. What was she doing?

"Watching her, huh? All the guys watch her."

He swung around to face Rose. "What?"

She gestured toward the window. "Camila. All the men watch her, but that's all they do."

"I've heard differently."

"Depends on who you listen to." She refilled his cup. "Once you get to know Camila, you'll soon realize the truth."

"Which is?"

Rose lifted an eyebrow. "Now, hon, you need to find that out for yourself."

His eyes strayed back to Camila with her arms full of lavender boxes. "Is she taking those somewhere?" The more he learned about Camila, the more curious he became.

"Boy, you've been gone too long. Camila bought out Millie's gift shop and she makes homemade soaps and quilts she sells over the Internet. She's going to the post office."

"Looks like she's doing very well."

"You bet, hon. Never seen anyone work harder."

The bell over the door jingled and Jilly ran in. She paused when she saw Tripp. "Oh, hi, Mr. Daniels."

"Hi, Jilly."

"Hi there, hon," Rose said. "What do you need today?"

"When I finish helping Mama, I'm going to put out Mrs. Shynosky's trash and I thought I'd take her a piece of your coconut pie 'cause she likes it."

"You got it, hon."

Jilly fished in the pockets of her jeans and pulled out some change. "Oh, wait a minute. I have to get more money."

"That's okay," Tripp offered. "I'll pay for it."

"No." Jilly shook her head. "I can't take your money. I'll get some from Mama." She darted out the door before he could stop her.

She talked to Camila and soon Jilly came running back. She laid the correct change on the counter and picked up the Styrofoam box. "Thanks, Rose." Then she was gone.

"Does she do that often?" Tripp asked.

"All the time," Rose replied. "We call her the angel of Bramble. I tried giving her the pie, but Camila makes her pay."

He remembered last night and Jilly's offer to help his parents. He thought that was unusual, but then, Jilly seemed to be an unusual girl. Then again, maybe not—Patrick had been the same way.

Tripp's grandmother had lived with them until her death. Their paper had been delivered to the mailbox at the road and Patrick would ride his bike every morning to get the paper so she could read it with her coffee. When Leona had discovered a rat in the house, she'd had Morris set a trap. Patrick had had a fit, unable to stand the thought of killing the rat. He'd promised to hunt it down and catch it, which he had. He kept it in a cage until the rat had died from old age. So many similar episodes ran through Tripp's mind. Patrick had been soft-hearted and kind and…

The bell over the door jingled again and Vance and Wallis Boggs came in. They had been in Patrick's year at school, but Tripp wasn't sure what kind of friends they'd been.

Melvin and Bert walked over and they all shook hands. "Damn. It's good to have you back in Bramble," Melvin said.

"Yeah, have a cup of coffee with us," Vance invited.

"Sure," Tripp replied.

"Got to get back to work," Melvin said. "Maybe another time."

"Me, too," Bert said, and the brothers left.

"Coffee, Rose," Vance yelled as they sat at a table.

"Keep your britches on, junior. I'll be there in a minute."

They talked about casual stuff and Wallis watched Camila out the window. Jilly climbed into the passenger side and they drove off.

"Can I ask y'all a question?" Tripp asked. He wanted answers, but doing this made his gut ache.

"Sure," they answered simultaneously.

"Do y'all believe that Patrick is Jilly Walker's father?"

"Hell, man," Vance snickered. "That's a million-dollar question. She could be anybody's."

"I was gone a lot back then so I don't know that much about Camila Walker."

"Every man in Bramble has had her," Wallis said. "Don't lose any sleep over it."

Rose placed the cups of coffee on the table. Tripp gripped his warm cup. "So y'all have slept with her?"

"All the time in high school." Wallis laughed. "Camila was always an easy lay."

Tripp stared at Wallis. "Patrick said just the opposite."

"What do you mean?" His voice became defensive.

"He said she was a nice girl." He'd heard Patrick tell his parents that many times, to no avail.

Wallis waved a hand. "Patrick believed that about everybody."

"Yeah." Tripp shoved back his chair. "Even you boys."

Vance glared at him. "What does that mean?"

"Anything you want it to." Tripp walked to the counter, paid for his coffee and the dinners Rose had ready for him. He thanked Rose, picked up the bag and left.

Once you get to know Camila, you'll soon realize the truth. That's what Rose had said. He doubted he'd find the truth listening to the rumors in this small town.

He drove through the residential area, taking a shortcut to Lady Luck. He stopped as he saw Jilly lugging a trash can to the road at Mrs. Shynosky's. Her bike was parked near the house.

As he watched her, something else became clear in his head. He didn't need a DNA test to prove that Jilly was Patrick's. All he had to do was look at this little girl and see her loving heart that was open to everyone—just like his brother.

Tripp stopped and got out to help her.

"You didn't have to do that," she said, blinking nervously.

"I know, but I wanted to."

She stared openly at him.

"What?" he asked.

"Did Patrick look like you?"

"Some. We have the same blond hair and blue eyes."

"That's what my mama said." She shuffled her feet. "I'm sorry I bothered you the other day."

"You didn't bother me," he assured her. "It was a pleasure to meet you."

"Really?" Her dark eyes opened wide.

"Yes. Really." He smiled. "And you're welcome at Lady Luck any time."

She smiled back. "Thanks. I gotta go. Mrs. Shynosky likes me to tell her what's going on in Bramble. I'll tell her the cowboy has returned. Bye."

"Bye, Jilly." He walked to his truck with a swing in his step.

Yes, Jilly was Patrick's.

Now he had to convince his parents of that.

Chapter Four

Camila locked up for the day and dropped her keys in her purse. Bert Boggs came out of the bank two doors down. "Had a good week, Camila?" he asked, a touch of sarcasm in his voice.

"Yes. Thank you," she replied as politely as she could. She disliked Bert intensely and his son, Vance, even more.

"Just make sure that all you're selling in there are homemade soaps and quilts."

Anger jolted through her. "Excuse me?"

"I know all about you, Camila. I'm not easily fooled like the other people in this town. I'm keeping an eye on you."

She swung her purse strap over her shoulder. "And I'm keeping an eye on you, Bert. If you get slack as mayor, I'll be running for your position next election."

"Why you—"

"Have a good evening." She walked to her car before Bert could say anything else. She'd parked out front earlier because it was her post-office day. If she'd just parked in back, this confrontation could have been avoided. But she wasn't hiding, even though she hated the way people like Bert made her feel—like a tramp.

Sometimes she wondered why she stayed in this town, although she knew it was because of Jilly. Jilly loved it here and everyone loved her. Camila started the engine and took a breath. It had been a stressful day. Tripp coming into her shop had sent her blood pressure into orbit. She just wanted him to go away and leave them alone. Jilly had said he'd been in the diner and her nerves had coiled into knots as she'd waited for another confrontation. He hadn't returned.

But she knew she hadn't seen the last of Tripp.

THAT EVENING SHE SPENT with her daughter. Since Jilly was grounded, Camila and Jilly made popcorn and gave each other a manicure and a pedicure. They laughed and giggled like teenagers and Camila realized this wasn't much of a punishment. When it came to her daughter, she was weak.

Later, she brushed Jilly's long hair.

"Mama?"

"Hmm?"

"Mr. Daniels helped me pull Mrs. Shynosky's trash can to the curb."

Camila forced herself to keep brushing even though her nerves were as tight as strings on a guitar. "Did he?"

"Yeah. He seems nice."

"I suppose he is."

"Mama?"

Camila knew what was coming next. It was like standing on a railroad track and hearing the whistle of a train and not being able to move or do anything, just wait for the inevitable. Wait for the pain.

The brush stilled in her hand. "What, baby?"

"You said I could talk to you about anything."

"Yes." The whistle shrilled louder.

They were sitting on the floor in front of the fire. Jilly had her back to her and she turned to face Camila.

"I want to go see my grandparents."

The train hit Camila then and she struggled to breathe, to

survive—for Jilly. She reached for her daughter and held her, praying that she could do this.

"Baby." She stroked Jilly's hair. "The Danielses believe that Patrick isn't your father and I don't want them to hurt your feelings."

Jilly raised her head. "It's okay, Mama. I just want to see if they're okay. If they're mean to me, I'll just come home. And Mr. Daniels said I could visit any time I wanted."

Camila couldn't speak.

"You said I could see them if I wanted to."

Now she had to eat those words. But she was wondering why Tripp had made such an offer if he didn't believe Patrick was Jilly's father. Why couldn't he stay out of their lives?

She swallowed. "Yes. I did." She couldn't stop this—just like she couldn't stop the train wreck of emotions. But it didn't make it easy.

"And Mr. Daniels will be there and he's nice."

Nice and dangerous.

Camila took a hard breath. "Okay."

Jilly gave her a kiss. "Thank you, Mama."

She pushed Jilly's hair back. "Do you want me to take you?"

"No. I can ride my bike."

"I don't like you riding alone."

"Mama." Jilly sighed in an aggravated way. "This is Bramble and everyone knows me. I'm not a baby."

"Still, take my cell phone so I can come and get you if anything happens." She had to have a way to stay in touch, with her daughter.

"Okay."

"When do you want to do this?" *Please, Jilly. Change your mind.*

"Tomorrow after I get through helping you in the store."

It was obvious Jilly had this all planned—probably for a long time. Now Camila had to let it happen. How did she do that? How did she make this easy for both of them? Camila soon realized there wasn't a set way, but she'd handle it as best as she could.

"I'd rather you went right after lunch. I don't want you on the road after dark and it gets dark early."

"Okay." Jilly hugged her. "I'll be fine."

Camila ran her finger down Jilly's nose. "You're growing up too fast."

Jilly smiled her beautiful smile and Camila wished she could freeze this moment in time—keep Jilly innocent and safe. Keep Jilly with her. But that was unrealistic.

"Oh. I almost forgot," Jilly said. "Mrs. Shynosky's daughter sent her some banana-nut bread and she gave me some. She said she couldn't eat the whole thing and she'd rather have the pie that I'd brought her. So I took it to Miss Unie."

"That was sweet of you."

"But I think she gave it to Lu Lu. Miss Unie doesn't eat much."

"I took her a gallon of milk and a loaf of bread earlier so she has some food."

"Why is she so stubborn about accepting things?"

Camila rubbed Jilly's arm. "Unie wants to be independent and she doesn't like charity."

"So you told her they were throwing the milk and bread out at the grocery store and she took it."

"Yes." Her daughter knew her well. Camila had pulled that trick on Unie before just to make sure she had something to eat.

"You're smart, Mama."

"Thank you."

Jilly settled comfortably in her arms. "Mama?"

"Hmm?"

"I'm worried about Benita."

Camila tensed.

"She hasn't called in a long time."

"Benita lives her own life, but she did call the other day. I was out, though. She'll come home when she's ready."

"Well, the next time I see Benita, I'm gonna tell her that's mean."

Camila wrapped her arms around her daughter, wanting to protect and shield her, but Jilly was fiercely independent. She'd always been that way.

Later, Camila curled up in bed dreading tomorrow. Dreading letting go of Jilly. Dreading the thought of anyone hurting her.

Before sleep claimed her, she drifted back through the years. She was seventeen and Tripp was holding her. She was floating on a cloud with her body pressed against the hardened muscles of his. Excitement mounted inside her, excitement like she'd never felt before. And she hated herself for that reaction. Never again would she degrade herself like that.

Never.

TRIPP LEFT MORRIS to finish cleaning the kitchen and followed his parents into the den. He turned off the TV.

"What'd you do that for?" Griffin frowned at him.

"Because it doesn't need to be on twenty-four hours a day," Leona snapped.

"I can watch sports if I want to." Griffin reached for the control.

"Dad, have a seat," Tripp said, holding the remote out of his reach. "I need to talk to both of you."

"What?" Grif eased into his chair. "You're going to leave so go ahead and tell us and get it over with."

"Oh, no." His mother began to cry.

"Wait a minute. I'm not going anywhere just yet." He handed Leona some tissues and guided her to a chair. He then sat facing them. "We need to talk about Patrick."

"No, no, no," Leona cried into the tissue.

"Son, why do you want to do this? Can't you see how much it hurts your mother?"

"Yes, and it hurts me, too. But I've met someone I think you need to meet."

"A woman?" Grif lifted an eyebrow.

Leona wiped her eyes and stared at him. "Who?"

"A young girl." He paused "Jilly Walker."

His father looked puzzled. "Who's that?"

"Camila Walker's daughter. Patrick's friend from high school."

Leona shook her head. "Oh, no, no."

"Yes, Mom. I feel Jilly is Patrick's daughter."

"Like hell," Grif scoffed. "Camila slept around—everyone knows that. How can you say such a thing?"

"Because I've met the girl. She has a lot of Patrick's characteristics."

Grif pushed to his feet. "Do not bring that girl into this house, Tripp. I forbid it." He picked up his cane and shuffled to his room. Leona got up and followed him.

Tripp buried his face in his hands. His parents were never going to accept Jilly.

That bothered him more than he ever thought possible.

THE NEXT DAY Jilly went back and forth from the gift shop to the coffee shop—not able to sit still or concentrate on anything. It was obvious Jilly was nervous. Camila was, too, but she hid it better than her daughter.

Camila folded a baby quilt and put it in a box for a lady. She rang it up and told Amber, one of her helpers, that she'd be back in a minute. In the coffee shop, she caught Jilly by the arm and pulled her to a table.

"You don't have to do this today. You can think about it for a while."

Jilly wagged her head. "No, Mama. I want to do it."

Camila wished she knew what to do, wished she could stop Jilly's thoughts about Patrick, wished she could've stopped Tripp from returning to Bramble. But she couldn't. Just like she had no control over the past. She chewed on the inside of her lip.

Just tell her you've changed your mind and she can't go. Just say no.

She couldn't do that, either.

"Well, go now."

Jilly perked up. "Okay." She launched to her feet.

Camila hugged her. "If they say anything mean to you, come home immediately."

"I will, Mama, and don't worry. I'll take Button with me."

"Get my phone out of my purse. I want to be able to call you."

"Okay. Bye." In a flash, Jilly was gone.

Camila opened her mouth to call her back, then closed it. Millie patted her on the shoulder.

"Please tell me I'm doing the right thing."

Millie shrugged. "I can't. I don't even know what the right thing is in this situation. We'll just have to wait and hope Leona and Grif still have a heart. I mean, who could look at that gorgeous face and not fall in love?"

Camila tried to smile, but failed miserably.

"Go to work," Millie suggested. "Staying busy is the best medicine right now."

Camila took her advice, but she kept wondering if Jilly was there yet. How were they treating her? What was happening? What were they saying to her baby?

Tripp had spent the afternoon riding over the ranch. It upset him that the place was in such bad shape. Pastures were overgrown, mesquite was growing wild again, fences were down and cattle roamed freely from Daniels land onto Boggs property. He'd called Earl several times, but the man never returned any of his calls.

After taking a shower, he changed clothes. He couldn't find any record of the payments Earl had made in the past year. They were going to talk about that, too. He checked on his parents. Grif was glued to the TV and Leona was listening to a book on tape that the nurse had brought her, so he didn't bother them. He'd tell Morris he was leaving, then…

There was a knock at the door.

It would be a waste of time yelling for Morris so he answered it himself. He stopped short when he saw who was standing there. Jilly. She held her dog in her arms, like before.

"Hi, Mr. Daniels. I came to visit like you said."

Oh my God! What should he do now? He couldn't hurt this young girl and he certainly wouldn't let his parents do that either.

"Tripp," Leona called. "Who's at the door?"

What the hell should he do?

"Tripp," Leona called again. Tripp made a decision, hoping Jilly had the same effect on his parents as she'd had on him.

"Come in," he said, stepping aside.

Jilly walked in and he closed the door.

"My parents are in the den. Please understand that they are old and say things that sometimes hurt."

Jilly nodded. "It's okay, Mr. Daniels. I know all about old people."

"Please call me Tripp," he told her. "That's a strong statement for someone so young."

"Tripp!" his mother shouted this time.

"Ready?" he asked Jilly.

"Yes," she answered, clutching the dog, and followed him into the den.

"Mom, Dad, we have a visitor. This is Jilly Walker."

Grif swung around, but didn't say a word. Leona pulled off her headphones, squinting, as if she were trying to see Jilly's face.

Jilly walked to her. "Hi, Mrs. Daniels. I'm Jilly and this is Button." She held up the dog.

"Button? What's a Button?" Leona asked.

"It's a dog," Jilly said. "A Chihuahua. Would you like to touch her?"

"Yes. I like dogs. I used to have a terrier." Jilly placed the dog in Leona's lap and Leona stroked it. Button shivered. "Oh, my. It's a little bitty thing."

"Yes, ma'am," Jilly said. "That's why Mama and me named her Button. I've had her for four years now and I take her everywhere, except when I go to school."

"How old are you, child?"

"I'll be twelve next Saturday."

"Let me see the dog," Grif said. Tripp stepped back and let everything happen naturally.

Jilly carried Button to Grif. "She's a little nervous, but she'll calm down in a minute."

"These type of dogs need a lot of care," Grif told Jilly.

"I give her lots of care and lots of love."

"Let me hold Button," Leona said and Jilly carried the dog back to her.

They did this for about thirty minutes and Tripp was sure Button was getting dizzy.

"How about something to drink?" he suggested.

"Coffee for me, son," Grif said.

"Tea, please," Leona added.

"And you, Jilly?"

"I'll help," she replied. "I'll leave Button with you, Mrs. Daniels."

"Why does she get to keep the dog?" Grif wanted to know. "She can barely see."

"That's not nice, Mr. Daniels," Jilly scolded.

"At my age, girlie, I don't have to be nice."

"Yes, you do."

"Aw," Grif scoffed.

"You can sit by Mrs. Daniels and you both can watch Button."

"I don't like it over there."

Jilly reached for his elbow. "Come on. I'll help you."

Tripp watched in astonishment as his father got to his feet and moved across the room with Jilly holding onto his arm. Once he was settled next to his wife, he reached for the dog.

"You have to be nice," Jilly reminded him.

"He doesn't know the meaning of the word," Leona said.

"I haven't been this close to you in years, Leona, so be careful, I might bite you."

Jilly giggled and his father smiled, something he rarely did. A miracle was unfolding before Tripp and he just watched the wonderful sight.

"I'll be right back," Jilly said, and followed Tripp into the kitchen. Morris was sitting at the table knitting.

"Hi, Morris," Jilly said.

"Ah, hi." Surprise filtered across his face.

"I'm Jilly Walker, remember? I sometimes help you put groceries in your car when you're shopping."

"Yes. I know." The surprise was still imprinted on his face and Tripp realized that Morris knew about Jilly. Probably knew a lot more, too.

"We're fixing tea and coffee for Mom and Dad," Tripp explained. "What would you like, Jilly?"

"Water, please. Mama doesn't want me to drink a lot of soft drinks."

Tripp wondered if Camila knew Jilly was here. He'd deal with that later. He placed everything on a tray.

"I'll carry it," Jilly offered.

He hesitated for a moment then let her carry the tray. Morris watched with a lifted brow as they left.

Jilly set the tray on the coffee table. "What would you like in your coffee, Mr. Daniels?"

"Black as sin."

Jilly grinned and handed him a mug. "Mrs. Daniels, what would you like in your tea?"

"Just a little honey, please."

Jilly stirred in the honey and held the cup out to Leona. When Leona didn't take it, Jilly took her hand and guided it to the cup.

"Oh, thank you."

Jilly sat cross-legged on the floor and Button jumped into her lap and curled into a ball. Tripp sat in a chair, watching, drinking a cup of coffee.

"What grade are you in?" Grif asked.

"Sixth," Jilly replied. "And I make all A's. I'm on the honor roll. I'm going to be a doctor."

"That's a mighty big ambition—and expensive."

"My mama started saving for my college education when I was born. She puts money in the account every month."

"Very wise," Grif murmured.

"And when I work, I put money in the account, too."

"You work?" Leona asked in shock.

"I help at my mama's store and she pays me."

"Do you work a lot?" Leona took a sip of tea.

"Only when my mama lets me. She works real hard and I help out all I can, but my schoolwork has to be done first."

"I see," Grif said and handed Jilly his mug.

Everyone was quiet for a while, then Grif asked, "Jilly, why did you come here today?"

Tripp was immediately on his feet. His one goal was to get Jilly out of the room before his father could say anything hateful or hurtful, but Jilly started talking and he listened like his mother and father did.

"Well, I used to see you in town a lot, but now I only see Morris. I thought you might be sick or something, but I never came out here to check because…" She trailed her fingers across Button's back. "Well, I know you're my grandparents, but I also know you don't believe that. That's okay, 'cause I believe. My mama doesn't lie."

Complete silence followed that statement.

"When I saw Tripp's picture in the paper, I came out here," Jilly continued. "People say that Tripp and Patrick favor and I wanted to see, but when I arrived I got scared and told him who I was and quickly left. My mama didn't know where I was and I didn't want to upset her."

"You've been here before?" Leona asked.

"Just that one time."

"So you believe you're Patrick's daughter?" Grif was stuck on that question.

Jilly turned to Grif. "Yes, sir. I not only believe. I know it."

"Because your mother told you and she doesn't lie."

"Yes, sir."

"Do you have any proof?"

Jilly got to her feet, clutching Button, her chin jutting out. "My mama's word."

"I'm afraid that's not enough for me," Grif said. "You came for money, didn't you?"

"Dad," Tripp reprimanded.

"No, sir, I didn't come for money. I don't need or want it and my mama wouldn't allow it anyway." Jilly gripped Button tighter. "My mama has always said that Patrick was soft-hearted and kind and I guess I came here to feel a part of that—to feel a part of my father. I won't bother you again." She bolted from the room.

"Jilly." Tripp went after her, but Jilly was already on her bike pedaling furiously for Bramble.

Damn. Damn. Damn.

Chapter Five

Tripp slammed the door a little harder than he should have and went back into the den. His parents were arguing.

"You didn't have to be so blunt," his mother was saying.

"Sometimes you have to be to get results."

"She's just a child."

"I agree with Mom," Tripp said. "You were way out of line, Dad. There was no need to hurt Jilly like that."

"They're after our money, son. Can't you see that?"

"Money?" Tripp choked out. "Have you checked your accounts lately? There's very little money left. Take a good look around you—the place is falling apart, the pool is covered with algae, as is the pond out front. The pastures are overgrown and unkempt and there's not much here to make a person think you have money. Jilly Walker just wanted to feel a connection to her father. That's it—no ulterior motive."

Neither had a word to say.

"I'm going after her to try and apologize. I'll be back later."

Tripp caught up with Jilly. He pulled the truck ahead of her, stopped and got out.

Jilly stopped, too, and her dark eyes were wet. He cursed himself for letting the situation get out of hand.

Button was in the basket and she raised up and barked, her

ears pointed, as if sensing Jilly's distress. Jilly patted the dog and looked at Tripp. "What do you want?"

"Thought I'd give you a ride into town."

"I don't accept rides from strangers."

Tripp drew a deep breath. "I'm not a stranger. I'm your uncle." At first, he'd been as stubborn as his father, but now he believed what he was saying.

Her bottom lip trembled and she caught it with her teeth.

"Come on, Jilly. Let me take you home to your mama."

That seemed to be the magic word. Jilly got off the bike and scooped Button into her arms. He lifted the bike into the bed of the truck and they climbed inside.

As they drove into Bramble, Jilly asked, "Do you really mean what you said?"

"Yes, Jilly. I believe you're Patrick's daughter."

"My mama's a good woman and she's kind and helps everybody and—"

"Just give my parents time," he interrupted, seeing how hurt she was. "Patrick's death shattered both of them and they haven't been the same since."

Her head was bent and she didn't say anything.

"Remember you said you knew about old people." He was trying to get her to talk.

"Yeah. But I didn't think it would hurt this much."

"I'm so sorry, Jilly."

She looked at him, her eyes clouded with tears, and he just wanted to make her pain go away. He was searching for the magic words when she spoke up.

"I like you. I think I'll call you Tripp."

"That would make me happy."

"But I'm not going back to see my grandparents."

"That's your decision."

He was hoping to change her mind, though. A few days ago, he'd been acting and thinking like his parents and, in time, he was hoping his father would change his mind, too. He felt his mother was already willing to accept Jilly.

But accepting Camila was another story.

CAMILA GLANCED at the clock and saw it was almost five. It would be dark soon and Jilly should have been back by now. She went into the coffee shop.

"Millie, Jilly's not answering my cell. I'm going home and if Jilly's not there in a few minutes, I'm going after her."

"Okay, sweetie. If you need any help, just call me."

Camila rushed home to an empty house and she felt empty inside. She ran her hands up her arms, her skin feeling sensitive and raw. She shouldn't have let Jilly go. It was too painful. She kept rubbing her arms, trying to dispel the feelings of the past. It was like a rash all over her body and the more she scratched it, the worse it became. And it was contagious. It had spread to Jilly.

All these years she'd protected Jilly, but now she felt so helpless. She couldn't just sit here. She had to do something. She grabbed her purse, then heard a noise. Glancing out the window, she saw Tripp's truck.

Oh my God. What had happened?

She dashed outside.

Jilly tore around the truck and into her arms. Camila held her tight and Button squealed between them. She eased her hold and kissed Jilly's forehead, her hair. "It's okay, baby. You're home."

Jilly darted into the house and Camila's protective instinct was to follow her, but first she had to deal with Tripp.

"What happened?" she asked in a cold voice.

Tripp set Jilly's bike against the garage and let out a long breath. "My father told her he didn't believe Patrick was her father."

She fought the rage ballooning inside her and turned away, but Tripp caught her arm.

She stared down at the fingers wrapped around her. "Let go of me."

His hand immediately fell to his side. "I'm sorry. I just want to talk to you."

"I have nothing to say to you or your family. Stay away from me and stay away from *my* daughter."

She ran after Jilly.

CAMILA FOUND JILLY in her bedroom, lying on the bed crying. Camila's heart broke and she sat down and took her in her arms. "Tell me what happened."

"He said Patrick wasn't my father," Jilly blubbered into her chest.

"Griffin?"

"Uh-huh."

Camila stroked her hair, which had come out of its ponytail. "I tried to prepare you for this."

Jilly raised her tearstained face. "I know, Mama, but it's okay. Now I won't worry about them."

She held Jilly's face with both hands. "Do you think that's possible?"

Jilly frowned. "Why do I worry so much about people?"

"Because you're you." Camila smiled. "Why don't we make spaghetti for supper and I'll call Betty Sue and see if Kerri can come over."

Jilly wiped at her eyes. "But I'm not supposed to see her except in school."

"Mmm." Camila gave it some thought. "That does present a problem, but since I'm in charge and I feel you've been punished enough, I say you're not grounded anymore."

"You're wonderful, Mama."

"I'll run out and get a movie and make popcorn and you and Kerri can have a fun evening."

"What will you do, Mama?"

"Oh, after supper, I'll pull the orders off the computer and fill them."

"But it's Saturday night. You shouldn't be working."

"I'll just be getting a jump start on Monday."

"But, Mama…"

"I'll go call Betty Sue." She stopped at the door. "Why didn't you answer the cell phone?"

"It didn't ring." Jilly fished it out of her pocket. "Oops. It's turned off."

Camila shook her head, walking out. She stopped for a moment. Tears stung her eyes and nausea churned in her stomach. What she'd worked so hard to prevent was happening—Jilly was being hurt. She shouldn't have let her visit the Danielses'.

But Camila knew that wasn't the answer. Jilly had wanted to meet her grandparents and there was no way to stop that. It wasn't easy watching her child go through this.

TRIPP WASN'T SURE what to do so he left—for now. He'd give Camila time to cool off then he'd try to talk to her again. He'd apologize to Jilly again, too.

He passed the Hitchin' Post, a beer joint, on the outskirts of town. Earl Boggs's truck was parked in front, so Tripp stopped and went back. He was in a mood to talk to Earl.

Inside, country music played loudly, smoke filled the room, and men sat at various tables and at the bar. He spotted Earl immediately at a table with his brother, Bert, and two of Earl's sons, Wallis and Otis. Tripp walked over.

"Howdy," he said.

"Tripp." Bert nodded, shaking his hand. "How are your folks?"

"They're doing fine." He glanced at Earl. "Could I speak with you?"

"Sure, boy, but I'm comfortable right here so say what

you have to. Dorie," he shouted to the waitress, "bring another beer."

"No, thanks. I'm not staying. I just wanted to talk to you about the lease you have with my dad."

Earl's eyes narrowed. "What about it?"

"I can't find a copy. Do you have one?"

"A copy." Earl laughed. "Hell, boy, your dad and me did business the old-fashioned way—with our word."

"I can't find any lease deposits either."

"I always pay cash."

"There aren't any cash deposits."

Earl's chair scraped against the wood floor as he pushed to his feet. Tall and slightly balding, Earl had a beer gut that hung over his belt. "Are you saying I'm not paying Grif?"

"I'm saying I want to see some evidence."

"Everyone calm down," Bert said.

"Stay out of this, Bert," Earl snapped and swung his gaze to Tripp. "A big rodeo star, huh? You think you can come in here and flex your muscle. That's bullshit. This is Bramble not Vegas and I don't give a rat's ass what you want to see."

The words were slurred and Tripp knew Earl had had too much to drink, but it didn't stop him.

"Get your cattle off my property."

"Go to hell."

Tripp nodded. "Fine. I'll just round 'em up and sell 'em at the auction. I believe that's on Wednesdays." He leaned in closer. "You see, that's what I learned in my rodeo days—how to round up cattle real good." He turned and walked out.

"You bastard. I'll call the sheriff."

"Go ahead," Tripp shouted over his shoulder.

Inside his truck, he had to take a couple of deep breaths. He couldn't go home. He was too wound up. As angry as he was, though, all he could see was Jilly's hurt face.

And Camila's.

THE GIRLS WERE in the living room eating popcorn and watching a Harry Potter movie that they had seen at least twice. Camila glanced in and saw them do a high five, bump their butts together and do a happy dance. Obviously they liked something in the movie. Jilly was smiling and happy again and that's what mattered to Camila.

She headed for the garage. She'd pulled the orders from the computer and printed the labels earlier. If everything went smoothly, she'd have them finished by midnight then she'd have plenty of time to take Jilly to her basketball game on Tuesday.

A covered walkway connected the house to the detached two-car garage. Camila hurried to the storage shed where she stored the wrapped and labeled soap in plastic containers. In the early days, she'd made the soap at home so she didn't have to leave Jilly. When Jilly had started school, she'd made it in the back room of the shop, but she still did a lot of the packing and mailing from home. That way, she was close if Jilly needed her.

She worked on, trying not to think about the Danielses.

Or Tripp.

THE LAST ORDER PACKAGED, Camila stacked the boxes neatly on the table, then went into the house to check on the girls. She pulled her coat around herself. The temperature had been in the fifties and sixties all week—mild for February. Now it had to be in the forties. She was glad she'd lit Unie's heater earlier. That way she knew she was warm. Since the gas company had turned off her gas, Unie had a hard time understanding it was now on again.

Jilly and Kerri were asleep on the floor. Camila turned off the TV and gently woke them. "Time for bed."

They staggered to Jilly's room in their big T-shirts and crawled into bed like zombies. They wouldn't remember this in the morning. It reminded Camila of when Jilly was smaller and would fall asleep in the car or on the sofa. She'd never remembered anything. She'd been just a baby—and to Camila, she still was.

She rushed back to the garage to finish up.

"Camila."

She swung toward the voice, knocking over a stack of boxes.

"I'm sorry," Tripp said. "I didn't mean to startle you."

"What are you doing here?" she asked, bending to gather the scattered boxes.

Tripp didn't answer. Instead, he squatted and helped. Their hands touched and fire shot up her arm. She jerked back. "Go away and leave us alone." She stood and placed the boxes on the table.

"We have to talk," he said.

"About what?" she asked, unable to keep her anger under control. "My past? My many affairs? My lurid lifestyle?"

"You're angry," he said, unnecessarily.

"Yes. I get angry when someone hurts my child."

"I'm sorry about that. When she showed up, I wasn't sure what to do. But things were going really well. They were talking about Button, about school, then…"

The sincerity in his voice got to her and some of the anger began to dissipate. Standing just inside the garage with the light behind him, he was a silhouette in a lined denim jacket, hat, snug jeans and cowboy boots. She'd seen him like this a million times in her dreams and in her foolish, girlish fantasies. But this wasn't a dream or a fantasy. He was so real it took her breath away.

"My parents have deteriorated since Patrick's death. They don't have any interests and it's like they're marking time. When Jilly showed up that first time, I was impressed with her spirit. She's like a ray of sunshine. Actually, I think she has a halo around her head. That's what gave me the nerve to come and see you. If Jilly could affect me that way, I was hoping she could do the same for my parents."

"You were nervous about seeing me?" She couldn't quite believe that.

"Yes, I mean, you have to have a lot of nerve to ask a woman who's the father of her child. I apologize again for being so rude."

"If you had asked nicely, I would have told you. But you used a tone similar to several people in this town—as if I might not know who the father was."

He winced. "Was I that rude?"

"Yes."

"I'm usually not that inconsiderate. People have told me that I'm quite nice."

Oh, yes, he'd been nice and everything she'd ever dreamed about. But that dream had turned into a nightmare and...

"Are these boxes to mail?" He looked at the boxes stacked on the table.

"Ah...yes. I was going to load them in the Suburban."

"I'll help you."

"No. I don't need..." Her words fell on deaf ears. Tripp had already gathered several boxes and was strolling to the vehicle. She unlocked the back and he placed them inside.

"Is that how you want them?"

"Yes. That's fine."

They worked side by side until all the orders were loaded.

"What's in these boxes?" Tripp asked.

"Lye soap."

"Excuse me?"

Camila wanted to laugh at his expression, but she hadn't gotten to the point of laughing with Tripp.

"You heard correctly. Lye soap, some of it scented with lavender, ginger, eucalyptus, rosemary—all natural fragrances. Some of it's just plain and some is grated to use in the washing machine."

"My grandmother used to make lye soap, but she was never that adventurous."

"I learned from Mrs. Baker, but now I've perfected my own recipe. Of course, I also make other kinds."

"Like the almond and olive oil?"

"Yes."

"Do you make soap at home, too?"

"When Jilly was small I did, but now I make all my soaps at my shop. I package a lot here so I can be home with Jilly."

"Then it sells well?"

"Yes. I have a Web site that details all my soaps and my quilts. The Internet has opened up a big market."

It seemed so odd talking to him standing in the moonlight. It was almost surreal. She didn't even feel the chill of the evening. And she should. She didn't need to get her emotions centered on Tripp again. Not ever.

"But I can make more on one quilt than I can on a week's worth of soap. Homemade quilts are rare and people pay big money for them, but I offer them at a fair price." Why was she telling him this? She'd gotten completely sidetracked. Distracted, was more like it.

"My grandmother has some quilts stored away at the house. Maybe one day you'd like to see them."

The silence became awkward.

"No," she finally said. "I don't want anything to do with the Daniels family."

"I understand, but I hope you'll continue to let me see Jilly."

She pulled her coat around herself, suddenly feeling the chill. "I don't think that's a good idea."

"Why?"

"Because I don't want her hurt again. Your parents can say anything they want about me, but not about Jilly. She doesn't deserve it. She's only a result of the past."

"Once they realize she's a part of Patrick they'll…"

Her gaze clashed with his. "Now you believe she's Patrick's?"

"Yes. I'm not sure what happened back then and it really doesn't matter. I'd like to get to know my niece…and you. If you'll let me."

Was he for real? She had to take a breath and the coolness of the night rushed into her lungs. The decision she made now would be final for Jilly—and her.

Say no. End it. Just say no.

"What about your parents?" came out of her mouth.

"It will take them a while to adjust, but eventually they'll see what a sweet person she is."

He was telling the truth. She'd learned the hard way how to judge people and she knew he meant every word he was saying. Still, she hesitated.

"Maybe you'll let me take her out for a burger or something."

She shoved her hands into the pockets of her jacket. "As I said, I don't think it's a good idea, but once Jilly gets something in her head, it's there to stay. If she wants to see you or her grandparents, I won't stop her. But, please, I would prefer it if you left her alone without any pressure."

"I see."

The chill in the air dropped several degrees and Camila felt it all the way to her heart.

He tipped his hat and walked to his truck

She watched, almost in a stupor. She was doing the right thing.

Or was she?

Chapter Six

Tripp drove home feeling as if things couldn't get any worse. Camila was defensive and angry, and she had a right to be. Although for a brief minute, he could feel her softening, especially when she'd told him about her work. He'd respect her wishes and not pressure Jilly, but he wasn't giving up either. He planned to work on his parents and soon they'd see Patrick in Jilly. Just like he did.

He shifted his thoughts to Earl and wished he hadn't lost his temper. He wasn't apologizing, though. Earl was taking advantage of his father's frailty and Tripp was putting a stop to it.

As he reached the Lady Luck entrance, bright truck lights beamed his way. He kept waiting for the person driving to dim them, but instead the truck picked up speed and headed straight for him, forcing him into the ditch.

Suddenly both doors were yanked opened and someone pulled him out into the grass, driving a fist into his stomach. He came up fighting and, after a brief punching match, he realized he was outnumbered. There had to be at least four men.

Three men held him while another punched him, over and over. A hard blow to his jaw brought him to his knees. They released him and he fell flat on his face, prone in the grass. He didn't get up, knowing there was no way he was going to win this fight.

"Rodeo man, you're not welcome in Bramble." He heard the gruff voice, but he didn't recognize it. A diesel engine roared away, backfiring a couple of times.

Tripp rolled over, gulping air into his bruised lungs. He blinked up at the bright, cold moonlit night, feeling the dull throb in his head.

He had to get up. He had to make it to the house.

His bumper was behind him and he reached back, wincing, and pulled himself into a sitting position. Then, using the bumper, he shoved to his feet. He gulped in more air. His hat was in the grass, but no way was he bending down to pick it up. Moving carefully to the driver's side, he managed to get in. Slowly, he drove to the house.

By the time he parked in the garage, he had his second wind—and he was angry, angrier than he'd been in a long time. He stumbled into the kitchen.

Morris turned from the stove. "Holy cow. You look like you've been whipped with a fence post and a few of the barbs were left on it."

Tripp collapsed into a chair. "I feel like that, too."

Morris filled a pan with warm water and brought it to the table. "Who did this to you?"

"Not sure. Somebody ambushed me at the entrance."

Morris soaked a cloth then began to clean the blood from Tripp's face. "Who's got it in for you?"

"I had a talk with Earl in town and I don't think he liked what I said."

"Earl's a tub of lard. He ain't got the muscle to do this."

"I figure it's some of the boys who work for him."

"Mm-mm-mm." Morris clicked his tongue as he worked. "How bad is it?"

"Your left jaw is turning blue and your eye is going to be black and it has a cut beneath it. I'll get some antiseptic and tape."

Tripp didn't think his ribs were cracked, just bruised. If Earl thought this was the end of it, he was badly mistaken.

Morris came back and finished the job.

"What do you know about Earl?" Tripp asked.

"He's bad—badder than a blue norther in the Panhandle in the dead of winter in a house without no heat and…"

Tripp turned to stare at him, at least with his one good eye. He was having a normal conversation with Morris, without shouting, as when he was a kid and Morris would say things that didn't make a lot of sense. But Tripp always liked to listen to him.

"You old dog. You've been faking," Tripp said. "There's nothing wrong with your hearing."

Morris plopped into a chair, his face slightly red. "Damn, and I was doing so good. Seeing your battered face got me off my rhythm."

Tripp touched his swollen jaw. "Why would you pretend not to hear?"

Morris shifted uneasily. "It started with the townsfolk asking questions, questions that were none of their business. If I said *what* repeatedly or gave some ass-backward answer, they'd leave me alone. Then you came home and I figured it would work really good. If you saw that I couldn't hear, then you'd realize your parents needed help, needed you, and you'd stay for a while."

Ah, guilt, the little chip on his shoulder, the footprint on his conscience. Tripp couldn't fault Morris for his motives or his concern, though. Morris had been a part of the family forever. He'd started working as a ranch hand before Tripp was born. He broke his leg one winter and Grif had brought him to the house to recuperate. A couple of months later, the housekeeper had quit and Morris had helped out with the cooking. He liked to cook.

Leona had been pregnant at the time and as Morris's leg had healed he'd helped out wherever he could. He also liked housework. Morris was an odd parody. It was a common sight to see Morris sitting and knitting, something he'd learned from his mother. He wore jeans, boots and a western shirt with an apron in the house, and drove Leona around in a Cadillac. Morris never did ranch work unless extra help was needed.

"Don't pull that on me again," Tripp said. "And I don't plan on going anywhere just yet."

Morris folded his hands on the table. "That's mighty good to hear." He looked at Tripp. "What was the Walker kid doing here?"

"She came to meet her grandparents."

"Well, if that don't knock me plumb off the fence." Morris reached for the pan of water and carried it to the sink.

Tripp watched him, knowing Morris acted as dumb as a post, but he was as shrewd as a fox. "You know Jilly is Patrick's daughter, don't you?"

"I don't know nothin'." Morris had his back to Tripp, pouring water down the drain.

Tripp decided to go at it from another angle. "How often did Patrick bring Camila out here?"

"Not often—just when your parents were away or you were home. Patrick wanted to impress her with his rodeo-star big brother."

Tripp winced, not from the pain of his battered face or his bruised ribs, but for not recognizing the signs—that Patrick had used him to impress Camila. Patrick had been eager to show Camila Tripp's awards and trophies and he'd asked Tripp all kinds of questions about the rodeo in front of her. Tripp should have put a stop to it.

Patrick had had low self-esteem and Tripp had known that. He'd also known Patrick had been in love with Camila, so he'd gone along with whatever Patrick had wanted, but Tripp had kept his distance from Camila. Sometimes that had been hard to do, especially when she'd asked questions about the rodeo.

But when he'd noticed Patrick's stormy face, he'd backed off immediately.

Tripp had never understood why Patrick had kept drawing him into their relationship. Maybe because Camila had seemed more interested in Tripp than Patrick. He was glad his parents hadn't allowed Camila at the ranch. That had kept the visits limited—only when Patrick could sneak her past his parents.

That's why it had been such a shock when Patrick had invited her to the graduation party.

That damn graduation party. He should have kept his cool and left the teenagers to their own devices. But he couldn't just let Camila fall to the floor. He still didn't understand what had happened next. He wondered if he ever would. Camila didn't seem like a tramp to him. She was a loving, caring mother—that was obvious to everyone. So what had happened that night?

"Morris, when Camila was here, did you ever see them—mmm—together?"

Morris wiped his hands on a towel. "Whada'ya mean? Doing the nasty?"

Tripp met his eyes. "Yeah."

"Patrick was like a lovesick pup over her, but she always seemed skittish, shy, except when you were here."

He suppressed a groan and thought it best to get off the subject. His aching body couldn't take much more.

"Tell me about Earl. When was the last time he paid Dad lease money?"

Morris took a seat. "A little over a year ago."

"That's the last entry I saw on the books. Did Dad ever ask Earl for the money?"

"Yep. Sent me, too."

"And what happened?"

"I saw Earl in town and I told him the lease money was overdue. He told me I'd better mind my own business if I knew what was good for me."

"Did you try again?"

"Yep. Several times. We were short on money and I had to let go of the cleaning and yard and pool people. At my age, I couldn't keep up with a place this size. I ain't never seen Lady Luck like this, but the last time I asked Earl for money, one of his boys twisted my arm behind my back and said if I asked one more time he'd break it. I couldn't let nothing happen to me—there was no one else to take care of your parents."

The guilt intensified. How could Tripp undo thirteen years? How could he undo the past? Holding the table, he pushed to his feet. "Where's Mom and Dad?"

"In their room."

"I'll check on them."

"How you gonna explain your face?"

"I don't think they'll notice."

"Maybe not."

He went along to his parents' room on the ground floor. His mother was lying in a lounger in her gown listening to the book on tape. Her eyes were closed but he knew she wasn't asleep. It was so strange seeing her hair, which had turned completely white within a month of Patrick's death.

His father sat in his pajamas on one of the twin beds, cursing at a basketball game on the TV. It was even harder to see his father this way. He'd always been active, up early taking care of the ranch, staying in the saddle most days. There wasn't a thing he didn't know about cattle or horses. He'd taught Tripp everything he knew about riding, how to accept defeat graciously, how doing his best was all that was expected of him. And how family was the most important thing.

That's why Grif saw Tripp's interest in Camila as betrayal. To Patrick. And to family. Even though Grif considered Camila trash, the very idea that Tripp would try to come between her and Patrick had angered him. Tripp had tried to explain that he'd had no interest in Camila and that Patrick had blown the whole incident out of proportion because of the drugs he'd been on. That had made Grif even angrier.

God. He had to stop thinking about it.

He eased into a chair by his mother. "Dad, shut off the TV. I need to talk to both of you."

"Son, I ain't in a mood to talk."

"Shut it off."

"Hmmph," Grif complained, but clicked it off.

Leona removed the headphones and sat up. "What is it?"

"It's about Jilly."

"Is she okay?"

"She's back with her mother, but no, she's not okay. Dad hurt her and there was no reason for that."

"Sometimes, son, you can't pull your punches."

"This isn't a damn boxing match. It's an eleven-year-old girl."

"She couldn't give me any proof," Grif muttered. "I want proof."

"Look into her eyes. Listen to her voice—you'll have your proof."

"I need more than that," Grif said with Daniels stubbornness. "All it takes is a simple little blood test to prove the girl is Patrick's. Camila Walker hasn't done that and never will because she knows the truth."

"Do you know the truth?" Tripp snapped.

Grif's eyebrows knotted together. "What do you mean?"

"The truth, Dad? Do you have proof Jilly is not Patrick's? That's what you're saying the truth is, right?"

Grif remained silent, but the creases on his forehead were deep enough to hold gravy, as Morris would say.

"If you're basing your conclusion on the rumors from those idiots in town, then you're not as smart as I've always believed."

"Rumors start somewhere."

Yeah. In every man's head who ever looked at Camila Walker—including myself.

Tripp got to his feet, managing not to wince. There was only one way to get through to his father—to be as hard-nosed as he was.

"Bottom line—that's what you've always taught me. Bottom line, son, look at the bottom line. Well this is the bottom line, Dad. Can you live the rest of your life knowing you rejected Patrick's daughter?"

Griffin didn't answer again.

"Stubborn old man," Leona spat. She went to her bed and crawled in. "I'm glad I don't have to share the same bed as you."

"Believe me, it's a blessing to me, too," Grif replied.

"I'm not listening to that TV all night, Grif," Leona warned. "Leave it off."

Tripp walked over to his mother. "Mom, do you believe that Jilly is Patrick's?"

"There's just something about Jilly," Leona answered, fluffing her pillows. "Every night when I go to bed I wonder if this is the night I'll join Patrick." A long pause. "To answer your question—no, I couldn't face Patrick if I denied his child. All I know is when I heard her voice, I just wanted to hold her. That's the only proof I need."

"Silly old woman," Grif grumbled.

Tripp decided to let the subject drop for now. It was some headway, though. Now he had to talk to his father about Earl.

"Dad, when was the last time Earl Boggs paid you?"

Grif looked at him. "So that's how you got that black eye, huh?"

Leona sat up. "You have a black eye? Oh, Tripp, are you hurt?"

"I'm fine, Mom."

"Leave Earl alone, son," Grif said. "He's mean—his sons are meaner."

Tripp frowned. "When have you ever run from a fight?"

"When I got knocked down so hard I couldn't get up."

His frown deepened. "Is that how you broke your hip?"

"Leave it alone, son."

"My God." Anger churned inside him once again. "Earl Boggs is not running his cattle free on our land one more day. By the end of the week, I'll have every head off Lady Luck."

"Son, please." Grif leaned forward and Tripp saw fear in his father's eyes. "I've lost one son. I don't want to lose another."

His stomach clenched at the pain in his father's voice. He never realized how bad things were at home or in Bramble. But he wasn't running from this fight.

"Don't worry. I can handle this," he said. "I'll call the sheriff first thing in the morning to let him know what's going on. Try to get a good night's rest." He paused in the doorway. "Did you have a contract with Earl?"

"No, son. He came wanting to lease the land and I said yes. He wrote me a check, like he did four times a year. Then he just stopped."

"Tripp, please be careful," Leona begged.

"I will, Mom. Good night."

TRIPP LAY ACROSS HIS BED and felt the weight of the years bearing down upon him. The weight of letting his parents down—letting Patrick down. Patrick had looked up to him and in return Tripp had coveted Patrick's girlfriend. He'd denied that a lot of times, but it was the truth.

That night of the party when she'd moved her body against his, he'd wanted her in the worst way. He let the thought run through his mind. It was the first time he'd done that. Usually he wouldn't even admit it to himself. But he was having to face a lot of hard truths today.

And they hurt like hell.

Earl had beaten up his father and Tripp hadn't been here

to help. The guilt suddenly became heavy, so heavy he had trouble breathing. There was nothing he could do now but try and make things right—try to make amends.

As he drifted into sleep, he saw Camila's flashing dark eyes. And felt the softness of her body.

SUNDAY MORNING, TRIPP WINCED and groaned as he moved, but after soaking in a hot tub of water, his body felt much better. Looking in the mirror, he did a double take. With a black eye, a blue and swollen jaw, and a cut that was already healing, he definitely looked like he'd lost the fight.

After breakfast, he called the sheriff, Wyatt Carson, and told him what was happening. He met him in town then they drove out to the Boggs ranch.

Tripp had known Wyatt all his life. They were the same age and had gone to school together until Wyatt's family had moved to Austin. Wyatt had become a police officer in Austin; his wife was an officer, too. She'd been killed in the line of duty and Wyatt had brought his small daughter home. He'd run for sheriff and had been elected three years ago. He now lived fifteen minutes away in Horseshoe, the county seat.

"Let me handle this," Wyatt said as they drove into Earl's yard.

The yard of the large Boggs home was well kept, as were the pastures. Obviously Earl took better care of his mother's place. Tripp noticed a diesel truck parked with two other trucks.

He and Wyatt got out. The front door opened and Earl and three of his sons walked onto the porch. Otis was the oldest, a couple of years older than Tripp, and probably the meanest, having spent some time in jail. But Thelma had always managed to get him out. Lewis, the middle son, was his age and had always resented Tripp because he'd been popular in school. Wallis was the youngest, Patrick's age. There had been a fourth son, Roger, who'd been killed a couple of years ago.

"I'd like to talk to you, Earl," Wyatt said.

"What'd you bring the rodeo man for?"

"Because this is about Daniels land."

"I lease it, period. Enough said." Earl turned away.

"Not so fast." Wyatt halted him. "Mr. Daniels doesn't have a contract with you. Do you have copies of receipts where you paid him?"

"Hell, Wyatt. This is Bramble. All I need is my word."

"This ain't 1960, Earl," Wyatt told him. "And a lot more than your word is required."

"Like hell," Earl replied, and spat.

"Yeah. Like hell." Wyatt stood his ground.

"C'mon, Wyatt, I was born and raised here like you. I ain't trying to cheat nobody."

Wyatt rubbed his jaw. "Well, Earl, this is how it is. You show me receipts and the cattle stay. No receipts, the cattle have to go. That's the law and I'm here to enforce it."

"You listening to that rodeo man, ain't you?"

Wyatt glanced at Tripp. "You mean Tripp?"

"Ain't nobody else standing there."

Otis spit tobacco juice onto the ground. "You run into a tree, rodeo man?"

"I ran into a yellow-bellied coward."

Otis's face turned red in anger. "Are you accusing me of something?"

"Enough," Wyatt intervened. "I take it you don't have any receipts, Earl?"

"Sure as hell don't."

"Then I'll give you and your boys until Tuesday to get the cattle off. I'm sure Tripp doesn't have a problem with that."

Tripp shook his head.

Earl's eyes narrowed to tiny slits.

"Don't make this any harder than it has to be," Wyatt said. "I'll check in on Tuesday to make sure the job is done. If there's any meanness going on, I'll come looking for you

Earl. Prison is not a place you want to spend your old age."
Wyatt turned his gaze to the sons. "Otis, tell your brothers
what it's like in jail, then give it a lot of thought before you
do anything stupid."

Wyatt turned, but Tripp wasn't through.

"Next time you ambush me, I'll be ready, and if I can ever
prove that one of you hit my father, this town won't be big
enough for all of us."

He followed Wyatt to the car.

"You just couldn't let it go, could you?"

"No." Tripp buckled his seat belt. "This isn't over, Wyatt."

"I know, dammit. A range war is just what I need in Bramble."

"I didn't start it."

"Just watch your back."

"Thanks, Wyatt."

When Tripp reached Lady Luck, he went into the house
and got his rifle and shotgun out of the gun cabinet. He made
sure they were in working order and clean, then he put them
back. Until this was over, he'd better be prepared.

CAMILA SPENT TUESDAY making soap. By mid-afternoon her
arms ached from handling the big stainless steel pots and
large quantities of lard and olive oil. She poured the soap into
the wood molds and covered them.

Jilly had a basketball game tonight and the coach was going
over their game plan, so Camila didn't have to pick up Jilly until
five. She poured a cup of coffee and sat down in the coffee shop.

"Would you like a *kolache?*" Millie asked.

"No, thanks. It's very quiet today." Few people were out
and the streets were almost empty.

"I was thinking that—"

Before Millie could finish, the door burst open and Jilly
flew in. Camila's heart fell to the pit of her stomach. Something had to be wrong for Jilly to be here instead of practice.

Camila jumped to her feet. "What is it? What's wrong?"

"Cameron Boggs said his father beat up Tripp and Tripp's in bad shape. I gotta go see how he is. Mr. and Mrs. Daniels might need my help. I gotta go."

Camila was dumbstruck. She didn't know what to say. She glanced at Millie and Millie shrugged.

Camila caught Jilly's arm. "Baby, calm down."

"I can't, Mama. They said he's hurt bad."

Camila's stomach tightened and she wondered how badly Tripp was hurt—and why. "Are you sure, Jilly? It could just be kids bragging."

Jilly drew in a breath. "Tripp got mad cause Earl wasn't paying any lease money to Mr. Daniels and Tripp told Earl to move his cows. Cameron said his dad showed the big rodeo star who's the boss. I'm going home to get my bicycle then I'm going to Lady Luck."

"Wait a minute." Camila grabbed her, not sure how to explain this. "Remember what happened the last time?"

"I don't care. I'm going." That stubborn chin jutted out.

"Jilly…"

"Mama, please, don't tell me not to go."

It was on the tip of Camila's tongue, but she could see how upset her daughter was. Nothing was going to stop Jilly, but at least Camila could be there to protect her.

"Okay. I'll drive you."

She couldn't believe the words coming out of her mouth. She'd avoided Lady Luck for thirteen years. But now, for her daughter, she'd have to go back.

She was dreading every second.

Chapter Seven

Tripp checked the pastures on Tuesday and the cattle were still there. There weren't any signs that the Boggses had even been on the property. Wyatt had called and said he was coming out to the ranch, so Tripp went to the gun cabinet and took out a rifle.

"I'm going with you."

Tripp turned to face his father, the rifle in his hand. "No, you're not. Wyatt will be here any minute and we'll take care of things."

"Why do you need a gun?" Fear flashed in his father's tired eyes and Tripp felt a moment of anger at what the years had done to a man he'd thought of as stronger and bolder than John Wayne.

He patted his shoulder. "Dad, relax. I'll handle this."

"Earl's mean, son, and he got even meaner when his son was killed. Don't know what happened to him, but he ain't the same."

Tripp had heard the news even in Mesquite. Earl's third son, Roger, had been working on a truck and the jack had slipped, causing the truck to fall on him. He'd died instantly at the age of thirty-two.

"I know what it's like to lose a son and I…"

Tripp took a breath, the anger turning to empathy. Now he knew why his dad was afraid. "You're not losing me. I'm just trying to get this ranch back into shape and I'm not letting Earl take advantage of you or me." He moved toward the kitchen. "I'll be back before you know it."

"Son, don't go," Grif shouted after him, but he didn't stop. He had to do this.

In the kitchen, Morris removed his apron. "I better go with you."

Tripp sighed. "I've just had this conversation with Dad, and you're not going either. Stay here and keep Dad calm. I'm going to saddle the horses."

Years of neglecting his parents tore at him and he tightened the cinch a little too tight. The horse moved in protest and he gently rubbed her neck. "Sorry, girl." Now he was taking his frustration out on the best quarter horse he'd ever ridden.

That wasn't the only thing that was eating away at him. He couldn't get Camila's hurt expression and those sad eyes out of his head. He had to find a way to see her again and try to explain.

"That's a mighty good-looking horse," Wyatt said, walking up and eyeing the red-chestnut mare.

"This is Cayenne." Tripp stroked the white stripe on the horse's face. "I named her that because she's the color of cayenne pepper and has a hot temperament, but she's the best quarter horse I've owned. She can turn on a dime and she's doesn't tire easily. I call her Cay." Tripp pulled the reins of another horse and she moved forward. "This is Daisy. I believe she's docile enough for you."

"Hey. I grew up riding—just like you."

"Yeah, but when was the last time you were on a horse?"

"Not for a while," Wyatt replied, swinging into the saddle with a groan.

Tripp opened the gate then mounted Cay and they rode into the pasture.

"Have you seen any activity today?" Wyatt asked.

"No. I've laid low like you asked me to."

"Good. Maybe we can resolve this peacefully."

They galloped to a ridge where they could look out on a valley with tall weeds and overgrown bushes and mesquite. Cattle munched on the grass beneath the weeds. To the south, riders were approached—seven, Tripp counted. His pulse quickened and he felt as if he were at his first rodeo, in a chute atop a horse meaner than the devil, waiting for the gate to open. Except this was no rodeo.

The riders didn't come to confront them—they began to herd the cattle south, toward Boggs land.

"I can't believe this," Tripp said.

"Me, neither," Wyatt added. "This seems too easy."

Earl cantered toward them, pulling up short beside Wyatt. "I'm moving the cattle like you asked me to."

"Thanks, Earl. I appreciate the cooperation."

Earl's eyes swung to Tripp, and he spit chewing tobacco on the ground. "Just stay out of my way."

Tripp nodded. "No problem."

Earl jerked the reins and galloped back to the herd.

Tripp and Wyatt turned toward the ranch.

"This doesn't feel right," Tripp said.

"Don't look a gift horse in the mouth. Earl knows he's in the wrong. It's just hard for him to admit that."

"Yeah, Wyatt." Tripp laughed. "That's why you're the sheriff—you can straddle the fence with a straight face. Me, I'm going to wait and see."

"Just be careful."

CAMILA DROVE INTO the circular drive with a knot in her stomach. Lady Luck was just as Jilly had said—run-down. Years ago, it had been a showplace, a two-story colonial with white pillars, and Camila had felt privileged that Patrick wanted her to visit his home. She'd been too young to realize, or maybe she hadn't wanted to, why Patrick had brought her here when his parents had been out. Patrick had been her friend, though; she'd trusted him.

That was then, this was now and she had to concentrate on her daughter. It had taken a while to get to the ranch because they'd had to go home and get Button, Jilly had insisted the Danielses would want to see her. Camila was at the end of her patience.

She turned to Jilly. "Go inside and see how Tripp is. Ten minutes and I want you out of there. Do you understand me?"

"Yes, ma'am." Jilly hung her head.

"And understand we're invading these people's privacy so be polite and—" she touched Jilly's cheek, unable to withstand that sad expression "—just be you."

"Okay, Mama." Jilly opened the door. "Button and me will be right back."

Jilly went inside and in a second she came running out, screaming, "Mama, Mama, Mama!"

Camila jumped out, her heart beating like a rhythm of a bongo drum, loud and hard. She met Jilly on the other side of the car.

"Come quick," Jilly shouted and charged back in the house.

Camila ran after her and followed her into the den area. She stopped for a moment to take in the scene. Mr. Daniels held a shotgun and Morris and Mrs. Daniels were trying to take it away from him. They struggled back and forth to no avail.

"What's going on?" she asked.

They paused in the struggle and looked at her.

Mr. Daniels frowned. "Who the hell are you?"

"Camila Walker."

His frown deepened. "Get out of my house."

She walked forward, trying not to let his tone get to her. "Not until you give me the gun."

"You can't tell me what to do, missy. My boy needs help and I'm gonna help him."

Camila glanced at Morris for an explanation. "Tripp and

Wyatt went to see if the Boggses were moving their cattle off our land. Wyatt left a while ago, but Tripp hasn't come to the house."

"Something's wrong. I know it. Now get out of my way." Mr. Daniels tried to move, but Leona and Morris wouldn't let go of his arms.

"Let me go," Mr. Daniels shouted.

"Stubborn old fool," Leona shouted back. "What can you do? You can barely walk."

"I can fire this damn gun."

"Everyone calm down," Camila said. "I'll go to the barn and see if I can find Tripp."

"Not without me, missy."

Morris groaned and rolled his eyes toward the ceiling.

She didn't know how to handle this, but she was sure Mr. Daniels was serious. "You can go with me and I'll carry the gun."

"Now you're talking, missy."

"For heaven's sakes, Grif." Leona threw up her hands and sank onto the sofa. Jilly went to her.

Camila took the gun from Grif without a problem. "Ready?" she asked.

"You might have to give me your arm," Grif said, and he appeared shaky.

"See." Leona pointed a finger at him. "Let Camila go find Tripp, you pigheaded mule."

"Shut up, Leona." Grif clutched Camila's elbow and they made their way to the kitchen.

"Jilly, stay with Mrs. Daniels." She wasn't sure what was going on, but she wanted Jilly where she was safe.

"Mama…" The plaintive cry shook her and she wondered how she'd gotten herself into this situation.

"I'll be fine. Just stay here with Mrs. Daniels."

As they passed Morris, she whispered, "Call Wyatt and get him back here."

"Gotcha. I'll be right behind you."

They slowly made their way out the back door and moved toward the barn and corrals. The gun felt heavy and awkward in her hand. She'd never fired a gun in her life and she was hoping she wouldn't have to today.

"This doesn't change a thing, missy." Grif let out a long, ragged breath.

She knew exactly what he was talking about—the fact that he didn't believe Jilly was Patrick's.

"I don't expect it to."

Stubborn old mule. Ornery cuss. Ungrateful bastard. The phrases burned her throat and she swallowed them back, concentrating on her task.

Where was Tripp?

TRIPP TURNED FROM PLACING his saddle on the rack and came to a complete stop. Otis, Lewis and Wallis stood in the opening to the barn.

"You didn't think it was over, now did you, rodeo man?" Otis snickered.

"No, Otis, but I didn't think you'd be stupid enough to try something today."

Lewis took a couple of steps into the barn. "This time we're gonna teach you a lesson you won't forget."

"You haven't got enough brain power to teach me anything." His rifle lay on a bale of hay and Tripp inched toward it.

Wallis laughed. "Don't worry about the brains, cowboy. You better worry about the muscle."

"Three against one. Is that supposed to be a fair fight?"

"Who cares about fair?" Otis said. "We're Boggses and our grandma pretty much owns this town. We do what we want."

"Well you'd better kill me this time because I will be filing charges."

"You heard him, boys." Otis made a dive for him with

Lewis and Wallis right behind. Tripp drove a fist into Otis's beer belly and he went down moaning. Lewis and Wallis hammered away at Tripp and he struggled to reach his rifle.

That was his only chance.

THE COOL AND BREEZY afternoon wind rattled the limbs of an old cottonwood tree by the barn. Wispy white clouds with dark underbellies rolled across a dull blue sky. Clear signs a thunderstorm was brewing. But an eerie silence echoed through the oaks and mesquite, interrupted only by the wind and the caw of a crow. It was a typical winter afternoon in Texas, but there was nothing typical about this day.

As they neared the barn door, grunting shuffling noises shattered the silence. Camila paused at the sight in front of her and fear zigzagged up her spine. A fight—the Boggses against Tripp. They had him down on the ground. Lewis locked an arm around his neck and Wallis was trying to drive a fist into Tripp's stomach, but Tripp kept kicking out with his feet. Otis sat a few feet away with a dazed look.

Mr. Daniels trembled on her arm. "Use the gun, missy," he said in a low voice. "They'll kill him."

Use the gun.

Her insides quivered but her hands were steady as she raised the shotgun and aimed it above their heads. It was up to her to stop this—to save Tripp. Her nerves buzzed, but she wouldn't give in to the fear. Without a second thought, she pulled the trigger and the butt of gun slammed against her shoulder and knocked her backward, but she stayed on her feet, keeping the shotgun pointed at the men. Her shoulder stung and it was going to hurt like hell tomorrow. She couldn't think about that now, as all four men stared at her.

Wallis and Lewis still held Tripp down.

"Let him go," she yelled, the feel of the gun giving her an awesome sense of power.

"C'mon, Camila, you're not gonna use that thing." Wallis smirked at her, not loosening his grip on Tripp.

She stared him straight in the eye, something she hadn't done in thirteen years. "Try me, Wallis. Just try me." She stepped closer, the gun pointed at Wallis's chest. "Move away from him." The thought of pulling the trigger again and feeling the kick of the gun wasn't something she really wanted to do. But she wasn't backing down. The fear that flashed in Wallis's eyes was worth a sore shoulder any day.

Wallis and Lewis slowly let go of Tripp and he rolled to his feet.

"You all right, son?" Grif asked.

"Yeah." Tripp reached for his rifle.

"You boys better leave and never come back," Grif warned. "It's easy to push around an old man and it takes a coward to ambush a man you know you can't beat in a fair fight."

"Old man—"

"Careful what you say, Otis," Tripp advised. "Unless you want to die here today. I'm not feeling too hospitable right now." He laid his rifle down. "On second thought we're going to do this the fair way—the way a man would do it." He stepped away from the gun. "One man at a time. Who's first?"

Wallis grinned, moving forward.

"What the hell…" Earl stood in the entrance. "I've been looking for you boys. What the hell are you doing here?"

"Taking care of business," Otis answered.

"Yeah, Earl. Your boys figured if they punched my lights out one more time, I might learn my lesson."

Earl stomped over to Otis and slapped him across the face. He staggered backward into Lewis. "You stupid idiot," Earl yelled. "I told you to leave the rodeo man alone."

Otis rubbed his face. "But you didn't mean that. He can't tell us what to do."

"No, but your grandma sure can," Earl told him. "She's

threatening to cut off all our expenses if we're involved in another ruckus. Is that what you want, to be without money?"

Otis hung his head. "No, sir."

"Then get your asses back home before I really lose my temper. And stay away from the Danielses."

They picked up their hats from the dirt floor and slowly made their way to their horses.

Grif trembled beside Camila—or was it her? She wasn't sure. Her hands were numb from holding the gun, but for the life of her she couldn't let it go.

Tripp took it out of her hands, his fingers brushing against hers. A warm electric current shot up her arm and their eyes met. They both felt it—the attraction that was always there between them. Forbidden, cursed attraction. "Take Dad to the house, please. I need to talk to Earl."

That soothing drawl relaxed her and she nodded, unable to speak.

"We'd showed 'em, son, didn't we?"

"Yeah, Dad. Now go to the house with Camila."

The walk back was slower and Camila didn't mind. It gave her a chance to calm down.

Morris ran toward them, panting. "Wyatt's on his way. I had to wait for him to call back."

"Everything's under control," Grif said.

"Good. Where's Tripp?"

"Talking to Earl. I need a damn cup of coffee with a shot of whiskey in it."

"I'll put on a pot." Morris ambled into the house.

"This doesn't change a thing, missy," Grif said when they were almost at the door.

"I know."

She knew that better than anyone. People like Mr. Daniels had to form their own opinion of her. Once he got to know her, he might change his mind, but she wasn't counting on it, nor did she need it. For Jilly, though, she would be nice and patient.

TRIPP PICKED UP HIS HAT and suppressed a groan. His jaw ached and his stomach wasn't feeling all that well either, but he wasn't taking his eyes off Earl. He didn't trust him for a minute.

Staring at Earl's set expression, Tripp tried to gauge what he was up to.

As if reading his mind, Earl said, "If I'd had my way, my boys would've hurt you bad."

Now the picture was clearer—Mama Boggs had applied some pressure and Earl wasn't happy. "What happened to you, Earl?" Tripp brushed off his hat and placed it on his head. "When I was kid, my dad used to take me to the rodeos on Harper's Road. I loved to watch you ride and I wanted to ride like that one day. You had heart and soul and knew how to have fun without hurting other people. What happened to all that heart?"

"It got ripped out, cowboy, and it's none of your damn business."

"It is when you take your anger out on me and my dad."

Earl reached into his shirt pocket and pulled out a piece of paper. He shoved it at Tripp and Tripp took the paper. It was a check for a year's lease signed by Thelma Boggs.

"Ma seems to think that we need to pay our bills, so you got lucky, cowboy."

"Or maybe you got lucky."

Earl's face darkened but he didn't say anything. At that moment, Tripp could identify with Earl's pain—a pain that had to do with his son's death.

On a gut instinct, Tripp decided to finish this with Earl here and now. "I know what it's like to lose someone you love."

"You don't know a damn thing."

"Not about your situation, but I know what it's like to live with guilt. That's what you're feeling, isn't it?"

Earl removed his hat and sank onto a bale of hay. Awkward silence filled the barn and Tripp waited for he knew not what.

Then Earl's voice came, "Roger said the jack wasn't working right and he needed a new one. I told him he wasn't buying a goddamn new jack. He had to fix the old one. Two days later it crushed him like a sack of potatoes."

"Earl, I'm sorry...."

Earl jumped to his feet and jammed his hat on his head. "I don't need your goddamn sympathy."

"But you do, Earl and—"

"Stay the hell out of my way, cowboy."

Wyatt hurried into the barn and stopped short when he saw Earl and Tripp. "What are you doing here, Earl?"

"Came to pay the back lease money. Got a problem with that?"

Wyatt's eyes narrowed. "No. But why didn't you do that earlier?"

"I wasn't in a giving mood then."

"Everything's fine," Tripp said.

Earl nodded and strolled from the barn.

Wyatt stared at Tripp. "If everything's fine, why is your face bleeding?"

Tripp dug out his handkerchief from his pocket and wiped away the trail of blood. "Earl's boys came back for another round, but we got it sorted out."

"Mmm. Guess I'll have to take your word for that, but if you want to file charges, you know where to find me."

"Yeah. Thanks, Wyatt."

Wyatt left and Tripp took a moment to gather himself, unable to get Earl's tortured words out of his mind. How many secrets were there in this small town? Earl was living with a mighty big one. He was eaten up with guilt, but he wasn't letting anyone help him. He was too proud and stubborn. No one would ever know Earl's pain and Tripp wondered why he'd shared it with him.

Tripp made his way to the house, trying to ignore the aches and pains in his body. Each step he took, he wondered what Camila was doing here. He didn't care. He just wanted to see her. Looking at her calmed him and excited him more than anything in his life—even the rodeo.

Today he was hoping for the calm.

IN THE HOUSE, JILLY RAN to Camila. "Everything's okay," Camila assured her. "Pull Mr. Daniels's chair forward. He needs to sit down."

Jilly turned the chair and Grif sank down, breathing heavily.

"Where's Tripp?" Leona wanted to know.

"He's fine," Camila said. "He'll be here in a minute."

"Where's my damn drink?" Grif yelled.

Morris rushed in with the coffee. "You're 'bout as jumpy as a long-tail cat in a room full of rockin' chairs with the door closed and—"

"Shut up, Morris," Grif growled, "and give me my drink."

"Yes, sir."

Morris set the cup on the end table.

"You put a shot of whiskey in it?"

"You bet."

Grif's hand shook as he drank the coffee.

"Are you okay?" Morris asked.

"Better than I've been in a long time. We showed those Boggses a thing or two."

Jilly moved closer to Camila. "Is Tripp okay, Mama?"

"Don't worry about Tripp," Grif answered before she could. "He's a Daniels and can take a bruising."

"Bruising?" Leona asked with a touch of fright. "What happened?"

"We took care of business," Grif spouted.

"You're being cocky." Leona stroked Button, her eyes on her husband.

"And ungrateful, self-willed and cantankerous." The words slipped out of Camila's mouth before she could stop them.

"How dare you!" Grif appeared shocked at her words.

"We better go," Camila said to Jilly, thinking she'd just ended the visit. And she'd rather not be here when Tripp returned.

"I want to hold the dog," Grif said, shifting his attention to Button.

Leona handed Button to Jilly. "Take her to the old fool."

Jilly obliged, settling Button in Grif's lap. "She's a little nervous," Jilly explained Button's trembling.

"That makes two of us." Grif rubbed the dog.

"Jilly, come sit by me," Leona invited.

Jilly walked over and sat by her. "Would you like me to hold your hand?" Jilly asked.

"Oh, yes, please."

"You're trembling," Jilly said.

"I'm a little nervous, too."

"It's okay. I'm here."

"You're a sweet girl."

"My mama's sweet, too."

"Yes, and very nice, considering."

Leona and Jilly's conversation dissolved into a foggy fuzziness. This was like a movie out of focus.

"Think I'll rustle me up a bottle of scotch," Morris said. "Can I get you ladies something?"

"No, thanks," Camila replied.

"Jilly, come sit by me," Grif said.

"No." Leona clutched Jilly's hand. "You have the dog. Jilly stays with me."

"We have to be nice, remember?" Jilly said.

"Aw, fiddle-faddle," Grif muttered.

Jilly whispered something to Leona and Leona nodded. Jilly got up and walked to Grif.

"Let me take Button to Mrs. Daniels. She's lonely."

"Okay, but hurry back."

The situation was surreal as Camila watched Jilly sprint back and forth, trying to dole out her attention and affection.

Griffin may not want to admit that Jilly was Patrick's, but at least he wasn't being mean to her. Now Camila found it hard to leave.

Then suddenly Grif shot her a look. "Are you after my money?"

"No," she answered without missing a beat. "I'm able to make my own money and I don't want yours or anyone else's."

"Grif, how could you?" Leona scolded.

"Well, I don't have any," Grif said as if Leona hadn't spoken.

"Thank you for sharing that, now Jilly and I really must go."

Jilly was standing by Grif and he reached out and caught her hand.

"Let's go," Camila said.

"I can't, Mama, he won't let go of my hand."

"Let her go," Leona shouted. "You stubborn old man."

"If I gave you three wishes, what would they be?" Grif asked Jilly, seemingly unperturbed by the other two women in the room.

"Well." Jilly thought for a minute. "I wish Mrs. Shynosky's daughter would visit her more often so she wouldn't be so sad and I wish Miss Unie wouldn't have to pick up cans anymore or eat cat food." She looked directly at Mr. Daniels. "And I wish people would stop being mean to my mama."

Grif frowned. "Those are some strange wishes for an almost-twelve-year-old. Don't you want to wish something for yourself? How about a new bicycle? New clothes? What would you wish for yourself?"

Jilly glanced at Camila then back to Grif. "I wish I could see what my daddy looked like."

Camila's heart sank to the pit of her stomach. Twelve years of being a mother came down to this, her one weakness, her one failure—of not talking about Patrick more so Jilly wouldn't have all these feelings and curiosity about her father. The silence became awkward and Camila just wanted to get Jilly out of the room before Grif could hurt her again.

As Tripp walked into the kitchen, Morris plopped into a chair with a bottle of scotch in front of him. Morris wasn't a drinker and Tripp wondered what he was doing.

Morris filled a shot glass and downed it, making a face and hitting the table with his fist. "Damn, that's good."

"Morris…"

"I got old," Morris said.

"And what?" Tripp lifted an eyebrow. "You're going to try and forget that in a bottle of scotch?"

"Naw. I just need a boost."

"It's gonna knock you flat on your ass."

Morris poured another glass. "Then you'll have to pick me up."

"Morris, what are you talking about?"

"I couldn't take the gun away from Grif. I got old and weak. Thank God for Camila." He downed another shot.

Tripp's heart skipped a beat. "Where is she?"

"In the den with the folks. That girl's got spunk. She can hold her own with Grif."

"I think she can hold her own with anybody." Considering what she'd done in the barn, Tripp knew that for a fact.

"Heard the blast. Anybody get hurt?"

"Just my pride. I'm getting old, too. I couldn't take three Boggses."

"Hell. Another ambush?"

"This time they showed their faces, but that problem is solved. We won't be bothered by them anymore." Tripp tapped his shirt pocket. "Got the back lease money, too."

"Hells bells." Morris poured another glass. "I'll drink to that. I'll drink to anything."

Tripp headed toward the den, then quickly went back and grabbed the scotch bottle. "I'm taking this. You've had enough."

Inside the den, he stopped short. Grif was holding onto Jilly's hand and Camila seemed nervous. His mother wore a frown, and tears glistened in his father's eyes.

"You're okay," Jilly said when she saw him.

"Yes." He tried to smile without wincing. "I'm fine."

"Son, son," Grif muttered, hearing Tripp's voice.

He went to his father, his eyes on Camila. "I'm right here."

"Everything settled?"

"Yeah. Earl and me had a talk. No more problems."

"Would you ask your father to let go of Jilly?" Camila spoke up. "We really have to go."

Tripp looked at Camila. "Thank you."

"You're welcome, now..." Tripp held up a hand, stopping her.

"It took a lot of guts to do what you did."

"I could see your father was upset and needed help."

"Like hell! I could have done it on my own."

"Like pigs can fly, huh, Dad?"

"Okay." Grif gave in with a snort. "But it doesn't change a thing."

Tripp sighed. "Let go of Jilly."

Grif obeyed and Camila pulled Jilly to her side.

Grif tried to push to his feet, but was unable to do so on his own. Tripp reached for his elbow and gently helped. Grif staggered and Camila quickly reached for his other arm.

"I'm fine," Grif said, his body trembling. "Just a little too much excitement for one day."

"Let's go to the bedroom so you can lie down."

The threesome slowly made their way to the bedroom with Leona and Jilly following.

"Foolish, foolish man," Leona murmured.

Grif sagged onto the bed then lay down.

"We'll go now," Camila said. "Hope you feel better, Mr. Daniels."

"I'm fine," Grif grumbled. "Jilly."

"Yes, sir," she answered, moving toward the bed.

Camila caught her arm. "Mr. Daniels, we've been through this and I don't—"

"You wanted to see what your father looked like—" Grif cut her off, pointing to a large picture on the wall. "There he is. There's Patrick."

Tripp was dumbstruck. What had changed his father's mind? He glanced at Camila and her olive skin turned a grayish color as she stared at Patrick.

When she walked out of the room, he followed her.

Chapter Eight

"Are you okay?"

Camila took a couple of deep breaths, trying to still her agitated nerves. It was so eerie seeing Patrick's picture. She could almost feel his presence, feel all the pain of that night.

"Camila, are you okay?"

Through the pain, she heard Tripp's voice. "Yes…yes," she lied.

There was a tense pause, then Tripp asked, "What happened before I made it to the house?"

She shrugged. "Nothing much. Your father asked if I was after his money, then he grabbed Jilly and wouldn't let her go." She told him about the wishes.

"So that's what that was about."

"Yes."

He watched her for a moment. "I'm sorry. My father can be tactless, but it seems he's coming around."

Her eyes flared. "Am I supposed to be happy about that—happy to have my child's paternity questioned at every turn? Happy to deal with all the…" She stopped unable to finish.

"I'm sorry, Camila. Jilly is a wonderful girl. I noticed that the first time I met her. Now my parents have, too. You've done a great job raising her."

Camila was feeling so many conflicting emotions being here at Lady Luck, and Tripp being nice to her made her want to bawl like a baby. But she would never let him see that weakness.

Her eyes narrowed. "Am I supposed to say thank you?" She could hear the anger in her voice and she didn't like it. This wasn't like her.

"I can see you're angry."

"Yes. I'm angry about your father's interrogation and your demands for a DNA test. Maybe I should have it done and put it in the newspaper and post it at the community center so everyone would know. But then I'd be sinking to your level and—" She clamped her lips shut, not able to believe the pathetic words coming out of her mouth. Why was she acting like this?

Her chin jutted out. "Jilly and I have to go."

"Seeing Patrick's picture has upset you?"

All the anger inside her seemed to dissipate with those compassionate words. She inhaled deeply, surprised that he understood a bit of what she was feeling. "Yes, it has. He looked just like that the day he died."

"My mother put away the rest of the photos. They were too painful to see every day. My father refused to take that one down. It was taken a few weeks before he died."

"I know. He hated having to go to the photographer."

"Yeah." Tripp stared at her. "I guess he shared a lot with you."

"He was my best friend."

There was a painful silence that was always going to be there between the two of them—because Tripp was Patrick's brother.

But it didn't stop her from reaching out to touch the bruise on his face. His stubble felt warm and masculine to her sensitive fingertips. She cleared her throat. "Hope they didn't hurt you too badly."

"Naw. I'm tough as nails, but I appreciate the help."

"Jilly had heard in school that you were hurt and I had to bring her out here so she could see you were okay. We arrived as Morris and your mom were trying to take the shotgun away from Mr. Daniels. He was reluctant at first, but then he gave it to me—as long as he could go with me to find you."

"You didn't have to do that, but I'm awfully glad you did."

She rubbed her shoulder. "I might have a sore shoulder tomorrow."

"Oh, no, I'm sorry. That old gun kicks like a mule."

"I'll survive. It…" Her voice trailed away at the softness of his blue eyes—soft as a cloud and as warm as any sunshine she'd ever felt.

"Jilly and I really have to go." She quickly turned toward the bedroom. "She has a basketball game tonight."

"We have to talk about Patrick." The words came out so low she almost didn't hear them. She kept walking, though. She wasn't talking about that now. She just wanted to leave.

That night was her secret and she'd never tell him. Not even when he looked at her like that.

Never.

SOON THEY WERE in the Suburban and headed for Bramble. Jilly was very quiet and Camila was still shaken about all that had happened. Not speaking seemed the best thing to do. The only thing she could do.

They were almost home when Jilly said, "Mama, I guess the Danielses now believe that Patrick is my father."

"Yes, but they need time." She pulled into the driveway. "It's been years since Patrick died, but the Danielses are still grieving."

"I'll go back tomorrow and try to cheer them up."

"No." Camila turned in the seat to face her daughter, hating the sternness in her voice. This time she had to be for both their sakes. "You have school and homework and tomorrow is your ballet class. I went along with this today because I could see how upset you were, but we're not invading their privacy again. We have to respect that."

"Yes, ma'am."

"You're not going back until you're invited." She hated to be harsh, but she had to set boundaries for Jilly for her own benefit. Camila needed a boundary, too—to keep her from thinking about Tripp.

"Okay." She glanced sideways at Camila. "Wallis did beat up Tripp like Cameron said. Why do the Boggses have to be so mean?"

"I don't know, baby. Sometimes people take great joy in being mean. It somehow makes them feel big and important." She knew that very well.

"I don't like Wallis Boggs."

Camila didn't, either. Nor did she like Vance Boggs. They were the boys Patrick had wanted to be friends with, but they had turned out to be his worst enemies. Camila saw them all the time and her stomach churned every time she did but she lived her life the best she could.

She glanced at her watch. "We better hurry or you're going to miss the game and Coach Smythe will be very mad."

They hurried and made it to the gym on time. Jilly went to change into her uniform and Camila rushed over to the concession stand she helped run with Betty Sue and Jolene Boggs. Jolene was married to Mason, the twin of Betty Sue's ex, but Betty Sue and Jolene were still friends.

"Sorry, I'm late," Camila said, tying on an apron.

"Busy day at the shop?" Betty Sue asked.

"No. I'll tell you later."

For the next thirty minutes, they were busy selling hot dogs, popcorn and soft drinks. When there was a lull, Camila told Betty Sue about her afternoon.

"Oh my goodness. Are you okay? Is Jilly okay?"

Jilly dribbled down the court, then leaped into the air and made a basket. Bramble was up by six.

"Yes. I think she's fine, but I'm so afraid my past is going to hurt her."

"Camila, nobody believes those rumors anymore," Betty Sue said, munching on popcorn.

"Oh, yes, some people still do."

"Just egotistical idiots.'

"I agree," Jolene said, coming back into the booth. She'd gone to check on one of her children. She fixed a soft drink for herself and leaned against the counter. "One night we were having dinner with Vance and Debbie at the Bramble Rose. You were working late and came in to get something to eat. After you left, Vance started bragging about how he'd slept with you. He'd had a few beers and was rather loud so I asked him where he slept with you and when. Mason gave me one of those looks that said keep my mouth shut, but I'd had a beer myself and I felt like calling his bluff."

Two girls came up for popcorn, interrupting the story. Camila served them, thinking it strange to be talking about her past with Jolene. They never had before.

When the girls left, Jolene continued, "Vance stuttered and couldn't answer and I told him that he was lying and that he'd never slept with Camila Walker. Vance told me to shut up and Mason said for him not to talk to me like that. It was a very sticky evening, but men just love to talk about their triumphs even when they're only in their heads. Believe me, that's where most of them are."

Betty Sue laughed and Camila joined in, letting her guard down, letting herself relax. "Thank you for doing that," she said, touched that Jolene had actually taken up for her.

"In school, you seemed standoffish," Jolene said. "Now I know you were just shy. The more I get to know you, the better

I like you, and anyone who could raise a child like Jilly is tops in my books. My son, Cody, has a big crush on her."

Jolene was right about Camila being standoffish. In those days, she never got close to anyone but Patrick.

"Look, who's coming," Betty Sue said before Camila could say anything. "The number-one bitch of Bramble."

Lurleen Boggs, Wallis's wife, headed for the concession stand. One of her twins, Dulsey, was on the team. The other twin, a boy, Cameron, played on the boys' team.

"Two Diet Cokes," Lurleen said to Jolene.

"Good game, huh?" Jolene said, filling the order.

Camila waited on another customer, but she could still hear the conversation.

"Yeah, but I don't understand why Dulsey doesn't get to play more. Jilly Walker plays all the time and she's only a sixth grader, too."

"Are you watching the game?" Jolene asked. "Jilly's making most of the points and that's what the coach wants. He wants to win. We all want to win."

"Or maybe her mama is sleeping with the coach. Why would he let a sixth grader play so much?"

Frissons of fire shot up Camila's spine, but before she could respond, Jolene set the Cokes on the counter then knocked one into Lurleen—the cold drink running down her blouse and jeans.

"Oh, I'm so sorry," Jolene said. "It slipped out of my hand."

"You bitch," Lurleen snapped. "You did that on purpose."

Jolene graciously handed her a towel. "Lurleen, you're about thirty pounds heavier than me, but I bet I could still kick your ass, so you'd better watch your mouth. And if I were you, I wouldn't believe everything Wallis tells you."

"Every man in this town has had her, Jolene, and you know it." Lurleen dabbed at her clothes.

"No…"

"Am I invisible that you don't see me standing here?" Camila had had enough. She didn't need anyone taking up for her, though, it felt good. "I haven't slept with the coach or any other man is this town. If Wallis told you that, he's lying."

"Stay away from my husband." Lurleen looked at her with contempt.

"That's a pleasure," Camila said. "I wouldn't touch him with a ten-foot pole."

"You're missing a lot of the action." Betty Sue prompted Lurleen to leave. "And Dulsey is playing."

The game ended and the Bramble Bobcats won. Shouts of joy echoed through the gym. After lots of hugs, the girls headed for the locker room. Camila, Betty Sue and Jolene sold a few more drinks then they cleaned up and closed the stand.

Out of the corner of her eye, Camila could see Tripp shaking hands and talking to some of the townsfolk. Jilly and Kerri came out of the locker room and Jilly spoke to him. Camila kept her distance, not ready for another meeting with Tripp.

ON THE WAY HOME, Camila stopped at Unie's and lit her heater. She knew Unie would never light it and Camila couldn't stand the thought of her being cold. Soon Jilly was in bed and Camila took a quick shower. Her shoulder was a purplish color and sore. She'd have a reminder of this day for a while.

She sat on Jilly's bed—which was their nightly ritual—to talk about their day. Jilly chatted about the game and how they might win their division this year. She didn't mention the Danielses and Camila was relieved. She'd had all of the Danielses she wanted for one day.

In her room, she brushed her long dark hair. With her head down, she brushed it over her face with long strokes. Jilly sometimes brushed Camila's hair and she loved it—she loved being with her daughter. Although there had been other people in their lives, it had been just the two of them facing life, facing everything. Now their lives were changing.

She was so surprised when Grif had shown Jilly Patrick's picture and she was almost afraid to think what that might mean. Jilly wanted to know her father's family and Camila had to accept that with dignity. She'd do anything to make Jilly happy.

Her hand paused. Tripp wanted to talk about Patrick, but she needed some breathing space. She'd rather not have that discussion at all.

Turning off the light, she curled beneath the covers. She was exhausted emotionally. She closed her eyes and drifted into sleep—drifted into her favorite fantasy of Tripp Daniels. Her eyes popped opened. What was wrong with her? She wasn't seventeen any longer.

And Tripp wasn't a fantasy.

He was very real—too real.

THE NEXT MORNING, Camila dropped Jilly at school and drove to her grandmother's house to check on things. As she entered the back door, loud music greeted her and she knew her mother was home.

Camila's first instinct was to turn around and leave, not in the mood for a confrontation with Benita. But she hadn't seen her mother in a while and she couldn't just walk away.

"Good morning," she called.

"Oh, my baby," Benita cried, hugging Camila in a cloud of Chanel perfume. "Look at your mama." Benita whirled around in a red skimpy nightgown, her long dark hair falling down her back. "Don't I look great?"

"Yes, you look great." At forty-eight years old, Benita still looked incredible, slim and trim, but curvy, although her olive skin was slowly beginning to show signs of aging around the eyes and mouth. Her mother's world revolved around herself. Camila had learned that at a very early age.

Benita was the only child of Alta and Charles Walker. They'd spoiled her terribly and Charles had doted on her. Benita was fourteen when he'd died and her whole world had changed.

Benita had gotten pregnant in high school, like Camila, and Camila had been born before Benita had turned eighteen. Alta had forced Benita to marry the father, Travis Holden. The marriage had only lasted a short while and Benita had never taken his name. People said Travis had wanted it that way because he didn't believe Camila was his.

Travis and his family had moved away and Benita had gotten a letter about a year later saying that Travis had been killed in an accident. So Camila had grown up without knowing her father or having a male role model in her life—just the many men her mother had dated. When Camila was ten, Benita had married for the third time and had planned to move to Houston and take Camila with her.

Alta had refused to let Camila go. There had been a big argument and, in the end, Alta had won. Camila had stayed with her grandmother, only seeing her mother on the odd occasion—like today.

Benita touched her face. "My little chickadee, you look so sad."

"I'm just shocked to see you, that's all." Her mother had always called her chickadee or chick. Charles Walker had been an avid fan of W. C. Fields and he used to call Benita that, and Benita had done the same with Camila.

"Ouch." Benita made a face. "Where's my Jilly?"

"In school," Camila replied.

"Dammit, I—"

"I've got to get to work," Camila said, suddenly feeling the need to get away. "I'll bring Jilly by after her ballet class."

"You better," Benita warned. "She's the only bright spot in this dreary town."

Camila hurried to her shop, not even wanting to speculate why Benita was home. She was sure it was the usual reasons—her husband had kicked her out and she was short of money. Camila couldn't think about her mother. It made her too emotional, too angry.

She spent the morning pulling orders from the computer and filling them, then she finished the plans for Jilly's party. With everything that was going on, she should have planned a quiet party in their home, but it was too late to change anything now.

In the afternoon, she worked on a double wedding ring quilt and Ione Farris, an older lady who loved to quilt, helped her. When Camila needed extra help, there were several ladies willing to lend a hand. She had the little fisherman and the cowboy boot to finish, too.

When Ione left, Camila kept working, trying to concentrate on something other than the Danielses, Tripp and her mother. Her shoulders began to ache and she quit for the day, walking into the coffee shop and sinking into a chair.

Millie placed a cup of coffee in front of her. "What's wrong, sweetie?"

Camila took a breath. "My mother's home."

Millie pulled up a chair. "You're kidding. I guess she couldn't stay hidden forever."

Camila dragged her hands over her face. "I don't know if I can take much more."

"Oh, sweetie."

"And I haven't told you what happened at the Danielses' last night."

As she relayed the evening, Millie's eyes grew bigger and bigger. "You fired a gun!"

"Yes."

"Are you okay?"

"I think so. My shoulder's a little sore."

"Life sure gets interesting here in Bramble." Millie clicked her tongue. "Griffin Daniels actually admitted that Jilly is Patrick's."

"In his own way." Camila rubbed her shoulder. "I keep thinking I shouldn't have to prove my child's paternity."

"Oh, sweetie."

"Just too many things happening and now Benita is back. I've been planning Jilly's party for weeks and I wanted it to be perfect and—" she looked toward the Bramble Rose "—this is going to sound terrible, but I don't want Benita there. I don't want her to embarrass Jilly."

Millie reached for Camila's hand and held it tight. "Or is it that you don't want Benita to embarrass you?"

She bit her lip, looking at Millie. "Probably."

Millie patted her hand. "You're a beautiful, talented, successful woman. Stop beating yourself up and enjoy some of that—enjoy the life you've built for you and Jilly. No one deserves that more than you."

"I'll try," Camila promised. "Thanks for listening."

"Any time, sweetie."

Joe Bob and Bubba came through the door.

"I better get these old coots some coffee."

"Hi, Camila," they said in unison.

"Hi, Joe Bob, Bubba." She tried to smile.

"Where's Slim?" Joe Bob dropped into a chair. "Thought we were having a domino game."

"Keep your britches on," Millie answered. "He'll be here."

Their conversation went over Camila's head. Tripp drove up to the Bramble Rose and her eyes were riveted on him. He strolled into the diner dressed in worn jeans, dusty boots and a cowboy hat. He had an easy, smooth way of walking that drew attention, or at least, it had always drawn hers.

She sat there pondering her fascination with Tripp and decided it was time to talk. That was the only way to get rid of all the guilty, conflicting feelings about the past.

Glancing at her watch, she saw she had about an hour before Betty Sue brought Jilly home from ballet class.

Enough time to talk to Tripp.

Chapter Nine

Camila went out the front door, her concentration on Tripp and what she'd say to him. Her attention was diverted by Unie, who was pulling two large plastic bags behind herself. Lu Lu was under her arm.

Camila walked over to her. "Unie, where's your cart?"

"Bert took it away from me," Unie snarled. "Said it belonged to the grocery store. Hateful old bastard."

"You can't be pulling these heavy bags around town. I'll see if I can find you something else."

"Bless you, child," Unie said, then leaned in close and whispered, "Bert's after my money. Is he watching us?"

"No, Unie. I don't see Bert." Unie was stressed and not making sense.

"He's watching." Unie's eyes darted around, clutching Lu Lu tighter. "He's a sly old bastard and he ain't gettin' my money and he ain't gettin' my cans."

"Unie, I'll go get my car and take you home."

"Is Bert gonna be with you?"

"No, Unie. Just me."

"You ain't gettin' my cans, either," Unie warned. "They're for my son."

"I'll be right back." Camila ran for her Suburban. Why Bert had to be so vindictive she didn't understand, but she'd have a little talk with him. There was no need to be mean to Unie just because she was different.

Camila loaded the cans in the back and Unie insisted on sitting with them. Camila didn't argue because she knew it would be a waste of time. Unie crawled into the back and sat cross-legged, her hands and eyes on the cans, her arms around Lu Lu. For someone her age she was very nimble.

Camila jumped into the driver's seat and drove off.

TRIPP WATCHED ALL THIS out of the window. He turned to Rose. "What's Camila doing?"

"Helping Unie. She and Jilly are the only ones who pay her any attention."

"Unie got into the back of Camila's Suburban." He was a little puzzled, to say the least.

"Unie won't leave the cans. She stacks them in her living room, all over her house. Slim takes her once a month to Temple to sell them. Slim wasn't too keen on the idea, but Camila asked him and he'd do anything for Camila."

Camila had that effect on all men. Tripp knew that for a fact. Her dark beauty was hard to ignore and he was just becoming acquainted with her kind heart.

"The cans don't bring much money, but Unie manages to live on it. She's always saying she's saving money for her son," Rose was saying. "Unie's never had children or a husband that anyone in this town can recall. So I guess she created one in her head."

"Who took the cans before?"

"Unie did, but her truck broke down and she didn't have any money to fix it. She shouldn't be driving anyway. Doesn't know where she is half the time and thinks people are trying to steal from her."

"But she doesn't think Camila's trying to steal from her?"

"No. She pretty much trusts Camila and Jilly."

Tripp settled on a bar stool at the counter.

"So what are you in here for today, hon?" Rose asked.

"Coffee, please."

Rose poured a cup, eyeing Tripp's face. "Earl's boys give you that black eye?"

"Yeah." He didn't see any reason to lie.

"You be careful, hon, and if all else fails—" she pointed across the street to the bank "—just tell Mama Boggs. Thelma's the only one who can control them."

"Yeah." Tripp knew that.

"You just be careful, you hear?"

Tripp was about to answer when the bell over the door jingled and Camila walked in.

"Hi, Camila," Rose called. "Did you get Unie home?"

"Yes. Bert took her cart away."

"Why would he do that?"

Camila shrugged. "Not sure, but I intend to find out. In the meantime, if you have something she could use, let me know. I have to find her another cart. She can't lug those plastic bags around."

"Will do."

Camila looked at Tripp. "I was coming to talk to you, but now I'm running short on time. Jilly will be home in about thirty minutes."

"I'll take it," Tripp said, getting up from the stool with his coffee in his hand. Would you like anything?" he asked.

"No, thanks."

"Let's sit at a table." They found one in a corner. Camila slipped off her jacket. "How's your face?"

He grinned. "How's your shoulder?"

She found herself grinning back. "A bit stiff and sore."

He took a sip of his coffee. "Yep. Know how that feels."

"Do you think your trouble with the Boggses is over?"

"Yeah. I had a talk with Earl and I believe we understand each other now."

"Good."

Silence followed.

Camila folded her hands in her lap and waited.

"My parents want to see Jilly again and I have to know how you feel about that. I told them we had to respect your decision."

A smile touched her lips. "I told Jilly she had to respect your privacy."

His eyes twinkled. "At least we're on the same page."

Her stomach flip-flopped at the light in his eyes and words tumbled from her mouth. "I thought Jilly and I talked about everything, but I was unaware she had these feelings about her grandparents. I would never stop her from seeing them. My only fear was her getting hurt. I'll admit, though, I'm rather paranoid about that."

"Under the circumstances, I can't blame you. My parents won't hurt her now. They'll probably smother her to death."

"I just want to take it slow. Jilly has school, her friends and…"

"And you're nervous as hell."

Her eyes flew to his. "Yes." He understood; the realization turned her stomach into a whirligig.

He leaned forward. "I understand, Camila." His words confirmed what she already knew. A slight pause. "We need to talk about Patrick."

Those exciting feelings stilled and she got to her feet. "I have to go."

"You can't keep running from that conversation." His eyes didn't waver from hers.

She slipped into her jacket, knowing he was right. She was running. "Maybe later," she said.

She took a couple of steps and turned back. "I don't know if you've talked with Nurse Tisdale who sees your parents weekly, but she said your mother has cataracts that need to be removed. Has your mother mentioned that?" This was none of her business. Why was she bringing it up?

He frowned. "Nurse Tisdale has been on vacation for a week. I'm waiting for her to return. The nurse who's filling in doesn't know a lot."

"It could help her sight tremendously."

Tripp stood. "Thanks for telling me. I was wondering about that, but neither Mom nor Morris has mentioned a thing."

Tripp was standing so close that his tangy aftershave wafted to her nostrils and familiar, forbidden feelings stirred inside her. She took a step backward. "I've got to go."

"Camila."

She stopped.

"When can Jilly see my parents?"

"I'll talk to her and let you know." Saying that, she hurried out the door.

"BENITA'S HOME," Jilly exclaimed when Camila told her. Betty Sue had just dropped her off. "I'm so happy. I can't wait to see her."

Happy—that should have been Camila's response, too. She wondered if she'd ever feel that way about her mother.

Jilly jumped out of the car as soon as Camila stopped and ran into Benita's house. Jilly and Benita were hugging when Camila walked in.

"Ah, Jilly baby, you've grown so much," Benita said, looking at her granddaughter.

"I'm going to be twelve on Saturday."

"That's the reason I came home," Benita whispered.

"Really? That's totally cool."

Benita was wearing lime-green stretch pants and a yellow stretch top—every line and curve was visible, nothing was left to the imagination. She looked like a hooker. Even as a child, Camila had been embarrassed by the way her mother dressed. That hadn't changed.

Jilly was looking at Benita, too. "That outfit is, like, way out there," Jilly said. "How do you breathe in that?"

Camila suppressed a smile.

"Very well, thank you, and all the guys love it."

Jilly made a face. "I'm not into boys yet."

"What!" Benita drew back. "You're going to be twelve. It's time to start dating."

"I don't think so," Camila said, taking a seat at the table

"We've been worried about you," Jilly said. "You have to start calling us more."

Benita sat down, crossing her legs. "You've been worried about me?" Her gaze was leveled at Camila.

"It would be nice if you phoned once in a while."

"I called the other day to tell you I was coming home, but I got that *puta.*"

Camila's lips tightened into a straight line. "Millie said you called."

Benita studied her long red fingernails. "How is the witch of Bramble?"

Jilly shook a finger in Benita's face. "You have to be nice. Millie loves us."

Benita kissed Jilly's cheek. "Yeah. That's the only thing that keeps me from—" Her voice stopped when she caught the look on Camila's face. "Now, Jilly baby, tell me everything you've been doing since I left."

Jilly rattled on and on, not leaving out much, and when she got to the part about the Danielses, Camila's stomach coiled into a painful knot.

"How dare that old man." Benita's eyes blazed with sudden anger. "Next time I see him, I'll give him a piece of my mind."

"No you won't," Jilly told her. "He's an old man and he misses his son."

"Dios," Benita groaned. "You're just like your mother."

"Thank you. Everybody tells me that."

Camila let out a long breath, not even realizing she'd been holding it while Jilly'd been talking.

"Your mama is one of a kind." Benita winked. "Is everyone hungry? Enchiladas are in the oven. Beans and rice are on the stove and there's a salad in the refrigerator. I made rice pudding for dessert."

"Oh, boy. Benita makes the best enchiladas and rice pudding." Jilly jumped up. "I'll help put it on the table."

For the next thirty minutes, there was no arguing, just quiet family conversation. But Jilly did most of the talking. For the first time, Camila acknowledged how much her daughter talked. She didn't get that from her or Patrick. They'd both been quiet, shy teenagers. She must get it from Benita. That was not a comforting thought.

"Benita, there's a lot left over. Can I fix a plate for Miss Unie?" Jilly asked.

"Jilly, are you still worrying about that old can lady?"

"Yes. She's alone and doesn't have a lot. Sometimes I think she eats cat food because that's all she buys besides bread and milk."

"Okay." Benita touched Jilly's cheek. "Anything to please my granddaughter."

Benita and Camila did the dishes in silence while Jilly looked for a movie on TV. Afterward, Camila and Benita sat at the kitchen table.

"Why did you come home?" Camila had to ask. It wasn't for Jilly's birthday, though, she knew Benita loved Jilly.

"To lick my wounds—as usual," Benita replied.

"So the marriage didn't work out?"

"No. I filed for divorce and came home. And I can see you're excited to see me."

Benita pushed every emotional button in her, but she didn't react. "I hope you plan to stay for a while, and please try to get along with Millie."

Benita lifted an eyebrow. "Like you do? Suppressing every emotion you have?"

Another button pushed. She wanted to scream, but she suppressed the feeling, just like her mother knew she would.

"Yes, Benita, that comes from being raised the way I was—never being secure about anything."

"It always comes back to me—the awful mother."

"It comes back to the truth."

"Same thing."

"I don't want to argue with you."

"Oh, chick." Benita got up and hugged her. "Something about being here brings out the worst in me."

"Jilly and I have to go. She has school tomorrow." Camila stood. "Do you know when you're leaving?"

"No, but I'll let you know before I do."

"I'd appreciate that—for Jilly's sake."

"Yes, for Jilly's sake," Benita murmured, following her into the living room.

They said their goodbyes and left. Camila drove to Unie's and Jilly took the food inside. Camila had lit the heater earlier so she didn't get out. Unie didn't like a lot of people in her house. Soon Jilly was back.

"Miss Unie wouldn't open the door and I had to scream real loud that it was me before she let me in. She said she thought it was Bert after her cans."

"It doesn't seem like Unie's doing too well."

"Can't we do something, Mama?"

"It's hard since she doesn't have any relatives. I guess we'll have to start checking on her more."

"Okay." Jilly nodded. "She said Bert took away her cart."

"Yes. I carried her cans home today."

"We have to find her another."

"I plan to do that tomorrow."

"Good," Jilly said. "If anyone can do it, Mama, you can."

"Ah, such faith."

"Mama's the greatest." Jilly raised her arms in a victory sign.

At that moment, Camila said a silent prayer that nothing or no one ever ruined her relationship with Jilly. She could survive a lot of things, but not that.

TRIPP WALKED into the kitchen. Morris was at the table polishing silver that had been neglected too long.

"Morris, have you talked to Nurse Tisdale?"

Morris looked around. "Is she here?"

"No, she's not here." He was trying very hard not to get annoyed. "I meant, have you talked to her about Mom's eyes?"

"Yep. Several times."

"And?"

"Your dad now, he's stubborn, but your mom takes it to a higher level. She's like an old coon dog that's been hunting all night and hasn't treed one coon, and when he finally gets wind of one he just lays down too tired to make the effort and—"

"Dammit, Morris, I don't understand what the hell you're talking about. Why hasn't Mom had cataract surgery?"

"Like I told you, the effort is too much for her."

"My mom is not a coon dog and we're talking about her sight."

"Well then, you ask her yourself because I never could get anywhere with her. Stubborn as a coon dog."

Tripp sighed and went to find his parents. They were in the living room doing their usual thing. Leona was listening to a book on tape and Grif was watching sports.

When Grif saw Tripp, he immediately clicked off the TV. "Did you see Earl in town?"

"No." He'd looked for Earl and had gone into the bank to thank Mrs. Boggs. She'd said that Earl was on the ranch and wouldn't be bothering the Danielses again. He'd thanked her and left, knowing the situation was over.

"Good. Maybe we've seen the last of him and his boys." Grif strained to see behind Tripp. "Did you bring Jilly?"

"No, Dad, but I did talk to Camila."

"What did she say?"

"She said she wouldn't stop Jilly from coming, but she has school and after school activities."

"What does that mean?"

"It means Jilly can come when she has time."

"We get to see her every now and then, is that it?"

"We can be patient," Leona said.

"No we can't," Grif snapped. "She's Patrick's daughter and I want her here."

"I do, too," Leona replied. "But we can't deny her for twelve years and then expect her to be an overnight grand-daughter. We have to be patient."

"Fiddle-faddle."

Tripp sat by his mother. "Wouldn't you love to see that granddaughter, Mom?"

Leona held a hand to her chest. "Oh, my, yes."

"Then why haven't you had the cataract surgery?"

"She's scared, that's why," Grif told him.

"There's nothing to be scared of and I'll be with you."

Fear and the stubbornness Morris had mentioned tightened his mother's jaw. But Tripp had a secret weapon. Jilly.

"Jilly has dark hair and beautiful dark eyes and they flash with a soft light when she talks. At times she has this expression—it's hard to explain—kind of like Patrick when he was at his computer. He was at peace with the world. Jilly has that same look—she's at peace with her world."

Leona hiccuped a sob.

"I'll make an appointment in the morning, Mom. What do you say?"

Her hands trembled. "Are you taking me?"

"Yes, ma'am. I'll be with you through the whole thing."

She hiccuped again. "I'm scared to death, but I want to see Patrick's daughter."

"Good, then I'll make the arrangements."

Tripp helped his parents to bed, feeling good about this victory. His mother was going to see again. How could she not want to do this? Depression. She'd given up. But now Jilly was bringing new life to Lady Luck—just like he knew she would.

He fell across the bed, wishing he and Camila had been able to finish their conversation.

Maybe soon.

Chapter Ten

"It's cool Benita's home, don't you think, Mama?" Jilly leaned against the headboard in a big T-shirt and pink flannel pajama bottoms, cuddling Button.

"Benita and I have a different relationship than you." Camila answered truthfully, like she always tried to do.

"But you love her."

Did she? At ten, when Benita had left, she'd hated her for not fighting to take Camila. She'd wanted to be with her mother. After that, their relationship had been strained and they'd never talked about that time. Maybe now that they were older they should.

She glanced at Jilly's expectant face. "Yes. I love her, but sometimes she makes me very angry."

"Do I make you angry?"

"No." Camila brushed Jilly's hair back. "You never make me angry."

Jilly fidgeted in the bed. "When you found out you were pregnant and my daddy was dead, were you angry you were going to have a baby?"

Her heart took a nosedive and it was a moment before she could answer. How could she tell her daughter about that awful time, the insecurities, the heartache and the pain? Camila kissed Jilly's cheek, still wanting to be truthful. "I can honestly say I was never angry at you, just overwhelmed with grief and worry. I didn't know how I was going to raise you, care for you."

"But you did good. You're the best mama in Bramble."

"That's because I have this wonderful daughter who's an absolute joy."

Jilly giggled and slid beneath the covers. "I love you, Mama."

Camila straightened the blanket. Hearing those words made everything she went through worthwhile. Jilly made everything worthwhile.

"I love you, too, baby."

She fiddled with the blanket knowing she had to tell Jilly about her talk with Tripp.

"I spoke with Tripp today."

Jilly's eyes sparkled. "You did? Is he okay?"

"Yes, and the Danielses would like to see you again."

"Really?" Her eyes grew brighter. "I can go tomorrow."

"You have basketball practice and you promised to help Mrs. Haskell."

"Oh." Jilly pleated the sheet. "Then I'll go on Friday. I'll leave right after school and take Button. Is that okay, Mama?"

Button, hearing her name, poked her head from beneath the covers and barked. Jilly gathered her close and Camila patted Button's head.

"Yes. That's okay, but I'll drive you. I don't like you going that far on your bicycle."

"Okay, Mama. Good night." Jilly gave her a quick kiss.

"Good night, baby."

SO MANY THINGS were crowding in on Camila. Most of all, she had this fear she was going to lose Jilly to the Danielses. That was irrational, but she couldn't shake the feeling of helplessness, of letting her child grow and make her own decisions. And it was very obvious Jilly wanted to be a part of her father's family.

Where does that leave me?

Alone—with a capital A.

She should go to bed, but she was restless and knew she wouldn't sleep. Maybe she'd go to bed in Jilly's room and just hold her. No, that wasn't the answer either.

A tap at the back door sounded and she jumped.

Who could that be at this late hour? She went to the door and pulled the curtain back. Tripp stood there.

Her heart jerked in her chest. What was he doing here? She wouldn't open the door and maybe he'd go away. But the lights were on; he knew she was still up. She was caught. She opened the door.

"I know it's late," Tripp said, "but I saw your light on and I thought we could finish our talk."

She stepped aside, giving in to the inevitable. "Yes, it is late."

He removed his hat and suddenly the room was too small. She wanted to push him out the door and not have this conversation, not have anything to do with Tripp Daniels. But that was childish. She had to talk to him—no matter how painful it was.

"Is Jilly asleep?" he asked.

She tightened the belt of her terry cloth robe, feeling self-conscious. "Yes. Have a seat."

He sat at her kitchen table, placing his hat in front of himself. "I apologize for the lateness of the hour, but I was passing by and—" He stopped. "That's a lie. I couldn't sleep so I came to see you—to see if you'd talked to Jilly."

"Yes," she replied, touched by his honesty. "She'll come on Friday afternoon." Camila was aware she must look a sight with her hair hanging down her back and her face scrubbed clean—not to mention the ratty bathrobe and fuzzy slippers.

"Thank you."

"I'll bring her because I don't like her going that far on her bike, but I won't stay."

"You're welcome to."

"No, thanks. I won't be going back to Lady Luck." She sat across from him, knowing she had to get this over with. "You wanted to talk about Patrick."

"Yes."

She clenched her hands in her lap. "What do you want to know?"

"That night of Patrick's graduation party—was Patrick taking drugs?"

Her eyes narrowed. "Why are you asking that?"

He took a moment. "You see, I blame myself for Patrick's death and my parents blamed me, too. That's why I've been gone so long. Dad said I wasn't his son anymore and told me to never come back."

Camila was shocked. She'd never dreamed he'd gone through anything like that. She'd just assumed he was over-wrought with grief and couldn't come home.

"Why would your dad say that?"

"Because that night there was a lot of drinking and bragging going on and a lot of tiny white packets floating around. I saw Wallis handing something to Patrick. Later when Patrick and you started acting out of character, I figured all the kids were doing drugs. That made me angry and I tackled Patrick about it, but he said for me to mind my own business. What happened at that party, Camila? Were all of you doing drugs?"

She swallowed the constriction in her throat.

Seeing her difficulty, he added, "That night I saw you coming out of Patrick's room. You looked bad so I went in to talk to Patrick. I asked him about the drugs again and he became belligerent. I'd never seen him like that before. I told him to sleep it off. The next morning, I told my parents what

I suspected and that Patrick needed help. They became angrier than Patrick, saying Patrick was a good boy and wouldn't do anything like that. Later Patrick came out to the barn angry that I had interfered and he took off in the new Corvette. That's the last time I saw him." He took a breath. "You're the only one who knows the truth. Was Patrick doing drugs?"

She licked dry lips. "Patrick didn't do drugs. He hadn't ever before." She saw his shattered expression and quickly added, "But there were drugs there that night so you had reason to be concerned."

"I see."

She looked past his shoulder to the blue frilly curtains she'd made. They were light, airy and fun—things she needed in her life. Back then it had been so different, so… Her defense mechanism kicked in and she suppressed her emotions just like Benita said she did. But then something unfurled in her. She couldn't suppress her emotions forever. She needed to let go, to share—with Tripp.

The pain tightly woven around her heart began to unravel. Tripp had a need for answers. She could give him those and in return find some for herself. But could she do it?

She took a long breath. "In school, I was very shy and didn't make friends easily." She spoke slowly and hesitantly, forcing the words out. "Someone told me I was standoffish and I suppose that's true. My mother had cut this path of disgrace before me and I had a hard time living it down. Looking back, I can see if I had just made an effort, things would have been different. I just assumed people didn't want to be friends with me. Patrick made the effort to get to know me and we became friends all through school. He was good in math and science and I was good in English. We helped each other."

She kept her eyes on the curtains. "In high school our relationship changed. Patrick wanted to hold my hand and he'd kiss my cheek unexpectedly. I was too young and naïve to recognize the signs. Patrick was in love with me."

"He'd been crazy about you forever," Tripp said.

Camila looked down at her hands and studied her white knuckles. "But I didn't feel that way about him. He was my friend—my very good friend."

"Did you tell him that?"

"Yes, but he said it didn't matter. We could still be friends."

"That's why you came to the party?"

"I didn't get an invitation, but Patrick insisted. That year he started tutoring some of the football players so they could pass. He changed then, wanting to be a part of the in crowd—the football jocks. He invited them all to the party, Vance, Wallis, and several others. They knew, as Patrick put it, that he was mooning over me. Wallis told him he could give him something to make him a he-man, take-charge-of-your-woman type man. Patrick took the drug and slipped something into my drink. I didn't know this until Patrick told me later."

Tripp felt anger mounting inside him. He'd wanted answers to alleviate his pain and now he'd opened Pandora's box and he couldn't close it. He had to hear the rest and he didn't know if he had enough strength to face what he was beginning to feel in his gut.

"Patrick became very affectionate and I just wanted him to stop touching me, but I couldn't get the words out. Then I was so dizzy and you were holding me and I… Patrick was angry with you for dancing with me. I tried to tell him we weren't dancing, but my mind was fuzzy and I…and I…"

"What happened next?" he prompted, now knowing Camila hadn't been coming on to him. She'd just been drugged and probably had been looking for an understanding person.

"I don't remember much, but Patrick took me to his room. He kept saying he loved me and we were going to get married.

I just wanted to lie down. I was having a hard time standing up and then…"

Her words trailed away into a vast vacuum of speculation and dread. He got up to ease the suspicion in him, but there was only one way to do that—to say the words out loud. He didn't know if he could do that, though. Looking at her pale face, the words slipped out of their own volition.

"Did he force you to have sex?"

She shook her head. "Patrick would never do that."

"Did you want to have sex with him?"

"No, but I gave in because…"

"Oh my God! Oh my God!" The words erupted from deep within him.

"It wasn't his fault," Camila cried. "The drugs made him another person and he was so sorry afterwards. He came to my house the next day and begged for me to forgive him. He wanted us to run away and get married. I told him no and he began to cry saying I was his best friend. That made me angry and I told him his football buddies were his friends. But they really weren't—they played a cruel joke on him and me, and they laughed about it. Patrick said he saw Vance earlier and he was eager to know what had happened. Patrick was just sick and couldn't believe what he'd done. But I couldn't forgive him then. I asked him to leave."

She took a breath, pushing out the rest of the story. "He said I was never attracted to him—that I was attracted to his older brother and he knew it. I…I…told him that was true. He crashed his car a few hours later." She drew in more air. "So you see you're not to blame for Patrick's death—I am."

Tripp jammed hands through his hair feeling as if the floor had just given way and he was falling, falling…. He yanked open the door and stepped outside, sucking cold air into his lungs, letting it cool the heated emotions in him. His legs felt weak and he sank down onto the step.

How could something like this happen? In a small town like Bramble? There were good people here, good kids. How did one party get so out of control? All he could feel was anger at what had been done to Patrick. To Camila. All for a joke— a good laugh. For years he'd known something hadn't been right, but he'd never imagined this depth of cruelty.

He said I was never attracted to him—that I was attracted to his older brother and he knew it. I...I...told him that was true.

Oh, God. He could have stopped everything that night if he'd just taken control of the situation, taken Camila home. But he hadn't. The thought was like acid in his gut. How did he make this right?

NAUSEA ROSE in Camila's stomach and she ran to the bathroom, drawing deep breaths. After a minute, the churning stopped and she wiped her face with a wet washcloth. She'd never told anyone that story and the aftermath was almost more than she could bear. The look, the shock, in Tripp's eyes was what she'd expected—that's why she'd avoided talking to him. He hated her. She'd killed his brother. She'd killed Jilly's father by not being more understanding. But she'd been incredibly hurt.

She wasn't going to think about this anymore tonight. It was driving her crazy. She went to the kitchen to turn out the light. The door opened and Tripp came back in.

"Neither of us are to blame for Patrick's death," he said, his voice hoarse. "Patrick made some bad decisions by getting in with the wrong crowd. He's to blame for that, not you. You're the victim in all this."

She blinked back a tear, hardly believing her ears. This was more than she'd expected. "Thank you, but if I had been more understanding, more…"

"He forced you, for God's sake."

Her hand touched her throbbing temple. "Please."

"Camila, these boys wanted to get back at you for rejecting them and it got way out of control. Patrick got caught up in that. I'm so sorry for all you've been through."

Words stuck in her throat.

"I think you've done a remarkable job putting your life back together."

"I had Jilly. Something good came out of it."

"She's the best of you and Patrick."

She looped her hair behind her ear. "I've always thought that."

Their eyes clung and neither could say what they wanted to. It would take time. He reached for his hat. "I'd better go. It's getting late and a lot colder."

"I haven't listened to the weather. How cold is it suppose to get?"

"It'll probably be freezing by morning."

"Oh no." She grabbed a big coat out of a closet. "Could you stay with Jilly for a few minutes? I don't like leaving her alone this late."

His eyes narrowed. "Where are you going?"

"I lit a heater for Unie earlier and sometimes she turns it off. I have to make sure it's still on or she'll freeze to death."

"Why doesn't she light it herself?"

"The gas company turned off her gas about a year ago because she couldn't pay her bill. I had it turned back on and pretended the gas company had done it by mistake. If she knew I was paying for the gas, she wouldn't use it. So when it's cold, I go over and light her heater. She won't light it because she's afraid she'll be arrested. I tell her not to worry that when she's used up all the money she's paid in, they'll cut it off. But she doesn't quite grasp everything. I just don't want her to be cold."

She buttoned her coat and pulled her hair back into a ponytail and slipped a band around it. "I'll be gone ten minutes tops."

She flew out the door and Tripp stood there with his mouth open. He'd never met anyone like Camila before—giving so much of herself and asking nothing in return. Patrick had known her good qualities though, that's why he'd been so crazy about her.

Tripp tried to sort through everything he'd learned tonight. But only one thing stood out. Camila was an incredible woman.

CAMILA PARKED IN FRONT of Unie's house, glad for the diversion. It gave her time to gather her wits, her emotions. "Unie, it's Camila." She knocked loudly on the door. "Open up. It's cold."

"Who is it?" Unie shouted.

"Camila."

"You alone?"

"Yes."

The door opened a crack and Unie peered at her. "You alone?" Unie asked again.

"Yes, Unie, I'm alone. I came to see if your heater works. It's getting colder."

Unie opened the door, Lu Lu in her arms. She had the same clothes on she had earlier in the day. "Gas company turned off my gas."

"I'll just check," Camila said, walking into the house, which was dark and very cluttered. One side of the living room was piled with plastic bags filled with cans. The house felt like an icebox. Camila sighed. Unie had turned off the heater. She pulled matches from her pocket and squatted at the only heater in the house. It roared to life within seconds.

"There," Camila said. "Now the room will get warmer."

"Bless you child." Unie came closer to the fire.

Unie sat in her chair close to the fire then jerked forward. "Is Bert outside?"

"No."

"You better leave, child. I can't have Bert stealing my cans."

"Okay. Don't turn the fire off. Just leave it on until you leave the house tomorrow. "

"It feels good."

"Unie, leave the heater on." Camila wanted to make sure Unie understood her.

Unie looked at her with a blank look.

"It's night and no one will know but you and me."

A thin smile touched her lips. "Good. No one will know."

"That's right so leave the heater on." She'd gotten through. Unie understood. "Good night, Unie."

WHEN CAMILA WALKED IN, Tripp glanced at the clock. "Wow. Ten minutes exactly."

Camila removed her coat. "Unie doesn't like anyone in her house too long."

"You do this every time it gets cold?"

"Yes." She hung her coat in the closet. "Thanks for staying."

"No problem." He placed his hat on his head. "How old is Unie? I remember her when I was kid."

"She's about ninety. No one knows that much about her. She took care of her parents until they died, then she became a recluse."

His eyes caught hers. "You're an incredible person."

A slight flush stained her cheeks and neither said a word for a moment.

"Thanks for telling me about that night. I know it was hard for you."

"I'd sworn never to tell anyone."

"Because of Jilly?"

"Yes. My main goal in life is to protect her."

He nodded. "From now on it will be mine, too. Your secret is safe with me."

"Thank you."

"Good night, Camila."

"Good night," she whispered, feeling as if he'd kissed her.

She walked into the living room and lay on the sofa. Tears rolled from her eyes and she didn't know why she was crying. She felt good and she felt bad. The two emotions together filled her with sadness. A sadness that one night had changed so many lives. A sadness that Patrick was gone. A sadness that she and Tripp would never be anything more than close acquaintances.

"Camila?"

Her mother stood in the doorway—the last person she wanted to see.

Chapter Eleven

Camila sat up. "What are you doing here?"

Benita flopped down beside her. "Just wanted to talk to my chick." She gestured toward the street. "Saw the cowboy leaving. Dare I hope you have something going with him?"

Camila glared at her. "I do not. Tripp came to talk about Jilly visiting his parents."

"Are you allowing it?"

"Of course. They're her grandparents."

Benita shook her head. "Camila, chick, this is where you stick the knife in and twist. This is where you get even for the way they've treated you."

Camila frowned. "Do you really believe that? Do you really believe that would be in Jilly's best interest? Everything I do, I do for her—to make her life better."

"Better than yours?" Benita lifted an arched eyebrow.

Camila sighed. "I'm not getting into that again."

"I was a lousy mother. I admit it."

Camila turned to face her. "Yes, you were. You never thought about me—just about what you wanted and a good time. You never cared how you embarrassed me. You—"

Tears slipped from Benita's eyes, forcing Camila to stop. All her anger vanished at the sight. She'd never seen her mother cry.

"You don't know what it was like," Benita cried. "Papa loved me and I worshipped him. I'd dance and he'd clap and laugh and we'd sing. I was happy, then he died suddenly and I was lost without him. *Madre* was like a drill sergeant, don't do this and don't do that. Dancing wasn't allowed anymore— it was sinful. Sometimes I was afraid to breathe, afraid of disappointing her. Then I discovered boys and they liked it when I danced. I could almost hear Papa clapping, saying, 'Have a good time, Benita. Enjoy life.'"

Benita brushed away a speck on her pants. "I guess I've been looking for a man like Papa—kind, loving and with a great sense of humor, who would make me happy. I haven't found him yet."

"What about my father?" Camila asked, surprising herself. "Did you love him?" They'd never talked about this and she suddenly needed to know.

"Ah, Travis Holden was about the most handsome man I'd ever laid eyes on. I couldn't concentrate in class for dreaming about him. He was my first sexual experience and I wasn't too wise about contraception and got pregnant. Travis wasn't happy about that, but he married me—mostly because *Madre* had a talk with his parents. We lived together about three months, then he went away to college in Lubbock and I stayed here to have you. We talked quite often at first, then the calls got fewer and fewer. He came back when you were born and asked for a divorce. He said he was going to seek custody of you, but I think he met someone else 'cause he never followed through."

"You've never talked about him before."

"I have a picture somewhere if you want to see what he looked like."

"Yes. I'd like that." Like Jilly, she wanted to see what her father looked like.

There was silence, then Benita said, "I wasn't even eighteen when you were born and I didn't know anything about babies, about love, about life. *Madre* took us from the hospital and took over—and I let her. I was young. I wanted to have fun. I didn't have those motherly instincts and I felt different and did stupid things—like getting married again, and again." She glanced at Camila. "But I loved you, chick. You were my little girl and probably the best thing I ever did was let *Madre* raise you."

"Why would you think that? It was the same environment that you grew up in, stern, strict, no fun, but I was completely lost when she died. When I discovered I was pregnant, I was so afraid. I don't know what I'd have done if it hadn't been for Millie. I needed you then. I needed a mother."

Benita began to cry again, but Camila didn't stop. "When I was ten, you planned to take me with you, but you gave in to *Madre* and left me behind. That hurt. I wanted to be with my mother."

"Dios."

"You say you don't have motherly instincts. How do you know? You've never tried. I was so nervous when Jilly was born. What if I held her wrong? What if she stopped breathing? She weighed six pounds and four ounces and she scared the life out of me. But no one was raising my child but me."

Benita buried her face in her hands, continuing to cry.

"You have a daughter, a granddaughter and we need you. It's time to grow up and stop chasing after a man you're never going to find and to be a part of this family. You always come back so that has to be a sign that there's something here that you care about."

Benita groped for Camila and held her tight. "I love you, chickadee." Then she jumped up and ran out the door.

"I love you, too," Camila whispered. But her mother was gone.

TRIPP GRABBED A BEER out of the refrigerator. Everyone was in bed so he went into the den and dropped to the sofa, propping his feet on the coffee table and resting his head against the cushions. He took a big swallow thinking of what those boys had done to Patrick. To Camila. His stomach churned with familiar anger.

But something wasn't right. It wasn't anything Camila had said. It was something about Patrick and the last time he'd seen him that day in the barn. He forced himself to remember. When Patrick had first come in, he hadn't been angry, he'd just seemed despondent. Tripp had been brushing down a horse and Patrick had sat on a bale of hay, watching him.

Patrick had said he didn't do drugs and Tripp shouldn't have mentioned anything to their parents. They would start watching him like a hawk. Then out of the blue he'd asked, "How do you make someone love you?"

Tripp had told him that it had to happen naturally. That had angered Patrick and what he had said was engraved in Tripp's mind.

All you have to do is be you and the girls fall all over you. She doesn't even see me for you. No girl does. It's the same way with them, too. They used me and I know how to get even and I will.

Patrick had run from the barn before Tripp could stop him.

He hadn't known what Patrick had been talking about and later, after they'd found out he'd crashed his car, Tripp had thought that he'd meant suicide—that he'd kill himself. But now that didn't sound right.

I know how to get even. That didn't sound like a person intending to commit suicide. It sounded like Patrick had wanted revenge. That was what Tripp wanted now in the worst way. But he'd bide his time and soon he and Vance and Wallis would meet. It wouldn't be at night and it wouldn't be an ambush. He would get some straight answers and he'd settle the score.

For Camila.

He took a big swig of beer, letting himself think about

Patrick and what he'd done to her. His actions didn't resemble the softhearted, intelligent boy Tripp had known, but then, Patrick had been swayed by other influences, and of course, his unrequited feelings for Camila. He'd wanted her to love him and she didn't.

That didn't excuse what he'd done. It only made it worse.

She doesn't even see me for you.

He'd been talking about Camila.

Here came the guilt. Tenfold. Camila had been looking at him and he'd been looking back. And Patrick had known. Tripp would never have done anything about the way he felt about Camila—and never would. She'd been hurt enough. Good God. What a mess.

And the worst part of all—he'd believed the rumors like everyone else in this town. He went to bed wondering how he could have ever done that.

THE NEXT MORNING, Camila felt disoriented from the night before. Too many revelations, too many heartaches, yet it had felt good to share the past with Tripp. She'd carried that night with her for so long, her secret pain. Now Tripp knew and she felt lighter, understanding the past a little more—if that were possible. She didn't think she'd ever really understand how that night had turned into a nightmare. But it was over and she had Jilly. That's how she'd handled the past—by loving her daughter.

She dropped Jilly at school and drove to Bramble's small grocery store to talk to Fred, the manager, about a cart for Unie. He had a broken one and said she could have it. She gave him five dollars for the cart and made him write out a bill of sale to Unie so Bert couldn't take it away from her. She talked Slim into welding it together.

"Benita's back," she said, knowing it would be all over Bramble soon.

"Hot damn." Slim wiped his hands. "That ought to liven up this town."

Camila looked down at her sneakers. "That's what I'm afraid of."

Slim grinned. "Benita is Benita. And that's not going to change."

Normally she'd want to crawl away in a corner when anyone spoke of her mother, but Slim was right; Benita was Benita. Maybe it was time Camila accepted that.

Camila painted Property of Eunice Gimble in red on the cart, just in case Bert tried to pull a fast one. Then she pushed it down the street and into the bank.

Thelma Boggs watched her. Camila rolled the cart up to Bert's desk.

"Why the hell did you bring that in here?" Bert asked, his brow knotted together.

Camila pointed to the name on the cart. "This cart is property of Eunice Gimble and if you take it away from her, I'll have you arrested for theft."

His eyes bulged out of his head. "Don't come in here threatening me."

"I'm just telling you, Bert. That's the way it's going to be." She pushed the cart outside with everyone staring at her. That was okay. She'd made her point.

TRIPP WORKED TIRELESSLY on the ranch, trying not to think about Camila, but she was in his every waking moment and most of his dreams. She should hate him because he could have stopped what had happened that night. But she didn't seem to blame him for anything. He did, though.

He had people coming to clean the fountain and pool. Jilly might enjoy the pool this summer.

But he might not be here.

That thought edged its way through all the worries about

his parents, about Camila. He couldn't stay away from his ranch much longer. He couldn't leave here, either. His parents needed him. What could he do? Work until he couldn't think.

The accident kept running through his mind and he still felt something wasn't right. There was more to it. It could have been that Patrick was distracted by revenge so he wasn't watching the road. As many times as Tripp told himself that, he didn't believe it. He'd talk to Wyatt as soon as he could. He hadn't been the sheriff then, but he might be able to answer some questions, to alleviate Tripp's mind.

That night in bed, as tired as he was, he could still see Camila's dark eyes. He wanted some sort of victory for her so she wouldn't blame herself for anything that'd happened.

Would he ever stop blaming himself?

TIME PASSED QUICKLY for Camila. Unie had her cart again and was pushing it all over town, picking up cans. Camila was expecting a visit from Bert, but so far he'd stayed away.

At the next city council meeting, she found out why. Bert had put Eunice Gimble on the agenda for discussion. He considered Unie a nuisance to the town and said she should be committed to a mental institution where she could get medical treatment. Since Unie had no relatives, he proposed the city hire an attorney to have the necessary paperwork drawn up.

While she agreed the town should do something, Camila disagreed on a mental institution and luckily the other members agreed with her.

She heaved a sigh of relief. For now, the city would not have Unie committed. Camila had more time to do something because she knew Bert was not going to let this drop.

CAMILA KEPT BUSY making soap and quilting, but Tripp was never far from her mind. Benita came by and helped with the packages to mail, but she was very quiet, very subdued, which wasn't like her at all. Camila didn't know if she liked her mother this way. Benita wasn't herself.

Her hands stilled over the fabric in her lap as she pondered that thought. She wanted Benita to be someone she wasn't. Looking back, Camila saw that she was like *Madre*— structured and molded in her behavior. Maybe if she'd been able to shrug off some of the rude remarks and laugh and joke, then maybe she wouldn't have felt things so deeply. That reality was hard to digest.

She couldn't go back and change the way she'd felt, but now she had an opportunity to get to know her mother. Talk as equals, be friends, and most of all, learn how to be mother and daughter.

That would make her happy.

THURSDAY, TRIPP TOOK his mother to the doctor in Temple and surgery was scheduled for Monday. Leona was still nervous, but Tripp knew she now had a purpose—seeing her granddaughter.

After he took his mother home, he drove over to the county seat to speak with Wyatt, who showed him the old file on Patrick's accident.

There wasn't much in the file. Notes said beer had been found in the car, and there were photos of the crashed Corvette and tire marks along Harper's Road, as if someone had been burning rubber. Then there was another note—Corvette hit the tree head-on and the front end of the car was pushed almost completely into the front seat. Patrick's body was on the passenger's side.

The passenger side.

That didn't make sense, so he showed Wyatt.

Wyatt shook his head. "Why are you dredging this up now?"

"I have a lot of unresolved issues about my brother's death."

"Let it go, Tripp," Wyatt said in a sympathetic voice. "It was an accident."

On the way back to Lady Luck, Tripp's mind was in a whirl. Patrick's body had been on the passenger's side. He couldn't get that out of his head. Yet there wasn't any evidence to support another person being at the scene of the accident. But his instincts told him there had been. Someone else had been driving Patrick's Corvette.

But who?

ON FRIDAY, CAMILA was nervous and she didn't understand why. Jilly visiting with the Danielses was constantly on her mind. She kept watching the clock and had to force herself to stop. It was a visit, nothing else. So why was she so on edge? She dropped a stitch and said a curse word under her breath.

She was acting like Jilly wasn't coming back. A pain shot right through her and she had to take a breath. What was wrong with her? It wasn't like she was losing Jilly.

Benita came into the shop. "Hi, chick, need any help?"

She sensed Benita was at loose ends and wanted something to do. "Do you mind watching the shop? I have to take Jilly to the Danielses'. The prices are marked."

"Sure." Benita looked at her. "You seem a little nervous."

Camila took a breath. "I guess I am, which is ridiculous."

"Would you like me to go with you? I can watch the shop if you'd rather, but I feel you need me more."

Camila did, and she was surprised Benita recognized it. "Yes. I'd like that. Millie will watch out for customers."

After a brief stop at her house to pick up Button, they headed for the school. Camila handed the dog to Benita and her hand shook a little.

"Relax, Camila," Benita said. "You wanted this for Jilly."

"This was actually Jilly's idea." Camila told her about Jilly's bicycle ride out to see Tripp.

Benita laughed. "That's my girl."

"I want her to be independent and stand up for herself, but sometimes she even surprises me."

"You were always very shy," Benita remarked, stroking Button.

"Yes. Painfully so."

"Because you were ashamed of me." The words came out low and hurt, but Camila heard them.

Camila parked at the school. "I've always loved you, Benita. I just never understood why you did some of the things you did."

"Me, neither," Benita replied, and Jilly came running and nothing else was said.

Camila waved to Betty Sue, Jolene and Rhonda, another mother. Jilly crawled into the back seat.

Button barked excitedly and jumped into Jilly's arms.

"Hi, Mama, Benita." She leaned over and kissed them, holding Button. "This is so totally cool—all of us together." Then she rolled down the window and waved at her friends as Camila drove away.

"Buckle your seat belt," Camila said.

"Mama," Jilly sighed. "I'm not five."

"Oops. I forgot. You're a day away from being twelve."

"Right. Benita, I'm glad you're here for my birthday. Mama makes it a special day. She even bakes my cake. That's the first thing I'll smell in the morning. Then we have my private birthday—just Mama and me. I don't know what I'll do when I grow up and go away to college and have to leave Mama. But don't tell my friends that."

"Your secret is safe with me," Benita said, glancing at Camila.

Those innocently spoken words made Camila feel so much better. She and Jilly had a good relationship; other relationships could only make it stronger.

She would see to that.

Chapter Twelve

When Camila drove into the circular drive, the front door opened and Tripp came onto the veranda. His shirt hung over his jeans and his hair was tousled, as if he'd been working. She felt that familiar flutter in her stomach.

"Bye, Mama, Benita." Jilly gave them quick kisses and was gone.

"I'll pick you up at seven," Camila called.

"Okay."

Jilly's thoughts were now on the Danielses and Camila experienced a moment of loneliness. She'd have to work on letting go.

"Doesn't feel very good, does it?" Benita asked as Camila drove away.

"What?"

"Leaving your child?"

She glanced at her mother, saw the pain on her face and wasn't sure what to say.

"I felt that way every time I left you, but I always thought *Madre* was better for you. Now I can see that I was wrong. I should have tried to be a mother instead of someone dropping in and out of your life."

Camila blinked away a tear. "I never knew you felt that way."

"Surprising, huh?" Benita brushed back her hair. "I see you

with Jilly and I envy that closeness. Jilly adores you and she thinks you can do anything. I wish we had a similar relationship. At least one where you liked me."

"We'll work on it." She held out her hand to her mother and Benita placed hers in it. Camila squeezed, as did Benita. "We don't really know each other, so spending time together should be a good starting point."

"I agree," Benita said, "but you're so busy."

"I can always use help."

"Deal," Benita replied.

Camila knew their relationship was changing for the better. Maybe because they were older. Or maybe because they were mother and daughter. Whatever the reason, they loved each other and Camila needed her mother.

Now more than ever.

BENITA HAD GONE HOME and Camila was working in the shop when the phone rang.

"Mama, we're having a cookout," Jilly said. "Can I stay until eight o'clock? I'm having a really good time."

No. No. I want you to come home.

"Sure, baby," came out of her mouth. "I'll pick you up at eight."

"Thanks, Mama. Tripp wants you to come, too."

She bit her lip, wanting to accept, but knowing that Tripp was just trying to be polite. "No, thanks. I have a lot of work to do. I'll be there at eight."

"Mama?"

"I'll be there at eight, Jilly." Her voice was stern and Jilly recognized it.

"Okay. Bye."

Camila took a moment to compose herself. Jilly was having a good time. That's what mattered. As she stood there staring at the phone, she realized something about herself. She wasn't good at sharing. Only because she'd never had to share Jilly before. She had a lot to learn.

Now she had time to finish preparations for the party. The domino game was at Slim's house tonight because Camila wanted to decorate the coffee shop. Everyone wanted Jilly to have a wonderful day.

"Need any help, sweetie?" Millie asked as Camila placed boxes of decorations on a table.

"My mother's going to help." She hadn't asked Benita, but she knew she'd come if she asked. This could be their time together.

"I guess miracles do happen," Millie replied, tongue in cheek, taking off her apron.

"Millie."

"Okay. I'm bad and too old to change."

"For me would you please try to get along with her?"

"For you, sweetie, I'd do anything. But don't expect too much." She picked up a tray of snacks. "I'll take these over to the domino players and I'll see you in the morning."

"Bye, Millie."

Camila locked the door behind her and sorted through the box of decorations. She glanced at her watch and decided to give Benita time to finish supper, then she'd call her.

She pulled out the helium machine she'd rented and began to blow up balloons and tie them together with colorful ribbons. Jilly liked balloons and Camila planned to fill the shop with them.

Absorbed in her task, she jumped when someone tapped at the door. She wondered if Millie had forgotten something or it could be her mother. She hurried to the door and stopped in her tracks when she saw who it was. Tripp stood outside.

The first thought that occurred to her was that something had happened to Jilly. She yanked open the door.

"What's wrong? Is Jilly okay?"

"Whoa." Tripp held up a hand. "Jilly's fine."

"Oh." She let out a long breath.

"I came to take you to the cookout."

She blinked. "What?"

"Jilly was very quiet after she talked with you and I know she wants you there so I'm asking in person. Please come to supper."

"Oh." Her pulse skittered alarmingly and she wondered what he'd say if she told him she'd never been on a date. Patrick had driven her out to Lady Luck several times and that was the closest she'd ever come to one. Of course, this wasn't a date—just an invitation. But she sensed it could be more.

"I really have a lot of work to do to get ready for Jilly's party."

Tripp glanced at the clumps of balloon floating on the ceiling. "I thought work was an excuse."

"No."

He grinned. "Tell you what, you come to supper and I'll help you decorate later."

"I really…"

"Jilly wants you there. I want you there." His eyes held hers. "Please."

All her common sense left her at the sound of that one word. The blue eyes so tempting didn't help either. "Okay," she heard herself saying.

He smiled and her knees felt weak. "Get your coat and let's go. Jilly's waiting."

"I…I can come in my car."

"I'll bring you back. Remember I have to help with the decorations."

"That's really—"

He held up one finger. "No arguing."

Before she knew it, she was in his truck heading for Lady Luck. There was something intimate about being in the cab with him, within touching distance, breathing the same air.

The cab smelled faintly of leather, old boots and a fragrance she couldn't define, unless masculinity had a smell.

Sunglasses rested on the dash along with a pair of leather gloves. On the back seat were a couple of ropes.

"Do you always carry ropes with you?"

He slanted her a smile. "Never know when you might need one."

She knew he was a championship calf roper. "The year you won the national championship, the whole town watched."

"Really?"

"Yes. Rose brought in a bigger TV and the place was packed with people watching."

"Did you watch?"

Like a fool. "Yes, I did. I thought you were great."

"Thank you. That year my friend, Colter Kincaid, won the bareback championship. We were feeling pretty good about ourselves."

"And you won it the next year."

He glanced at her. "So you keep up with the rodeo?"

"It's hard not to do with everyone in town talking about it. You've put Bramble on the map and everyone is proud of you."

"Are you?"

They drove into the circular drive and Jilly came running out, preventing Camila from answering. She was more than grateful for that reprieve.

"Mama." Jilly hugged her. "I'm glad you changed your mind." Jilly took her hand and led her into the house. "We've been real busy cleaning. Mrs. Daniels is getting her eyes done and Tripp wants the house similar to what it used to be when she sees it clearly again. Tripp didn't want me to help, but I told him I know how to clean. I've dusted everything and Mr. Daniels says the staircase sparkles like a brand new silver dollar. Mrs. Daniels is taking care of Button." Jilly pulled her into the living room, chattering nonstop.

"Camila, I'm so glad you came," Leona said, sitting on the sofa, holding Button.

"Now maybe we can eat," Grif added in his grumpy voice.

Jilly wagged a finger at him. "You have to be nice."

"Fiddle faddle."

"Balderdash," Jilly countered.

"Poppycock."

"Hogwash."

"Dang-nab it, girl," Grif growled with a grin on his face. "You're not supposed to talk back."

Jilly placed her hands on her hips. "Are you going to be nice?"

"Aw. Okay." Grif glanced at Camila. "Your daughter is running me ragged."

"Yes. I can see." Jilly was so comfortable with them, as they were with her. Any awkwardness had completely vanished. But Camila wasn't so sure about the Danielses accepting her.

"We'll eat on the patio if that's okay with everyone," Tripp said.

"Isn't it too cold out there?" Grif asked with his usual impatience.

"The temperature is in the sixties, but it's pleasant outside. Jilly has the table all set."

Leona got to her feet and Button jumped out of her arms and trotted to Camila. "By all means, we'll eat on the patio," Leona said.

Camila picked up Button, glad of something to hold. "What can I do to help?"

"Nothing," Tripp replied. "Jilly, Morris and I have it under control."

Tripp took Leona's elbow and they went through the French doors to the patio. Morris stood at a grill with a large white apron covering him.

"Miss Camila, it's good to see you," Morris said.

"Thank you, Morris. Can I help?"

"Yes, ma'am. You can sit down and stay out of my way. Don't like women telling me what to do. You've been working all day so take a load off."

Camila took a seat by Leona. "I apologize for the men in my family. Manners are not a strong suit."

"I'm working on them," Jilly said, standing between Leona and Camila.

"You're doing a marvelous job," Leona replied.

Camila glanced at the table with the blue napkins and a bright colored ribbon tied around each, like Camila did at home. "The table looks wonderful," she said to Jilly.

"I did everything like you do, Mama."

"Yes. I see."

"How do you want your burger, Miss Camila?" Morris asked.

"Well done."

"No blood in mine," Jilly said.

"Yes, Miss Jilly, you've already told me that."

"Just wanted to make sure."

The meal passed in a flurry of chatter—mostly Jilly's. It was as if she'd known the three older people all her life.

"Mrs. Daniels is having surgery on Monday, Mama," Jilly announced.

"That's wonderful," Camila replied. "It's going to make a world of difference."

"That's what my son tells me."

Camila sensed Leona's nervousness. "I know several ladies that have had it done and it's quite simple. It's an out-patient type thing and then no bending or lifting for a few days. You'll be able to see much better."

"Oh, I hope so."

"I'll come keep you company," Jilly promised.

"I'll look forward to that."

The wind grew chilly and Leona and Grif went inside with

Jilly and Button while Tripp and Camila cleared the table and carried the dishes to the kitchen.

"I'll do the dishes," Camila offered.

"No, no, no," Morris snapped. "Don't want a woman in my kitchen. I ain't gotten so old to where I can't do a few dishes."

Tripp caught her elbow and guided her out onto the patio. "We could use a bottle of Prozac around here every day."

Camila smiled, sitting in a chair. "That's just older people. They're quite candid."

Tripp pulled up a chair and sat facing her, their knees inches apart. It was almost too close for comfort, but it was nice— just the two of them alone with the night surrounding them.

"By the end of the day, I'm feeling as if I need a shot of whiskey or just wishing for someone to shoot me."

She suppressed a laugh. "You're doing very well and the place is looking much better."

"I have aches and pains to prove that, but I want the place halfway decent by the time my mother can see again."

"That's very nice."

Silence grew heavy.

"How are you?" Tripp asked.

"Fine." Her gaze centered on his face. "Your bruises are healing."

He touched the fading darkness around his eye. "Yeah. My aches are about gone, too."

There was silence again.

Tripp shifted uncomfortably. "I know how hard it was to talk about Patrick the other night."

She linked her fingers together. "I've never told anyone what really happened."

"I just keep thinking I could have stopped everything."

Her eyes shot to his. "How?"

"When you were dizzy and I caught you, you moved your body against mine and I thought you were coming on to me."

"Oh," slipped from her lips.

"I knew you were either drunk or drugged, but still I did nothing."

"Why?"

He took a long breath. "Because I believed the rumors and when I saw you coming out of Patrick's room, it confirmed everything I was thinking. Or so I thought." His eyes held hers. "I'm so sorry."

She swallowed hard, trying not to let that hurt. Her cowboy had feet of clay. He was human. She cleared her throat and glanced up at the stars, needing to be honest but knowing this truth would not come easy. "I was probably coming on to you. I remember seeing you and wishing I could dance with you."

He shook his head. "Why do you do that?"

"What?"

"Take the blame for everything."

She chewed on the inside of her lip. "Maybe because it's true."

"It's not." His eyes darkened. "You should be angry that I didn't take you home right then and there."

She lifted an eyebrow. "Now who's taking the blame?"

He sighed and ran his hands through his hair, leaving it tousled and making him that much more attractive. "I'm just impressed that you've handled everything so well—impressed that you're not filled with anger and hatred."

Her fingers tightened. "I was for a while. I just wanted to crawl away and die, but then I discovered I was pregnant—an innocent little baby—and I had to rise above everything I was feeling and make a life for her."

"I'm totally blown away with all you've accomplished."

She moved uneasily. "Thank you."

He looked into her eyes. "Something about Patrick's accident is bothering me."

"What?"

"I'd always thought Patrick was angry at me for mentioning the drugs to my parents and for coming to your aid, but as I think back over our conversation that day, Patrick seemed more bent on revenge. He said they used him and he knew how to get even. I'm just recalling some of this because I've been fixated on blaming myself. Did Patrick mention any of this to you when he was at your house?"

Camila scooted to the edge of her seat. "No. He just wanted me to forgive him."

"This has been driving me crazy and I finally went and read the report on the accident. I learned something that was really puzzling."

"What?"

"Patrick's body was on the passenger's side, and there was no evidence anyone else was in the car."

"You feel there was?"

"Yes." He stood and paced. "But no one could have survived that accident."

"Maybe his body was thrown to the other side."

"Could be, but I don't think so. I think someone else was driving."

"But who?"

"I haven't got a clue."

"When Patrick was at my house, he said it was Wallis and Vance's fault. He shouldn't have listened to them, but…but he wanted me to love him so badly that he let them persuade him to take the drug."

"So if anyone was driving, it has to be one of them."

"Maybe," she said and got to her feet. "But it's not going to do either one of us any good to keep speculating. It happened so long ago and there's no way to prove anything now. It's time to go forward—not backward. Stop blaming yourself."

He moved so close she could feel his breath on her cheek, her skin and everything in her melted into a warm fire fueled by nothing but his breath.

"Patrick said you couldn't see him for me."

She breathed in the scent of him. "Yes...I...I had a terrible crush on you and Patrick picked up on it." She pulled her coat tighter around her. "I guess you're used to hearing that."

"No. Not from someone I couldn't take my eyes off of. Patrick saw that, too."

She was unable to speak.

"It's true. Patrick knew it wouldn't take much for me to fall hard for you."

"I've got to go," she said in a hurry, suddenly not able to handle this.

He grabbed her arm. "I'm being honest, Camila. That's all."

She licked her lips. "This is very difficult for me."

He watched her tongue and his head bent. Her insides quivered with expectation, with longing and with a need too long denied. She stood on tiptoes to meet his lips.

"Mama?"

The moment was gone. Camila turned to her daughter, her breath lodged in her throat like a block of wood, restricting her breathing.

"Are you through cleaning out here?" Jilly asked.

"Yes, baby, and it's time for us to go home."

Goodbyes were said, but Camila didn't remember much of anything. All she could think about was the look in Tripp's eyes. It wasn't guilt or blame. It was emotion, passionate emotions—for her. She wasn't sure she was ready for that.

Why not? ran through her mind all the way into town. *Why not?*

Chapter Thirteen

Tripp pulled up to the back of Camila's shop.

"I had a really good time. Thanks for asking me." Jilly crawled out of the double-cab truck.

"You're welcome," Tripp replied. "We'll do it again real soon."

"Okay. I'd like that. Bye, Tripp."

As Camila reached for the door handle, Tripp whispered, "I'll meet you here in thirty minutes."

Her eyes met his. "There's no need."

"A deal's a deal. I'll be waiting."

Jilly was outside, so Camila couldn't argue the point. She got out feeling as if her emotions were either going to take a nosedive or skyrocket to the moon. Either way, she wasn't prepared.

And she should be. She was thirty years old, but in some ways she was as naïve as Jilly about men—in other ways she didn't want to think about. So much had been taken from her by a night of reckless behavior. She could stay in that vault she'd built for herself or do something about it.

Patrick knew it wouldn't take much for me to fall hard for you.

Tripp had actually said those words, and they bolstered her courage and scared her at the same time. Her mind was bouncing back and forth with such swiftness that she just realized her daughter was very quiet on the drive to the house.

Unlocking their back door, Camila said, "You haven't mentioned what you want to do for your birthday."

Jilly flopped down at the kitchen table. "After what I did, I thought I didn't get to choose anymore."

Camila pinched her cheek. "We'll think of something. Now go take a bath and get ready for bed."

"It's good that Mrs. Daniels is going to have surgery, isn't it, Mama?"

"Yes. Very good."

"But she's so scared."

"Tripp will be with her."

"I suppose." Jilly headed for the hall, then turned back. "What kind of cake are you gonna make?"

"That's a surprise."

"Just so it's chocolate."

"I know."

Jilly looked sad and Camila walked over and put her arms around her. "What is it, baby?"

"They're so lonely, Mama, and it makes me sad."

"Your visit cheered them up."

Jilly drew back. "Can I go back tomorrow and spend some of my birthday with them?"

"You have to be asked, baby, and besides Benita will want to spend time with you, too. It's going to be a busy day."

"Yeah." Jilly hugged her mother then went to her room.

Camila's heart broke seeing her child in such distress, but Jilly had been that way since she was small—worrying about other people.

After Jilly had her bath, they talked and laughed about their day. Jilly was feeling better, getting excited about her birthday.

Camila kissed her. "I have to go back to the shop to finish up an order. Benita will be here."

"I'm not a baby. I don't need a sitter and why do you have to go back to the shop? You work too much."

"Shh." Camila placed a finger over her lips. "Go to sleep."

Benita walked in as Camila entered the kitchen. "So where are you going that you want me to stay with Jilly?"

"I haven't finished the decorations."

Benita lifted a dark eyebrow. "That's not like you. You always do things ahead of time. One of those annoying little habits of yours."

Camila slipped into her coat. "I went to supper at the Danielses with Jilly."

"Wahoo! That's something."

"Yes. So now I have to finish before morning."

"Millie can stay with Jilly and I'll help you. That way it won't take so long."

Camila picked up her purse. "Someone else is helping me."

"Oh. Who?"

"Tripp Daniels."

"Wahoo!" Benita winked. "So there's a reason the cowboy's been hanging around."

Camila sat down, needing to talk to someone. "I've had a crush on him forever. I mean—" she pushed back an errant strand of hair "—I never felt about Patrick the way I did for Tripp. Looking at Tripp did these weird things to my stomach and I just wanted to be around him, to soak up the same air. I never quite understood that because he didn't even know I was alive, or at least I didn't think he did."

Benita took Camila's hands into hers. "Chick, that's called attraction, chemistry, between a man and a woman. Sometimes there's enough electricity to light up the Astrodome— raw human energy and it's a wonderful thing. I take it you didn't have that combustion with Patrick."

"No," she answered, not wanting to tell Benita what had really happened. It would only make her feel bad.

"So go with the flow and enjoy yourself." Benita squeezed her hands. "For heaven's sakes, enjoy yourself."

"It's not like that. He's helping me because of Jilly."

Benita sighed. "Chick, go look in the mirror and see if you can tell yourself that lie. Tripp ain't helping you because of Jilly."

"This isn't easy for me."

"I know, chick, and I wish I could give you a manual or something."

Camila grimaced. "I don't think I need a manual."

"Just let things happen naturally and if I see the sky light up, I'm just going to smile."

Camila stood. "There won't be fireworks. It hasn't reached that stage."

"All it takes is a spark and you've been simmering for a long time."

Camila slung her purse over her shoulder. "It's really strange talking to you about this." She paused. "Doesn't it bother you that I might be having sex with a man I barely know?" It would bother her if it were Jilly.

"What bothers me is that you're so repressed. You're not living or experiencing any of life's pleasure of a fulfilling relationship with a man. You only live for Jilly. Tripp Daniels is a good man and he won't hurt you. I'd have to hurt him if he did that."

"Benita, you'll never win mother of the year."

"No, chick, I'll leave that up to you. I fell off the other end of the scale a long time ago."

"I better go or I'll never be ready for tomorrow."

When she reached the shop, Tripp wasn't there. It had been longer than thirty minutes, so maybe he'd gotten tired of waiting. Just as well, Camila told herself. Lighting up the Astrodome wasn't on her agenda.

She continued blowing up the balloons, feeling a little disappointed. She thought about their conversation earlier. Had someone been with Patrick that day? If so, how could that person have gotten away so easily, and without a trace?

It didn't make sense, but it bothered Tripp, and Camila couldn't get it out of her mind. She tried to remember some of the things Patrick had said that morning. *He was sorry he'd hurt her. He didn't want their first time together to be like that.* He'd been angry at Vance and Wallis, but he hadn't said anything about getting even. When he'd left, he'd said that he would give her time and they'd talk again.

But she never saw Patrick after that.

She thought she'd driven him over the edge, but could other things have been going on?

WHILE TRIPP WAS filling up his truck with gas, Wyatt drove into the station.

"You don't have to worry about Earl for a while," Wyatt told him.

Tripp screwed on the cap. "Why?"

"He had a heart attack and he's in a Temple hospital."

"Is he okay?" Tripp had looked for him several times in town, but he hadn't seen him since that day in Tripp's barn. Now he knew why.

"I think so. He's had surgery and has to slow down and change some of his bad habits, especially the heavy drinking."

"I'm sorry he's ill."

Wyatt lifted a skeptical eyebrow. "Really?"

"Yeah. Really. I don't believe Earl's all bad. He just had some hard knocks that's changed his way of looking at life." Tripp glanced at his watch. "I've got to go. Night, Wyatt."

Damn. He was running late. Parking his truck, he hurried to Camila's shop. He opened the door and stared. Camila sat on the floor with a clump of balloons in her hands. She was tying them together with a bright red ribbon. Balloons covered the ceiling and the ribbons trailed down, but all he could see was her. She had to be the most beautiful woman he'd ever seen. He'd thought that years ago and his opinion hadn't changed. She wore a white long-sleeve knit top with jeans. Some hair had come loose from her clip and dark tendrils hung around her face.

Sitting under a light, an iridescent glow seemed to reflect from her dark hair. To him, it looked like a halo. To him, it *was* halo. Camila Walker was about as close to an angel as he'd ever met.

She looked up and let go of the balloons. They floated to the ceiling. "Oh. I thought you'd changed your mind."

I'll never change my mind about you.

"No." He closed the door and walked in. "I was at the gas station, had to fill up and have a tire fixed and I ran into Wyatt." He sank down onto the floor, removing his hat and jacket. "What are you doing?"

"Blowing up balloons. I intend to fill the place with them."

He glanced at the ceiling. "You've made a good start. So what do you want me to do?"

She handed him the tube from the helium machine. "You blow up a balloon and give it to me and I'll tie the end into a knot and put a ribbon on it and connect several together."

"Got it. Are these going to stay blown up until tomorrow?"

"Some might not, but the majority will be fine." They worked until the ceiling was covered, then they hung streamers and a banner that read Happy 12th Birthday, Jilly. Camila made bows for finishing touches.

Tripp leaned against the counter. "I take it Millie's not going to be opened tomorrow?"

"She's closing at eleven and then I'll decorate the tables. The party starts at two."

"Am I invited?"

Startled, she glanced up from putting ribbons in a box. "It's mostly for kids, but of course you're invited. I have a feeling several older people will stop by."

"Am I considered older?"

She grinned. "Yes. Older than twelve."

For a moment, he watched the glow on her face, then knelt to help her. He placed the lid on the box and stared at her.

"What?" she asked at his gaze.

"There's dust on your nose."

"Oh. I must have gotten it when I stapled the banner to the ceiling." She immediately tried to wipe it away.

"Nope. Still there."

He reached out with his forefinger and brushed it away. She froze.

"What's wrong?" he asked, fearing he'd insulted her.

She sank back on her heels. "You…you make me nervous."

"Why?"

She picked up a piece of ribbon from the floor. "Because you're Patrick's brother."

His gut tightened. "Are you afraid of me?"

Her eyes flew to his. "Oh, no."

"Then what is it?"

"I'd rather not talk about it."

"But we have to. We have to talk about Patrick and what he did to you."

"No. I…"

He could see the torment on her face and knew they both had to face the truth. "Say it, Camila. Say what really happened that night."

"I can't. I'd rather…"

"Patrick raped you." He said the words she didn't want to hear.

"It wasn't his fault."

"Yes. It *was* his fault." The truth tightened his gut more, but he had to be honest. "He took the drug and he put something in your drink, too."

She gazed at the bow on the door. "Patrick kept saying he loved me and asked why couldn't I love him? My head was fuzzy and I just didn't have the strength to resist anymore, so I…I…gave in." Tears streamed down her cheeks.

"Did you ask him to stop?"

"I don't remember. I just remember feeling so dirty afterward." It was the first time she'd admitted that to anyone and she felt the horror and the revulsion of what had happened to her. Felt it in ways she didn't want to feel. "But it was my fault, too. I couldn't love him the way he wanted me to."

He swallowed. "It wasn't your fault, Camila. Please believe that."

She brushed away tears with the back of her hand. "Why are we talking about this? It's over and we can't change a thing."

"You can stop blaming yourself."

She blinked. "Yes. Maybe I can—for Jilly. I never want her to know about that night. I want her thoughts of Patrick to be good ones."

"She's very lucky to have you."

"And I'm lucky to have her. It doesn't matter how she was conceived."

"No," he agreed, watching her face. "So why do I make you nervous?"

She shrugged. "It's rather silly."

"Tell me."

"When I was a teenager, other girls had fantasies about rock stars. I had fantasies about you and it's rather disconcerting to have you within touching distance."

He lifted an eyebrow. "What kind of fantasies?"

"Very mild compared to what goes on today."

"That's a pity. I was hoping they were more risqué."

"They weren't."

"Did they include anything like this?" He leaned over and licked her nose.

Her mouth fell open. "You licked dust from my nose."

"I'd lick a lot of things from your body, Camila Walker."

"Ooooh."

He caught the sound with his mouth and her lips softened under his. He cupped her face, kissing her slowly and gently. "Did your fantasy include that?" he whispered.

"Oh, yes."

He deepened the kiss and her mouth opened and he lost himself in her sweetness.

A balloon popped with the force of a cannon going off in the confines of the room. They jumped apart, then burst out laughing when they realized what it was. Laughter rippled from Camila's throat like an enchanting chord of music, filling the room, filling him.

Almost in slow motion, he lifted her to her feet and slipped his arms around her waist, pulling her body against his. His mouth covered hers and she moaned softly, trailing her arms up to his neck. The kiss deepened and changed intensity and Tripp knew he'd been waiting for her touch most of his life. His hands tangled in her hair and the kiss went on.

Camila had fantasies and dreams and they were nothing like the real thing. She wanted to absorb herself into him, to feel all those things she'd wanted to feel as a young girl. But as a woman, the emotion was stronger, more intense.

His touch, his kiss, erased all the painful memories and she let herself feel, enjoy this discovery inside her—the discovery of raw human emotions between a man and a woman.

It could have been seconds, minutes or hours when Tripp ended the kiss and rested his forehead against hers. "I've been wanting to do that for thirteen years."

"Me, too," she whispered.

"We have no reason to feel guilty now."

"No." But reality was slowly seeping back into her mind, urging her to take it slowly. She had Jilly to think about. She took a step backward. "I'd better go. I have to get up early to make Jilly's cake."

"Do you do everything?"

"Yes. I try to make the day as special as I can for her."

"You're wonderful, Camila Walker." He reached for her hand. "Come on, I'll walk you to your car."

She slipped into her coat, grabbed her purse and they made their way outside into the cool night. Camila locked the door and Tripp followed her to her Suburban. She now knew what it was like to walk on a cloud.

"Do you have to light Unie's heater?"

"No. I did it earlier."

He touched her lips with his forefinger and her senses exploded with tiny frissons of heat that shot all over her body.

"See you tomorrow," he said and strolled to his truck.

Camila's knees quivered like Jell-O; her stomach was warm and fuzzy and her head was floating among the stars. She'd had this feeling before—when she'd had the flu. But this was so much better. And she didn't need medication.

She got into her car and headed home, trying not to let one, no two, incredible kisses get the best of her. A cool head was required and she was old enough to know a kiss was just a kiss. What happened next would be up to her.

Chapter Fourteen

Camila breezed into her kitchen and stopped short. Benita sat at the table with a towel tied around her head and a green mud pack on her face, painting her fingernails bright red.

"You're home, chick," she said without looking up.

Camila laid her purse on the table. "You gave me a scare. I thought I had a monster in my kitchen."

"Very funny. I had this stuff in my purse and I'd been wanting to try it and there was nothing on the tele—" Her voice stopped as she stared at Camila. "Where's the clip out of your hair?"

Camila touched her long hair, not even realizing it was hanging loose. Tripp's fingers had loosened the clip, so it was probably on the floor of the coffee shop. She'd retrieve it tomorrow.

"I guess I left it at the shop."

"Why did you take it out? Or did the cowboy do it for you?"

"I'm tired and I'm going to bed. Besides, with that stuff on your face, I can't talk seriously. I just want to laugh."

"Your day is coming, chick," Benita said. "Now everything is supple, but in a few years those perky breasts and everything else will go south."

"Well, then, save me some of that stuff." Camila found herself smiling.

Benita looked down. "Wonder if it will work on my breasts?"

"Why?"

"To lift them up."

"You'd need a block-and-tackle to lift those babies."

Benita looked at her. "Are you drinking?"

"Of course not."

"It's not like you to be humorous."

"I'm just feeling—" she thought for a minute "—young. I'm feeling young and a little silly tonight."

"A certain cowboy have something to do with that?"

Camila turned toward the hall. "Thanks for sitting with Jilly. Good night."

"Night, chick," Benita called.

THE NEXT MORNING, Camila and Jilly had their private party and her daughter loved the ballerina cake she'd made. As Jilly opened her gifts, the phone rang.

"Good morning, Camila." Tripp's voice was so clear, it felt like he was in the room and her pulse quickened.

"Tripp, good morning." She sounded breathless, even to her own ears.

"Do you need any help today?"

Yes. No. Yes.

"No. I have everything under control," came out of her mouth.

"I'll come early anyway just in case you do."

"Okay. Thank you."

"Do you have any idea what I can get Jilly for her birthday?"

"I'll let Jilly tell you." Jilly and some of the girls on the basketball team were having a fund-raiser to raise money to renovate the gym. Nothing had been done to it in years and there wasn't any money in the budget for repairs. So when anyone asked Jilly what she wanted for her birthday, she'd say a donation to the fund.

Camila handed Jilly the phone, wishing she could stop the fluttering in her stomach. But she would see Tripp later and she couldn't believe how much she was looking forward to that.

TRIPP HUNG UP AND LEANED against the cabinet. Camila sounded fine this morning. He worried he might have stepped over the line last night, but once he'd gotten past the nervous part, it had been pretty terrific. He'd been thinking about her ever since and he couldn't wait to see her again.

Morris tugged on his boots. "Why you grinning like a cat in a creamery who ain't had a morsel of food in days and the watch dog is all tied up in—"

"I'm not grinning," Tripp interrupted, knowing Morris would go on and on.

"Looks like a grin to me, unless you got a stomachache. When you was little we called it gas."

Tripp took a big swallow of coffee, trying to be patient with Morris and his weird sense of humor. "Are the folks up?"

"Yeah." Morris put on an apron. "They're on round, hell, I've lost track, but I'm sure I'll have to blow a whistle pretty soon."

"They seem to argue a lot."

"Besides grieving, that's all they've got to do."

"I'll go see what they're arguing about." Tripp headed for the door. After he played referee, he called Brodie, then he helped Morris with lunch.

When his parents went to take a nap, Tripp asked, "Morris, do you know what happened to the Corvette after Patrick's crash?"

Morris paused in the process of opening the refrigerator. "Lordy, why'd you want to know something like that?"

"I'm curious."

"You notice that tarp over an object by the old barn?"

"Yes. Isn't that Dad's boat?"

"Nope. Sold that a long time ago. The Corvette is under it."

"What!"

"It was impounded by the sheriff for a while, then the tow truck brought it here. I didn't know what to do with it so I just covered it up. Didn't want Grif and Leona to have to look at it."

Tripp hurried out the back door.

"What…"

But Tripp wasn't listening. He headed straight for the barn and stopped when he saw the tarp. Weeds had grown up around it and it took a while for him to see beneath the tarp. Morris had it tied down and he undid the knots and pulled the tarp away. There it was—the red Corvette.

For a moment he had trouble swallowing as he stared at the twisted and crushed metal and steel. The front end was mangled and pushed into the front seat, like he'd seen in the photo. The windows were broken out and he could see black spots on the leather seats and inside the car, which had to be blood. Patrick's blood. He swallowed the lump in his throat.

One thing caught his attention—the passenger side was almost completely caved in. But there was room on the driver's side—room for a person.

JILLY'S PARTY WENT OFF without a hitch and the place was packed with kids. The stereo was blasting and the kids were dancing and laughing. The older generation sat in Camila's shop eating cake and watching the younger ones. People spilled out onto the street and it seemed everyone wanted to wish Jilly a happy birthday.

Camila was busy serving cake and punch, but she was disappointed. Tripp still wasn't here and she'd begun to think he wasn't going to come at all. So much for fantasies. Her feet were now planted firmly in reality. But it had been nice while it had lasted—less than twenty-four hours.

She worried about Jilly, though. If Tripp didn't come, she was going to be so disappointed. She knew the Danielses wouldn't be able to make it, but Jilly definitely expected Tripp to be here.

So did Camila.

TRIPP HAD SPENT too much time going over the Corvette, looking for he knew not what, and now he was running late. Patrick's death was an accident. He had to accept that. Something good was happening between him and Camila and he didn't want to do anything to mess that up.

When he arrived at the party, he couldn't believe his eyes. People were everywhere and he couldn't find a parking spot. He finally parked in back and walked to the front.

He spoke to several people on the sidewalk, wondering if he was going to be able to get in. Boys stood around the door. He recognized Vance's son Dillon, Wallis's son Cameron and a couple of more boys, but Tripp didn't know their names.

Unie pushed her cart full of plastic bags, topped with her cat, down the sidewalk. People stepped back to let her pass. When she reached the boys, Cameron shoved her cart, saying, "Get out of here, you old bat."

Unie held on to her cart mumbling under her nose, but she steadily made her way to the door.

Dillon got in her way. "Didn't you hear him, you old witch? Get out of here."

"Yeah. Beat it before I call the cops," Cameron added, shoving her cart again.

Unie had a stick in her hand and she poked it into Cameron's chest. "Back off, you little weasel."

Cameron jerked the stick from her and drew it back. The cat gave a menacing hiss. Tripp took off at a run, grabbing the stick before it hit Unie.

"Like she said. Back off, boys."

"You're not my daddy," Dillon snapped. "You can't tell me what to do."

"You either back off or I'm going to mop this street with you. Your choice."

"You can't threaten us," Cameron said. "My daddy'll give you another black eye."

Tripp handed Unie her stick. "Really? Well now, Cameron, you see I was ambushed in the dark by four guys I couldn't identify. Are you saying your daddy did it?" Tripp was trying to make him nervous and it worked.

"Huh, huh…I didn't say anything."

A coward, just like his father.

Cameron's face darkened. "Why you picking on me? My daddy says she's—" he jabbed a finger at Unie "—a nuisance and should be put in a mental institution."

Camila opened the door. "What's going on?" She glanced from Tripp to Unie to the boys.

"The boys and I are having a little disagreement."

Unie fished for something in her pocket and handed it to Camila. "For Jilly," she muttered.

Camila looked at the crumpled five-dollar bill in her hand. "You don't have to give Jilly anything."

Jilly came outside. "Hi, Miss Unie. Hi, Tripp."

"Hi, Jilly," Tripp replied.

"I brought you something," Unie told Jilly, and Camila gave her the money.

"Oh, no, Miss Unie," Jilly protested.

"It's for the gym. I want to do my part."

The boys snickered.

"Thank you, Miss Unie," Jilly said, glaring at the boys.

Unie turned to push her cart away when Camila said, "Wait. I'll get you some cake."

Benita came up behind her with a plate of cake. "Thanks," Camila said and gave it to Unie.

"Bless you child." Unie placed the cake in her cart. The cat immediately tried to lick through the plastic wrap as Unie pushed the cart on down the street.

Jilly's glare intensified as she stared at the boys. "You were cruel."

"Come on, Jilly," Dillon said. "We didn't mean anything."

Jilly didn't say a word, just went back into the shop. This upset the boys and Tripp was stunned.

"See what you did," one of the other boys said. "Now she's mad at us."

"Who cares?" Cameron said. "I didn't want to come to her old party anyway. Let's find something else to do."

Cameron and Dillon disappeared around the cars. The other boys went into the party.

Before Tripp could move, Bert came charging up the street. "What the hell is going on here? All these cars are blocking the highway and people are double-parked. This is against city ordinances, not to mention the noise. Where's Horace? He needs to do something about this."

Horace, the police chief, came out munching on a piece of cake. "You looking for me, Bert?" Slim, Joe Bob, Bubba and Billy Clyde followed him.

"Yeah, goddammit. Why aren't you doing something about all this congestion? People can't get through Bramble."

Horace took a glance at the street. "Looks like they can get through to me."

"You idiot. I'm calling the sheriff."

"I'm right here," Wyatt said, walking up with his five-year-old daughter.

The little girl ran around the men to Camila with a twenty-dollar bill in her hand. "Where's Jilly?" she asked. "I got her present."

"She's inside, sweetie." Camila opened the door and the child went in.

"What's the problem, Bert?" Wyatt asked.

"Look at the damn street. Can't you figure out the problem?"

Wyatt also took in the street. "Looks like a busy day in Bramble."

"What the hell is she doing for y'all that you're so hot for her?" He gestured toward Camila.

Before Tripp knew what he was doing, his fist connected with Bert's jaw. Bert went flying backward on the pavement.

"You bastard. You goddamn bastard." Bert scrambled to his feet, rubbing his jaw. "Arrest him, Horace. He assaulted me."

"Take a deep breath, Bert," Horace suggested. "And we'll talk about this. First, you need to watch what comes out of your mouth. You just slandered a very nice young woman. Second, are you filing charges?"

"You're damn right I am."

Horace turned to Tripp. "Are you filing charges?"

"What the hell for?" Bert spluttered.

"For slander and for basically being a public nuisance," Tripp replied before Horace could.

"Yeah," Slim added, "I'll file charges, too. Any way we can shut Bert's foul mouth, I'm for."

"Me, too," Bubba, Joe Bob and Billy Clyde chorused.

"Everybody calm down and I'm sure we can sort this out." Wyatt stepped in.

"I can handle this," Horace said with a touch of resentment.

Wyatt stepped back. "Sure."

Horace took a step toward Bert. "I got some traffic tickets at my office for you parking illegally in front of the bank. So now I guess I'll have to enforce the law. Come on down to the office if you're filing charges against Tripp. I have to warn you, though, I'll be arresting you until the traffic tickets are sorted out."

Bert's face contorted with rage. "You just lost your job."

Horace shrugged. "Maybe, but until you get it through the city council I'm still police chief."

Bert stormed back to the bank.

Wyatt patted Horace on the shoulder. "Great job."

"Thanks, Horace," Tripp added, and turned and saw the shattered look on Camila's face.

She quickly went back to the party and Tripp hurried inside. The place was packed with giggling teenagers and he couldn't locate Camila. He finally saw her behind the counter with Benita and Millie. He weaved his way to where she was. She was making a bowl of punch. Millie and Benita were handing her ingredients.

"Hi there, cowboy," Benita said. "It's a bit crowded back here."

"I'd like to talk to Camila."

"I'll talk to you later," Camila said, not looking up from her task. "I'm busy."

Benita and Millie shared a glance and quietly returned to the party.

Tripp moved closer to Camila so she could hear what he was saying. Before he could find the right words, she said, "I don't need you to take up for me. I can handle Bert and people like him and I don't appreciate you making a scene on Jilly's birthday." She picked up the bowl. "Now if you'll excuse me, I have a lot of thirsty kids."

Damn. Damn. Damn. He cursed himself for letting his temper get the best of him. He'd driven a wedge between them, but before this night ended he'd make sure he'd removed it—even if he had to apologize until he was hoarse.

He stood there with the noise and the crowd all around him and realized that what he was feeling for Camila was stronger than anything he'd ever felt for any woman. It'd probably always been that way, but he could never admit it until now.

And now Camila didn't want anything to do with him.

Chapter Fifteen

Tripp realized the moment he'd smacked Bert, he'd made a big mistake. Camila had put up with gossip and rumors about her for years. She could take care of herself. The people of this town knew who Camila Walker was by her steadfast love and dedication to her daughter, her friends and the town of Bramble.

Wyatt walked up to him. "You'd better come outside."

"Why? Is Bert back?"

"No. Your parents are here."

"What?" He immediately trailed through the maze of kids to the door. His parents' fifteen-year-old black Cadillac was parked in the middle of the street. Cars were backed up behind them. His dad got out of the passenger side and Morris helped his mother from the back seat.

What in blazes? Tripp hurried to help.

He took his mother's elbow. "Move the car, Morris, it's blocking traffic."

"Couldn't find a dat-blasted parking spot and I didn't want them walking too far."

"Okay. Just move it." He guided Leona up the steps. "Mom, what are y'all doing here?"

"We wanted to wish Jilly a happy birthday. We went to Camila's house, but no one was there."

"Yeah," Grif said behind them, walking slower with his

cane. "Then old Unie Gimble told us there was party down here for Jilly. Why didn't you tell us, son?"

"I didn't think you'd want to come. It's mostly for kids." Tripp had never thought for one minute that his parents would want to come. They never went anywhere but to the doctor.

"Then what are all these people doing here," Grif spouted. "We're her grandparents. We should be here."

That didn't seem to matter all the years before, but Tripp wasn't getting into that. He was sure Jilly would be glad to see them. "Okay, okay," he said. "Let's go through this other door where it's not so crowded.

They went into Camila's shop where the older generation were sitting. Grif started shaking hands. "Joe Bob, Slim, Bubba, damn it's good to see you. Ione, Millie, Rose, you women are looking as good as ever."

Rose laughed. "Grif Daniels, you're the biggest liar in the county."

"Biggest flirt," Leona said and everyone laughed. "Where's Jilly?" she whispered.

Tripp wasn't sure how to handle this and he glanced at Camila, who walked in with Benita behind her. Luckily she came to his aid.

"I'm glad you came," she said. "I believe you know my mother."

"Yes. How you doing?" Grif asked.

"Very well," Benita replied. "Glad you could make it."

"Would have been nice if we'd been invited," Grif grumbled.

"Now that you're here, you're very welcome." Camila smiled slightly and Tripp admired her strength of character in not getting angry at his father's attitude. He could learn from her on how to control his own temper.

If she ever spoke to him again.

"Camila, I have something for Jilly." Leona held something wrapped in tissue paper. "Do you mind if I give it to her?"

From the size of the object, Camila had a very good idea what it was and she braced herself to be as cool as possible. She took Leona's elbow and her eyes met Tripp's and she quickly looked away. She was angry at him and she wasn't quite sure why. She'd figure it out later.

"Yes. She's right in here." She led Leona into the coffee shop with Grif and Tripp following.

Someone turned off the music and the kids stopped dancing and moved aside so the Danielses could reach Jilly.

Jilly's eyes opened wide. "Mr. and Mrs. Daniels," she said, surprise on her face.

"I brought you a birthday present," Leona said, handing Jilly the object.

"You didn't have to buy me a present. Really."

"We couldn't let this day pass without bringing you something," Grif told her. "We're your grandparents."

Jilly's eyes were huge. The room became very quiet; no one spoke or made a sound as everyone strained to hear what was said next.

"Unwrap your present," Leona urged.

Jilly removed the tissue from a silver frame and gasped.

"It's a picture of your father," Grif said. "We want you to have it so you can see him every day."

Jilly gently touched the face in the photo. "Thank you Mr. and Mrs. Daniels." She gave Leona a hug.

Leona stroked Jilly's hair. "Do you think one day you might call us Grandma and Grandpa?"

Jilly glanced at Camila and Camila could see her nervousness. She put an arm around Jilly's shoulders and Jilly seemed to gain strength from her touch.

"Okay. I'd like that." Jilly's smile was priceless.

"Now if someone will find me a chair—" Grif looked around "—I'll sit in here and talk to these pretty women."

"Behave yourself," Leona scolded.

Benita brought him and Leona a chair and they chatted with friends they hadn't seen in years. The kids started dancing again and Jilly was showing her picture to everyone. Camila felt that stab of loneliness again and she didn't understand why. It was a nice thing Leona and Grif had done and she was trying to see it that way. But after twelve years, a part of her was feeling a lot of things she didn't want to feel.

The afternoon came to a close and slowly the people began to leave. Parents arrived to pick up their children and Tripp left with his parents. His eyes caught hers across the room, but she quickly looked away.

Millie dropped Jilly and several girls at Camila's house. They were having a sleepover. Benita and Betty Sue stayed behind to clean up. It took over an hour to get the coffee shop back into shape.

"It was nice what the Danielses did today in front of the whole town," Betty Sue said, slipping into her coat.

"Yes," Camila replied, still having doubts.

"I'll pick up Kerri in the morning," Betty Sue called, going out the door. "See you later."

Camila carried the remaining cups to the trash, wondering why she was having so many conflicting feelings about this day.

"You okay, chick?" Benita asked, helping her bag the trash in the kitchen.

"Sure. Why?" She tied a plastic bag.

"You seem a little down."

"It's been a busy day."

"And eventful."

"Yeah."

Benita put a clean bag in the trash can. "Earlier you were a bit hard on the cowboy."

"I'm used to the nasty things people say and I can take care of myself. I don't need Tripp fighting my battles."

"Hey, there, wait a minute." Benita caught her by the forearms. "It was a pretty heroic thing Tripp did knocking Bert on his ass. Everyone out there wanted to do the same thing. Tripp just beat them to it."

"You saw what happened."

"Yes. I was trying to keep Jilly inside."

"Thanks. I'm glad you did that."

Benita lifted Camila's chin. "So what are you so angry about? It has to be something more than Tripp throwing a right at Bert."

"I don't know."

"Yes, you do."

Camila inhaled deeply and sank onto a stool. "Everyone keeps saying how nice it was what the Danielses did today. I'm sorry, I just keep thinking about all the years they denied who she was—about all the years they thought I was a tramp and didn't know who was Jilly's father. Am I supposed to forget all that now?" She heaved a sigh. "I can't believe I'm saying these things. I'm happy for Jilly. I really am. It's what she wanted but…"

"But you're feeling left out, hurt and a little lonely," Benita finished for her.

Camila looked at her mother. "How'd you know that?"

"Oh, chick." Benita sat on the stool beside her. "Even though my situation is different than yours, I've been through those emotions—every time you'd run to *Madre* instead of me, every time people would say what a good job *Madre* did raising you, every time you looked at me with those critical eyes. Of course, I deserved all that, but, Camila, you're a wonderful mother and you've built your life around Jilly and there's nothing for you to feel lonely about. Your relationship with Jilly is solid. And the people in this town, well, did you see all the people who were here today? They weren't here just for Jilly. They care about you, too."

"Yes. There are nice people in Bramble."

"The others—they just don't count."

"No. They don't count," Camila agreed, glad she could talk to her mother.

"I'm sorry your childhood was so stressful because of me."

Camila blinked away an errant tear. "I'm sorry I wanted you to be someone else." It hadn't escaped her notice that Benita had dressed in black pants and a dark colored blouse that hung loosely instead of being tucked in to show off her breasts. Her hair was up and she wore very little makeup. "You didn't have to dress down today to please me."

"It's about time I did something to please you."

"Thank you." She smiled. "Just be yourself. That's what I plan to do—to be the best mother and to love and to support Jilly."

"Don't forget about the woman in you."

She frowned. "What?"

"You already are the best mother, but what about your needs?"

She sprang to her feet and began to wipe the counter.

"Are you going to keep repressing her for the rest of your life?"

"I'm not like you. That part is hard for me."

Benita watched her. "You were pretty happy last night, but now it's a different story. What happened to change that?"

She turned around. "I let myself dream."

Benita lifted an eyebrow. "About what?"

"About happiness. About love."

"And that's a bad thing?"

"Yes, when it's not reciprocated."

"How do you know it's not?"

Camila folded the cloth and laid it on the counter. "It was very nice last night and this morning he called and said he'd come by early to help, then he arrived late. I think he's made it very clear that he's changed his mind."

"Camila, chick, he does have two elderly parents."

"They didn't even know he was here and I don't really care. I made a fool of myself acting like some pining spinster. One kiss and I had stars in my eyes and I let myself dream that I could have a relationship with a man—with Tripp. But I'm happy the way I am and that's the way I'm staying."

Benita slipped off the stool. "For crying out loud, let the man explain."

Camila glanced around. "Do you see him here?"

"No, but trust me. If I know anything, it's men, and Tripp Daniels will be back."

"Of course he'll be around to see Jilly, but I won't get caught in an emotional grinder with him."

"Chick, that grinder hasn't even been turned on yet." Benita patted her cheek. "Now, I think I'll go home and put up my feet." Benita stared at the ceiling. "What are you going to do with all the balloons?"

"Those that are still floating I'll take home and put in Jilly's room for when she wakes up in the morning. I'll pop the rest. I really did too many."

"Yes, but it was very festive." Benita kissed her cheek. "See you tomorrow."

The door opened and Slim came in. "Benita, how about if I buy you supper at the Bramble Rose?"

"Slim Gorshack, you take my breath away."

Slim grinned. "It takes a lot more than supper to take your breath away."

"You got that right." Benita winked. "I'll go if it's okay with my daughter."

"What?" Camila looked up, surprise on her face. Benita had never asked her that question before and she was a bit taken aback. "Oh. Sure." Things were definitely changing.

"Just don't think I'm easy," Benita said, going out the door.

"Never crossed my mind."

"If you're breathing, it crossed your mind."

Camila heard Slim's laugh as the door closed.

CAMILA STARED at the balloons, then went into her shop to get a pin. She pulled a clump of balloons down and started popping. Pop. Pop. Pop. The sound and the action released some of the pent-up emotions in her. "This is for Tripp Daniels," she muttered under her breath. Pop. Pop. Pop. "This is for being a fool." Pop. Pop. Pop. "This is for dreaming." Pop. Pop. Pop.

She sank to the floor with the busted rubber and ribbons around her. Now she had a mess and she felt like laughing. This was better—much better. She'd clean this up and go home to her daughter.

And Tripp could go to hell.

TRIPP STOOD OUTSIDE watching her through the glass in the door. What was she doing? Before his imagination ran away, he turned the knob and walked in. She glanced up, startled.

"Hi," he said.

She got to her feet, gathering the debris on the floor. "The party's over."

"I'm aware of that." He could feel the chill in the room and it had nothing to do with the weather outside.

She carried her load into the kitchen and came back for more, kneeling on the floor.

"I'm sorry I upset you by hitting Bert." He tried to explain, thinking that would be a good starting point.

"Bert's an idiot and most of the time he deserves to be hit." This puzzled him more. "Then why are you so angry?"

She leaned back on her heels, her dark eyes clouded. "I'm angry for allowing myself to dream."

He squatted down. "What are you talking about?"

"Last night, when I went home, all I could think about was seeing you again. I kept watching the door and when you didn't come, I realized I was putting a man before my daughter—like my mother had so many times in my life. I can't do that. I can't put my daughter through that kind of emotional turmoil." She didn't even realize what she was feeling until she heard her own words. She would not put Jilly through an emotional hell. That had been her goal since Jilly had been born and for a brief moment she'd lost sight of that.

She pushed to her feet and he did, too, catching her hands. "You're not your mother and Jilly would want you to be happy. Besides Jilly knows how much you love her. It's a totally different situation."

"Still, I will never do anything to embarrass her."

"You make it sound as if we're having sex in front of the whole town."

Her eyes flared. "That's—"

"Silly—just what I was thinking."

Camila put a hand to the throbbing in her temple, feeling foolish.

"Don't you want to know why I was late?" he asked.

"No. It doesn't matter."

He told her anyway.

"What difference does it make about the Corvette or who was driving it?" she asked. "Patrick is dead and nothing will bring him back."

Tripp stared at the remaining balloons. "I've had all this guilt about that night, about you and me."

She took a deep breath. "You have no reason to be guilty. There was never anything between you and me."

And never will be.

His eyes caught hers. "Are you asking me to let this go?"

"I'm asking you to let the past go, to let Patrick rest in peace."

He jammed his hands into his pockets. "For thirteen years

I've been lost, wandering from town to town to the next rodeo. I had good friends and that's what got me through, but in the back of my mind I was just waiting to come home. Now that I'm here it's—"

"Different?"

"Yes, everything's changed, except the guilt. It's still there."

"Only you can change that by letting go of all the heart-ache and pain and start living again."

He gave her a knowing look. "But you're not doing that."

"Yes, I am," she insisted. "I live every day for my daughter and try to make her life as good as I can."

"But what about you?"

She looked away. Her mother had asked the same question and she still didn't have an answer. At least not one she could explain.

"How do you feel when I do this?" He leaned forward and lightly kissed her lips, then her jaw, and breathed a kiss on her neck. Her heart hammered against her ribs and her body ached for more.

He drew back and watched her face, but she couldn't speak so many emotions churned through her. Desire. Guilt. Denial. Seconds ticked by, then the words came.

"When you do that, I remember that night."

His face paled.

Suddenly all those inner fears came to the surface. "That's always going to be between us. Patrick will always be between us."

"I see," he murmured.

She licked her sensitive lips. "Under the circumstances, I feel it's best if we try to have an amicable relationship for Jilly."

"If that's what you want."

"Yes, it is."

No, it isn't. You've loved him most of your life, but you're too afraid to admit it. The thought was like an escaped prisoner darting through her mind looking for a safe haven. But she would never harbor it. It would only bring heartache and she'd had her share of heartache.

Tripp nodded. "I hope you'll allow us to continue to see Jilly."

"Of course. I want Jilly to form a relationship with Patrick's family."

He turned and walked toward the door. Everything she ever wanted was walking away. Did she have the courage to stop him? No.

There was no future with Tripp Daniels.

Patrick's brother.

Chapter Sixteen

The next morning, Tripp left early for Mesquite. He had to talk to Brodie in person, and he needed to get away. He told his parents where he was going and he assured them he'd be back on Sunday evening. They seemed down about him leaving, but they had to trust him to come back.

He had to make a choice and in the end he only had one choice he could live with—being here for his parents. Now he had to tell Brodie his decision.

All the way to Mesquite, he kept seeing Camila's dark eyes, feeling her skin against his. He wasn't ever going to get her out of his head. But he'd be living on Lady Luck now and he'd get to know Jilly better. Somewhere along the way he was hoping to spend time with Camila and break through her defenses. Or he was going to turn into a very grouchy cowboy.

He crossed a cattle guard and sped down the dirt road to the house. Brodie was at the corrals, unloading some Hereford bulls.

"Hey, Tripp," Brodie called, slamming a gate and strolling toward him.

Brodie, a champion bull rider, was muscled and strong with black hair and blue eyes. Known as a smooth-talking charmer with the ladies, Brodie's reputation had followed him around the circuit. But Tripp knew him for the man he really was, an honest, loyal friend. They'd doctored each other's scrapes and bruises, been there for every win, every loss and the heartache and joy. They were closer than brothers.

They sat on the tailgate of Tripp's truck.

"Since you're here, I guess the news isn't good," Brodie said.

"My parents need me and I have to be there for them."

Brodie shrugged. "I'll buy you out."

Tripp knew he could count on Brodie to understand and to be supportive. They'd both suffered through estrangement from their families and knew how important that bond was, even when it was broken. But still, Tripp hated to disappoint his friend.

He looked around at the new pipe corral with swing gates he and Brodie had designed for easy access when working cattle. "We planned this ranch together."

"Things have changed," Brodie said. "You were estranged from your family and you thought you'd never see them again."

Tripp rubbed his hands together. "I really hate to do this to you."

"C'mon, Tripp, we're men now and we should have families of our own—like Colter. We can't stay rodeo cowboys forever."

"But we can stay friends." Tripp held out his hand.

Brodie gave him a bear hug. And Tripp loved that about him. Brodie was never afraid to show his affection.

"How are things going with the woman who had your brother's child?"

Tripp told him about Camila and how he felt. He didn't leave out much.

"So she's another reason you want to stay in Bamble?"

"She's the most wonderful woman." Tripp heard the wistfulness in his voice. "I hope you meet her one day—that is if she ever allows me into her life."

Brodie slapped him on the back. "You're hopeless. Women trip over themselves, no pun intended, to get to you and you're standing there like you don't even see them. Take my word for it, Camila Walker will let you into her life."

"There's a lot of heartache from the past."

"So get rid of it." Brodie jumped to his feet. "Come look at these bulls I just bought. You might want to take one back to Lady Luck."

When Tripp left, he felt better about the situation with Brodie. He didn't want to let his friend down. Brodie just wanted him to be happy. That's what they all wanted. Colter had found his happiness and Tripp's was just within his grasp. He just had to make it happen. How he wasn't sure yet.

AFTER CHURCH AND DINNER, Camila spent the afternoon trying to figure out a way to help Unie. That was easier than thinking about Tripp. She couldn't let Bert have her committed. She had to improve Unie's life so a judge could see that Unie could take care of herself.

Jilly stayed with Benita, and Camila went to Unie's, taking her food. But she was determined that Unie would take a bath and put on clean clothes.

Unie, of course, resisted, saying it was too cold. Camila didn't give up, knowing this would be a battle. She lit the small heater in the bathroom and it soon warmed up.

She took Unie's hand and led her into the bathroom. "See, it's warm in here."

"Yes, it is." Unie looked at the water Camila had drawn in the bathtub. "A bath would be nice. I need to wash my hair."

Camila was in shock for a moment at the easy acquiescence, but she quickly recovered before Unie could change her mind.

"Good," Camila said, going to the bag of goodies she'd brought. She handed Unie a bottle of shampoo.

Unie shook her head. "Don't want that. Want my lye soap."

"Got that, too," Camila said, digging in the bag and handing the bar to Unie.

"You watch my cans so Bert won't steal them. They're for my son."

Camila heaved a big sigh and went into the bedroom and gathered Unie's clothes. She carried them to the washer and dryer in the kitchen, which were covered with dust and cat food. Clearly they hadn't been used in a while and Camila wondered if they worked.

She put the cat food on the floor, then filled the machine with clothes and added lye soap. Holding her breath, she turned the knob and water started running into the tub. She felt like giving a cheer. They worked. She then got a pan of water and soap and cleaned the outside of the machines.

She was putting the clothes in the dryer when Unie came out of the bathroom in a long robe, her wet hair hanging down her back.

Unie stiffened. "What's that noise?"

"Just the dryer."

"Thought it didn't work. Gas company turned off my gas."

"It's working now."

"They'll arrest me for using their gas."

"No, Unie, it's okay. Remember I told you the gas company will turn it off when they're ready. So far they haven't."

Unie frowned. "Sometimes I forget."

"It's okay."

"You're a sweet child."

"Thank you. I brought my dryer so I can dry your hair."

"Don't like those newfangled things." She looked around. "Where's Lu Lu?"

"She's asleep on your bed."

Camila dried Unie's hair then Unie put on clean clothes without one word of protest. Camila then stripped the bed and washed the sheets.

Unie responded to love and attention like everyone and she would make sure Unie had a bath and clean clothes. Camila would work it into her schedule somehow because she wasn't letting Bert put Unie in a mental institution.

Camila had been busy all day and she'd pushed Tripp from her mind. But as she crawled beneath the covers, he was there. She could see his face, feel his touch on her skin. Flipping onto her side, she told herself she'd done the right thing. But her heart told her something else.

Monday passed quickly and Camila never seemed to have enough time. Leona was having her surgery today and she kept waiting for Tripp to call, but he didn't. When she picked up Jilly from school, it was the first thing she asked and Camila knew it was going to be a long evening.

THE SURGERY WENT WELL and Tripp was relieved. Since the doctor did both eyes, Leona had to stay overnight in the hospital. Tripp stayed with her. In the morning the doctor would take off the bandages and his mother would be able to see a whole lot better. He wanted the first face she saw to be Jilly's.

They had sedated Leona and she was sleeping soundly. He'd talked to his dad and Morris, and he sat staring at the phone, knowing he had to call Camila.

He picked up the receiver and dialed. Jilly answered.

"Hi, Tripp. How's Mrs. Daniels?"

"The surgery went really well. She's sleeping now."

"Totally awesome."

"Can I speak to your mother?"

"Sure."

Camila's soft voice came on the line and he paused for a second. "I…I…just told Jilly that everything went well."

"I'm so glad."

I wish you were here.

"I have a favor to ask."

There was a long pause on the line. "What is it?"

"They're taking the bandages off in the morning about ten.

I'd like Jilly's face to be the first thing she sees, but if you have a problem with that I'd understand."

"No, no. I'll take Jilly out of class and we'll be there at ten."

"Thank you, Camila."

He hung up knowing she'd say yes. That's the type of person she was.

NOW TRIPP HAD SOMETHING else he wanted to do. Earlier, he'd asked for Earl's room number so he could visit. Earl was alone. He lay still, his skin pale, and there were heart monitors attached to him.

"Hi, Earl," he said, walking farther into the room.

"Rodeo man," Earl said past dry lips. "What are you doing here?"

"My mom had eye surgery and I heard you were in here. Are you okay?"

"Could use some whiskey and a dip of snuff."

"I don't think you'll be doing any of that for the rest of your life." Tripp took a seat in the chair next to the bed.

"That's what they tell me."

An awkward silence followed.

"I keep thinking what you told me about your son."

"Don't. It doesn't concern you."

"Maybe not, but I carry around a ton of guilt over Patrick's death."

The awkward silence came again.

"How do you live with all that guilt?" Earl suddenly asked.

"By not blaming yourself. Accidents happened. A new jack could have done the same thing."

"Yeah, but whiskey helps. Now what the hell am I gonna do?"

"Forgive yourself."

Earl moved uneasily in the bed. "You know, rodeo man, that's one thing that irritates the hell out of me—your nice pearly-white attitude. Sometimes things are black and white and just plain ugly and forgiveness ain't even an option. So if you came here looking for a changed Earl, you ain't gonna find him."

Tripp stood. "That's a pity."

"I've taught my boys to be rough and tough, not taking crap from anyone. That's the only way to survive in this world."

Tripp rubbed his jaw. "I'm well acquainted with your boys."

Earl snorted. "Took three of them and a hired hand to bring you down. That's pitiful."

"It's pitiful that you think those kind of tactics are needed."

"Don't preach to me."

"What I don't understand is why you tried to cheat my dad. All you had to do was ask your mother for the money."

"There's that pearly-white attitude again," Earl snapped. "Can't you figure it out? Ma gave me the money and I used it to gamble. I was heavily into betting on football games and there was no way I wanted her to find that out."

"So your mother knows now."

"Yep. You and Wyatt coming to the ranch asking questions let the cat out of the bag. So you see, rodeo man, you're not one of my favorite people."

"Why did you tell me about your son?" Tripp needed to know that.

"Got me. That's about the stupidest thing I've ever done. Just forget my lapse."

Tripp nodded. "Hope you get to feeling better."

"I'll ride again, rodeo man, you can count on it. I'm not out yet."

Tripp nodded again and started out the door.

"Rodeo man."

Tripp looked back.

Earl waved a hand. "You know."

"Yeah, Earl. I know." Tripp walked out knowing exactly what he meant. Earl was sorry and he didn't know how to say it—probably never had in his whole life. Earl was learning lessons the hard way. All in all it had to be the sanest conversation he'd ever had with Earl. Usually Earl was three sheets in the wind and none too cooperative. Earl might not want to admit it, but he was changing.

That wasn't a bad thing.

JILLY WAS EXCITED about seeing Leona, and Camila had to calm her down several times. Tripp waited for them in the lobby and Camila's heart accelerated at the sight of him. She didn't think she'd ever be able to curb that reaction.

They went upstairs to the room and Jilly held Leona's hand as the doctor removed the bandages. The doctor checked both eyes and Leona blinked, turning her head to look at Jilly.

"Oh, my, my, my."

"Now don't get upset," the doctor cautioned.

Leona touched Jilly's face. "You're so beautiful."

"Thank you. I look like my mama."

"Yes, but there's something about your eyes—that soft quality. Oh, my, my, my."

"Don't cry, Mom," Tripp said.

"I'm going to put these patches over your eyes," the doctor intervened. "Just leave them on until you get inside your house, then your son has the instructions about care and the drops. I'll see you at your next appointment." The doctor walked out.

"Thank you, Camila," Leona said. "Thank you for bringing Jilly."

"You're welcome and I hope you continue to improve."

"You were right about it being so easy. I don't know why I hesitated all these years."

"It's done now and you'll see so much better."

"Yes. I'm looking forward to seeing more of my granddaughter—that is if you'll allow it."

"Mama's cool, Grandma," Jilly spoke up. "She'll let me visit."

Leona groped for Jilly's hand. "Thank you for calling me Grandma."

"We better be going," Camila said, avoiding Tripp's gaze, and they quickly left.

Camila was still resisting change, but she was trying very hard not to—for Jilly. During the week she took Jilly several times to see her grandmother. She always dropped her off and picked her up later. She thought that was best. She and Tripp hadn't talked again and she thought that was best, too.

Camila's relationship with her mother was changing for the better. Benita now helped her in the shop and customers loved Benita's craziness. There was a lot of laughter when Benita was there and Camila regretted the times she'd shut her mother out with her coldness and the judgmental attitude of a child. A child who was now seeing life so differently—as a woman, a mother and a daughter.

She wasn't sure what had changed, except maturity and knowing Benita loved her seemed to make a world of difference. The fact that she could accept Benita for who she was and not want her to change was a big step forward.

Jilly wanted to spend the weekend with her grandparents to help Leona, and Camila allowed it. On Friday afternoon, Jilly had a suitcase in her hand and Button under her arm, waiting for Tripp to pick her up.

He arrived on time and Jilly put down her suitcase and hugged Camila. "Bye, Mama. I love you."

"Love you, too. I'll see you on Sunday afternoon." Jilly had spent the night at Kerri's and Millie's, but she'd never spent two nights away. This was going to be a long weekend for Camila.

She waved goodbye and Tripp waved back. As the cowboy drove away, she'd never felt so alone in her life. Or afraid. And she wasn't sure of what. *The future. The unknown.* That wasn't it. She was afraid of love and all the emotions she felt for

Tripp. She was afraid of getting hurt. It was easier to suppress what she was feeling. That's what made her so afraid. How much longer could she continue to do this?

To deny the woman in her.

To deny love.

Chapter Seventeen

Camila worked until midnight then fell into bed exhausted. She was at the shop early to finish two baby quilts while waiting on customers at the same time.

Jilly was usually in the shop on Saturdays and everyone was asking for her. Camila missed her like everyone else, but she'd talked to her three times already. Being away from home wasn't easy for Jilly either.

Camila closed up the shop and took Unie some food so she could turn on her heater. Unie looked so much better in clean clothes and Camila sensed she felt better, too. She even asked how to use the washing machine. Camila showed her then drove to Benita's for supper.

Benita sat on the living-room floor going through old photos. "Hey, chick," she called. "I've got something for you."

Camila sank to the floor by her mother.

"I found his picture," she said, handing the photo to Camila. "That's your father. Travis Holden."

She stared at her father for the first time. He looked so young. But what surprised her the most was that she felt no connection to this man. She wondered if Jilly felt the same way when she saw Patrick's photo. They hadn't talked about it except to say the Danielses had made a nice gesture. Maybe they needed to talk more because Camila noticed that Jilly kept the photo in a drawer, not on her nightstand where Camila thought she'd keep it.

"What do you think, chick?"

"He's very young and handsome."

"You bet—blond hair, blue eyes. Us Puerto Rican women love those blue eyed blondes."

Normally a remark like that would have Camila frowning, but today she only smiled, accepting Benita and her tawdry language.

"Whatever happened to the Holden family?" Camila asked, curious. Benita and Travis had been married such a short time that not only had Benita not taken his name, she hadn't put it on Camila's birth certificate either.

"As I told you, Travis went to college in Lubbock and his parents moved there to be near him. He went to work for an oil company to help pay for his education. Something came loose from the rig and hit him in the head. He died instantly. He was twenty years old and Claude and Mavis never got over it. Mavis had a nervous breakdown and Claude drank himself to death."

"How sad."

"Yeah." Benita put the rest of the photos in the box.

"Did you love him?"

"Chick, I didn't know what love was, not sure I do now." She touched Camila's cheek. "But I know I love my chick and her little chickadee."

Camila choked back a tear. "You never used to talk this way. You're different."

Benita shrugged. "Maybe. Facing fifty, I'm taking a cold hard look at my life and, well, I'm thinking of staying in Bramble and being a mother and a grandmother."

"I'd like that."

They ate supper and then Benita showed Camila some of her beauty secrets. They laughed and talked like mother and daughter, and it felt good. Camila had a question and she felt comfortable enough to broach the subject.

"I haven't seen you drink anything."

"Nope. Gave up the hard stuff—too many bad decisions made under the influence. And that stuff is hell on a woman's looks." Benita launched to her feet. "But there's something I haven't given up."

"What's that?"

"Dancing."

Visions of that night she'd danced with Patrick at the graduation party flashed through Camila's mind and a chill spread over her body. Would that night always have this effect on her?

Benita ran into the kitchen and came back with a radio. She plugged it in and found a Latino station. A sensuous beat filled the room.

She held a hand out to Camila. "C'mon, chick."

"I don't think so."

Benita placed her hands on her hips. "It's just you and me. We can let our hair down and do what we want. This is a step to conquer all those repressed feelings. C'mon."

Benita twirled and moved to the beat of the music. Camila sat there for a minute then rose to her feet. To conquer all the bad feelings she had to make an effort to change. She joined her mother in the living room and they swayed to the music, and Camila moved her arms and hips the way Benita had taught her.

"Oh, yeah, chick. You got it now. It's all in the hips. One, two, move it here. Three, four, slide to the floor. Oh, yeah, we still have it."

Benita swung her around. "One, two, move your hips, circular motion, now the other way. Go with the flow, the movement, the feeling."

And they danced—the two of them oblivious to everything but the bond they were forming as a family, as mother and daughter—for the first time.

Finally the music stopped and they sank to the floor, arms wrapped around each other. The tears came then and they cried for all the years they'd been strangers and all that they'd lost.

The music started again and Camila helped her mother to her feet. "We have to keep dancing. No more tears, only happiness. Now the cha-cha. One, two, cha, cha, cha." She swung around and came to a complete stop. Tripp and Jilly stood in the doorway. Tripp had his hat in his hand and Jilly carried Button.

Camila smoothed her blouse, feeling self-conscious.

"I wanna dance," Jilly shouted and ran to join Benita.

Camila took a breath and walked to Tripp, unable to take her eyes from his face, and she hated herself for that reaction. But inside she knew something was wrong. Jilly wasn't supposed to be back until tomorrow.

"Is something wrong?" Camila asked, doing up the top button of her blouse, which had come undone.

His eyes watched her fingers. "Jilly…ah…she was very subdued and I asked what was wrong. She said she wanted to go home. She missed her mama."

"Oh." That surprised her. She didn't expect that from Jilly, who was usually very independent.

"We'll do it again another time."

"Yes, of course."

"Good night."

He walked out the door and she had that weak-kneed, Jell-O feeling again. She dragged in another breath and glanced at her daughter. Jilly was now laughing and dancing with Benita. Button barked and jumped up and down between them. Jilly was as far from subdued as she could get.

What had happened at Lady Luck?

TRIPP STOOD OUTSIDE and took several deep breaths. God, Camila was beautiful, especially when she didn't think anyone was looking. She'd looked uninhibited, her body free-flowing and sensuous, moving to the beat of the music. He wanted to take her in his arms and press his body against hers and… His thoughts skittered into something X-rated, but that was a movie he'd never see. Camila wasn't ever going to see him as anyone other than Patrick's brother.

And Tripp was in love with her.

He stopped in the process of opening the door of his truck. There. He'd actually let himself admit the truth.

But what good did it do him?

CAMILA SOON TOOK JILLY home because they had to talk. Jilly had her bath and Camila went in to kiss her good-night.

"It was fun dancing tonight, wasn't it, Mama? Benita seemed happy. She's really got the moves."

"Yes. Benita's very graceful."

Camila pushed back Jilly's hair. "Why did you want to come home, baby?"

Jilly pleated the edge of the blanket. "Tripp let me ride his horse and Cay, that's the horse, is totally awesome. I like to ride and Tripp did some roping, which you have to see. He can make the rope go exactly where he wants it to."

Camila had seen him rope on TV and he was very good.

"Sounds as if you were having a good time."

"Yeah, then I helped Tripp and Morris wash windows. We had the radio on and were laughing and working. It was fun."

"Where were Mr. and Mrs. Daniels?"

"They were taking a nap. That's why I was helping. I didn't want to sit around and do nothing."

"And…" Camila prompted, not having a clue where this was leading.

"I went into the house to get more rags to dry the windows and Mr. and Mrs. Daniels were awake and in the den talking. I wasn't eavesdropping. They were talking really loud."

Camila swallowed. "What were they talking about?"

"Mr. Daniels was on the phone talking to a lawyer and Mrs. Daniels was saying what a fool he was and for him to hang up. But he wouldn't."

Her chest felt tight and a sense of foreboding gripped her. "What were Mr. Daniels and the lawyer talking about?"

Jilly clutched the blanket. "He wants to get custody of me."

Camila's chest caved in and she had trouble breathing. She strove for control, not wanting Jilly to see how upset she was.

"Mr. Daniels said that you work all the time and I need to be in a family environment. When he hung up, Mr. Daniels told Mrs. Daniels that they had a good chance of getting me. She said he was an old fool and she wasn't supporting him in such a thing. He told her that was fine, Tripp would help him." Tears slipped from Jilly's eyes. "I don't want to leave you, Mama."

Camila reached for her daughter and held her tight. "No one is taking you from me. No one."

"Promise."

She kissed her forehead. "I promise."

Jilly rested her head on Camila's shoulder. "I should never have gone there."

"Oh, baby." She stroked her hair. "You have such a big heart and I'm sorry you had to hear what you did, but now we're forewarned and you don't have to worry about anything. I'll take care of it."

"I like Tripp."

Camila did, too, but he had to be aware of what his father was planning—to take Jilly from her. And he'd done nothing to stop him. How could he do that?

"You go to sleep and tomorrow we'll have one of our days together, doing whatever you want."

"I just want to be with you, Mama."

Jilly sounded as if she were five years old again, needing her mama. Camila kissed her once more. "Go to sleep, my precious."

She walked into the living room fuming because they'd hurt her child. Jilly had been nothing but nice to them and she didn't deserve this. Camila wasn't letting them get away with it. They could do whatever they wanted to her, but not to Jilly.

Glancing at the clock, she saw it was almost ten, but she didn't care. She had to go to Lady Luck and let them know how she felt—let them know that Jilly was staying with her. Camila called her mother. Benita came through the back door within minutes in her nightclothes.

"What's wrong?" Benita asked.

"Sorry to bother you so late."

"No problem."

Camila told her what had happened.

"*Santa Maria madre de Dios.*" Benita sank into a chair.

"I have to sort this out tonight." Camila grabbed her coat. "If Jilly wakes up, tell her I'll be right back."

Benita pushed Camila toward the door. "Go, chick, go. I'll take care of Jilly."

On the way to Lady Luck, Camila cursed herself for ever trusting Tripp. He could have stopped this. Why hadn't he? Why had he allowed Jilly to get hurt?

Chapter Eighteen

Tripp rode into the barn and unsaddled Cay. After seeing Camila, he needed to work off some restless energy. Riding always did that—took him away to his own private world. Most of the time Camila was there with him—like she was tonight with her beautiful eyes, long gorgeous hair, just out of his reach.

Like she always would be.

He walked in through the back door and the house was quiet. Everyone was in bed. He grabbed a bottle of water out of the refrigerator and twisted off the cap, taking a big swallow. The quietness seemed to echo around him and it gave him an eerie feeling. When Jilly was here, the house was alive with excitement, the way it should be.

He took another swallow. He still didn't understand why she'd wanted to go home. They'd been having a good time. She'd ridden Cay and she'd asked about his roping and he'd had to show off a little. In the afternoon, the weather had been a little warmer and he'd taken off all of the screens and had sprayed the windows with a water hose. Sometimes he'd squirted Jilly and she'd run shrieking.

When his parents had taken a nap, she'd wanted to wipe the windows, so he'd let her. He'd climbed the ladder and had done the higher ones. She'd run into the house for more rags and when she'd come out, she'd been very quiet. Had she called Camila while she was in the house? Maybe she'd just gotten homesick. Maybe…

The doorbell rang, interrupting his thoughts. He hurried to answer it, wondering who was calling this late. To his surprise, Camila was standing on the doorstep.

"Camila, come in."

"No, thank you. What I have to say I can say out here."

"That's ridiculous," he said. "It's getting colder. Come on in." He opened the door wider, and she marched into the den and turned to face him.

"I trusted you with Jilly. I trusted you not to hurt her."

He did a double take. "What are you talking about?"

"Jilly's heartbroken and you could have stopped it, but you didn't."

Tripp ran a hand through his hair. "Camila, I don't know what you're talking about. I'd never hurt Jilly and I'd stop anyone who tried."

Her eyes narrowed. "Are you telling me the truth?"

"Yes. Now tell me what you're talking about."

"I'm talking about the lawyer your dad hired."

His eyebrows shot up. "Lawyer? What lawyer?"

"The lawyer he hired to get custody of Jilly."

"What!"

"Jilly came into the house and heard him talking on the phone to a lawyer about getting custody of her. When he hung up, Leona said she wouldn't support him in doing that. Grif said that was fine. You would help him."

"Like hell!" Tripp couldn't believe his ears. What was his father doing? More to the point, what was he thinking?

"Why didn't Jilly say something to me?"

"Because she's scared she's going to be taken away from me."

"Oh, God, Camila, I'm so sorry. I'll get this straightened out."

"There's nothing to straighten out," she told him. "Jilly is my daughter and she stays with me—always. Out of the kindness of my heart, I let her come here, thinking it was the right thing to do. But Jilly won't be coming back to Lady Luck."

"That's where your wrong, missy." Grif shuffled into the room in his pajamas, holding on to his cane. Leona was behind him. "Jilly's a Daniels and she belongs here."

"She belongs with her mother," Tripp said.

"Not anymore. Frank said we have a good case."

"What are you doing, Dad?" Tripp asked with barely controlled anger. "What the hell are you doing?"

"Getting my granddaughter."

"You've scared Jilly so bad she doesn't want to come back."

"She'll come back," Grif boasted. "The law will make her."

"That's what you want? For Jilly to be forced to visit you?"

"She belongs in a family environment." He pointed his cane at Camila. "She works all the time and is never there for Jilly."

"You don't know what the hell you're talking about. You don't know anything about Camila and Jilly's life. Camila has been there twenty-four hours a day since the second Jilly was born. Jilly is her life and Camila has created a business where she can come and go as she pleases. She's completely involved in Jilly's school activities. She's there if Jilly needs her. Hell, she's there if anyone in this town needs her. You won't get anyone to testify for you. You're making a fool of yourself."

"I'm not the only one, am I, son?"

Tripp closed his eyes for a brief second, not wanting to have this conversation in front of Camila. She didn't need to hear this.

"She played you and Patrick against each other and you still want her. Every man in town wants her and I will not have my—"

Before anyone knew what she was doing, Leona reached out and slapped Griffin across the face. His cane clattered to the floor and he fell backward into his chair, a shocked expression imprinted on his face.

Leona stood over him, shaking a finger in his face. "Don't you dare talk about her like that. Don't you dare, Griffin. I'll put your insane body in a coffin and slam it shut without one regret."

"Mom." Tripp tried to calm her, but she shook off his arm.

"If you want to throw slurs at someone, throw them at yourself." Leona wasn't through as she rounded on her husband.

Camila didn't want to be a witness to this and desperately wanted to just slip away. But her daughter was a part of this family and something in her wouldn't allow her to leave until she got her point across.

"Patrick was a dear, sweet boy, but that wasn't good enough for you. You have to be a man, Patrick. That's what you always said to him. You have to be a man like your brother. You have to ride a horse, you have to be stronger and you have to be a winner. Well, Patrick wasn't like that, but you couldn't accept it. You just kept at him."

"You made him a sissy," Grif shouted, rubbing his face.

"Maybe I did, but I loved him and supported him in everything he did, even his love for Camila."

"She used him to get to Tripp."

"Camila didn't love Patrick and she told him that. She was honest with him."

"Then why did she have sex with him?"

"Because he forced her to!"

The room became deadly quiet.

"What?" squeaked past Grif's lips.

Tripp reached for Camila's hand and she clutched it tight, feeling as if she were going to need something to hold on to. She'd never dreamed Leona knew what had happened that night.

"You just had to go to the principal and get Patrick to tutor the football players. He didn't even like those boys and they filled his head with a lot of nonsense. But he had to be a he-man and he wanted to please his daddy. It got out of control, though. Those boys did drugs and they told Patrick they could give him something to make him a man." Leona took a breath. "That night of the party, we went out to dinner so the kids could have the place to themselves, but later Patrick told me everything. They gave Patrick some feel-good drug and they gave him something to put in Camila's drink. It took away her inhibition, her ability to reason. When Camila became drowsy, Patrick took her up to his room. Patrick did a bad thing to Camila and he was so sorry afterwards. He cried and cried, but there was no way to change it. He just wanted Camila to forgive him. Patrick was such a naïve boy. He thought if he and Camila made love, Camila would love him. He said that's why he did it."

"Why did she hold out on him—sleeping with other boys and not him?" Grif asked.

"You foolish old man," Leona shouted. "Camila was a virgin. I changed the sheets on the bed that morning and I'd be very surprised if she's slept with anyone since. But you made it worse, Grif. Patrick wanted to marry her to make everything right, but you said your son wasn't marrying a tramp. You'd disown him. He ran out and I never saw my son again. You killed him with your control and your bigot ideas. I hate you. I hate you." Leona slapped at Grif's face over and over.

Tripp pulled her away. "Mom, please, don't do this."

"It's long overdue. I've been quiet too long." She looked at Grif who seemed turned to stone. "To make matters worse and I didn't think there was any way for my world to completely disappear, but you got rid of our only remaining child. You accused him of killing his brother by spreading lies about the drugs and coming on to Camila. You told him to leave and never come back and Tripp didn't even know what was going on. Tripp didn't kill Patrick. Camila didn't kill Patrick. You did by wanting him to be someone that he wasn't."

Grif didn't respond and some of the things Leona had said were sinking in. If Leona knew Camila had been a virgin, then she knew that Jilly was Patrick's. But not once in the past twelve years had she made a move toward Jilly. Or had even tried to acknowledge her.

As if reading Camila's mind, Leona turned to her. "I knew Jilly was Patrick's and I'm ashamed that I never did anything about that. But I grew up where a wife was obedient to her husband and I adhered to all Grif decreed like a weak, helpless woman. But to be honest, after I lost Patrick, I stopped living. I just existed in my grief and I wasn't any good to anyone, especially a child. But the moment I touched her, I knew she was going to be my salvation." Leona took a step toward Camila. "I'm so sorry for all the pain Patrick caused you."

"I loved Patrick," Camila said, "but I wasn't in love with him. I've known him since kindergarten and we were the best of friends. He was kind and good to me and that's what I remember about Patrick—all the good times we had—not that one night that changed so many lives."

"Thank you, Camila. I hope you will continue to allow Jilly to visit me."

"No, Leona, Jilly will not be coming back here. I don't want her to face any of this unpleasantness."

"Yes, she will. I'll see to that," Grif spoke up, but his voice wasn't as strong.

Tripp confronted his father. "Why, Dad? Why are you doing this?"

"Because Patrick would want his daughter here."

"Patrick loved Camila and he'd be very upset that you were hurting her."

"He's not the only one who loved her. You did, too."

Camila's stomach clenched tight, but she couldn't force herself to leave.

"Camila was Patrick's girlfriend and I respected that.

There's never been anything between Camila and me. She's an attractive woman and I recognized that—that's all. You accused me of flirting with her and upsetting Patrick to the point of him crashing the car. I lived with that guilt for thirteen years. But I'm not to blame for Patrick's wreck."

Silence crept into the unspoken questions, the unspoken pain.

Tears trailed down Grif's aged face. "It was my fault," Grif muttered. "But I couldn't admit that so I blamed you and I blamed Camila. I could live with myself that way." He gulped in a breath. "My son is gone and I killed him. I killed my son."

"Dad." Tripp knelt by his chair. "It's time to stop placing blame. Patrick made some bad choices, but now we have to go forward."

"To what? You don't want me to have my granddaughter. I thought if I could do that for Patrick some of the guilt would go away."

"The only way the guilt is going away is to do like Jilly told you—to be nice, and you start by apologizing to Camila and to Jilly."

"Ah, fiddle-faddle. I'm not good at that."

"Dad."

Grif looked at Camila. "Missy, this pretty much changes everything. I blamed you for a lot of years for teasing my son and leading him on, but I learned today that's not what happened."

"No," Camila said, surprised she could speak. "I was always honest with Patrick about my feelings. I suggested that we not see each other in school, but Patrick said he could handle his feelings. I learned later that he couldn't, but it was too late."

Grif swallowed with difficulty. "Like Leona said, I'm sorry, too, for the pain my son has caused you and for…for my callousness. Please let Jilly come back."

She took a long breath as the past loosened its grip. "I'll leave that up to Jilly. Whatever she decides, I'll support her."

"Fair enough," Leona said.

"I have to go." Camila headed for the door, needing some space, some time.

"Camila." Tripp caught her at the door.

"Please." She pulled away. "I can't do this right now,"

She hurried to her Suburban before he could stop her. She had to think clearly for Jilly and she couldn't do that when he was within touching distance.

TRIPP WATCHED THE TAILLIGHTS of her car until they disappeared. He went back into the house feeling as if he were walking through a nightmare and couldn't find his way out. He never wanted Camila to be hurt again, but his family couldn't seem to stop hurting her.

"How's Camila?" Leona asked.

"She's upset, understandably so."

"What in tarnation is going on?" Morris asked, walking into the room in his pajamas, scratching his bald head. "Why is everyone up?"

"Go back to bed, Morris. Everything's under control."

"Suits me." He turned away. "My tails draggin' the ground and I ain't awake enough to beat my gums to make any sense in a Texas truck stop on a…" His voice trailed away into his usual nonsense chatter.

Tripp just shook his head. "Now let's go to bed. And Dad, don't do anything like this again."

Grif struggled to his feet. "Just wanted to do something for Patrick."

"I know, but next time talk things over with me first."

"Ahhh," was the response Tripp got and he took it for a yes.

Tripp glanced at his mother. "No more slapping."

"Don't know if I can promise that," Leona replied. "I want to slap him about three times a day. Might make it part of my daily routine."

"Since she can see, she's gettin' mean," Grif said. "She's a mean old woman."

"You should recognize the symptoms," Leona snapped back. "You're a mean old woman. My face hurts."

"It should after what you did."

"Listen up, you two, this arguing is going to stop. Camila's not going to let Jilly come into this tension-filled atmosphere. She wants Jilly to be happy and so do I. It's time for some fun and laughter in this house."

They both remained quiet.

Tripp handed his father his cane. "So I guess Jilly's not important enough to make a little sacrifice."

"I'm sorry I hit you," Leona said.

"Never knew you had a mean right," Grif responded.

"Just remember that."

"Bed," Tripp intervened before he lost every ounce of his patience.

He finally trudged up the stairs and fell across the bed. He didn't bother with the light or removing his clothes. What a night! He was totally spent.

Why did his father have to bring up Tripp's feelings for Camila? Tripp hadn't lied. There wasn't anything between them—not then. But now he'd tried on several occasions and Camila had made her feelings very clear. When did he accept defeat? When did he give up and get on with his life?

When he could stop thinking about her, every minute of every hour of every day. That sounded like never, and all Camila wanted to do was get away as fast as possible.

From his crazy family, and from him.

ALL THE WAY HOME, one thing resounded in Camila's head over and over. The Danielses knew she had feelings for Tripp—feelings she would never admit to because it would only cause more pain. Why? she suddenly asked herself.

Why would loving Tripp cause more pain? So many truths had been revealed tonight and she had to dig deep to dredge up her feelings. And it had nothing to do with Jilly. Trip had believed the rumors about her. When he'd admitted that, she'd said that it didn't matter, but it did. If he could believe that about her… Her head pounded from all the insecurities and doubts.

"You loved her, too," Grif had said. *Camila was Patrick's girlfriend and I respected that.* That's what she was to him and always would be. But she'd never been Patrick's girlfriend the way Patrick had wanted, and she'd suffered so much over that. She'd paid a high price for not being in love with him, but she had Jilly and that was a very big reward.

She needed time to regroup and get herself together and sort through the confusion. She was sure that nothing else would be done about custody of Jilly. That would be an enormous relief for Jilly. And her.

She walked into her kitchen and removed her coat. She could hear the TV in the living room and she made her way there. Benita sat on the sofa, her feet propped up on the coffee table, munching on popcorn watching an old W. C. Fields movie. For once in her life, Camila was grateful for her mother.

She stepped over Benita's legs and plopped down close to her.

"Hey, chick, is this the only place to sit?" Benita teased.

"Yes. I need to be close to my mother."

Benita reached for her hand. "How did it go?"

"Bad, disturbing and good all rolled into one, but the custody thing over Jilly is settled. Grif just wanted a bit of Patrick in his home." Holding Benita's hand, she made a decision. "I need to tell you something and it won't be easy." She took a breath. "I want you to know how Jilly was conceived. And no guilty feelings."

"Okay, chick," Benita said.

She told her every little detail of that night.

"I wasn't here for you," Benita wailed. "I should have been here for you."

"No guilt, Benita, remember? I had to stand on my own two feet and I became a stronger person able to raise my daughter. I'm only telling you this so all the secrets are out in the open and we can start living as a family—a real family."

"I'd like that," Benita said. "But I'm feeling a lot of rage at the moment and it might take me a while to get over that."

"But you will."

"For you, I'll give it my best shot." Benita set the popcorn bowl on the coffee table. "If we're not going to have any more secrets, I need to tell you something, too."

"Okay." Camila sat sideways to face her mother.

"I know the rumors about my less-than-stellar reputation hurt you."

"Yes," Camila admitted.

Benita looked at her. "Do you know how many men I've slept with?"

Camila shook her head. "You don't have to tell me that."

"Four. I've slept with four men and I was married to all of them. Travis was the only one I slept with without a wedding ring."

"But…but the gossip and the men bringing you home."

"That's all they did—buy me coffee and dinner after my shift ended and bring me home. The guys were the ones who embellished the evenings into something more. Men do love to brag."

Oh no. Camila was no better than the other bigots in this town. She'd believed everything she'd heard. She reached for Benita. "I'm so sorry. Why did you never try to talk to me?"

Benita wiped the tears from Camila's face. "Would you have believed me?"

Camila couldn't answer because she didn't really know.

"Don't worry about it, chick. I gave them plenty of ammunition. I wore my clothes tight and I danced and drank, but there was always a stopping point for me. I'm what's known as a tease, a flirt."

Camila still was speechless, seeing her mother so differently. Taking Benita's hand, she raised it up. "To trust, family and happier times."

"Hear, hear," Benita said.

Later, Camila sat in bed with her knees drawn up, staring into the darkness, letting all the insecurities and shame from her childhood rise to the surface. Benita's confession was like opening a window into her inner self. She had judged her mother because of the gossip and her mother's behavior. And it had all been false.

Camila's one goal in life had been never to be like Benita. So she'd lived her life accordingly, always putting Jilly first, never wanting her to experience shame. Unlike her relationship with Benita, Jilly had faith in Camila. She would never believe anything bad about her mother, and she was always the first to tell people how nice Camila was. She didn't even falter in telling that to the Danielses. They had a strong bond and nothing was ever going to break that. Camila wished she'd had that same kind of faith in Benita.

She sighed, leaning back against the headboard and seeing her life so clearly now. Determined not to be like her mother, she'd become quiet and shy, not interacting with the other kids. She'd repressed her emotions, but that night when Patrick had put the drug in her drink, she'd become like her mother—wanting Tripp and tempting Patrick. She'd blamed herself for everything because—she took a deep breath— she'd believed the rumors about herself. Because she was Benita's daughter.

Oh, God! She sucked in a breath.

She wasn't to blame for anything. She didn't deserve what had happened and Patrick had hurt her more than she could ever admit. Until now.

It had hurt when Tripp had said he'd believed the rumors about Camila, but she'd given him reason to believe. She could see that now with more insight. She'd done the same thing—believed the spiteful gossip about her mother. Benita wasn't the tramp Camila had envisioned in her head. And Camila wasn't either. Maybe there was hope for Camila. Maybe there was hope that she could love Tripp.

She sat there for a long time realizing she had to shed the shackles of the past to accept a future with Tripp. And she wanted that. She wanted to start living and experiencing life the way that she should—as a woman with a man she loved.

The night of Jilly's party, she'd told Tripp that Patrick would always be between them. It wasn't Patrick. It was her fear of being like her mother. She would let go of that fear now.

She ran her fingers through her long hair, feeling out of breath from all the inner revelations. The window, her heart, was wide open now. One thing niggled at her. How did Tripp really feel about her?

It took a minute, then she picked up the phone and dialed the ranch. Tripp answered on the second ring. For a moment she couldn't speak as she struggled for the right words.

"Hello, is anyone there?"

"It's me, Camila," she managed to say.

"Are you okay?" A concerned, loving note was in his voice that she was beginning to recognize.

"Yes. I'm much better."

"I want you to know I would never hurt Jilly or betray your trust in me. I had no idea what my dad was up to."

"I know." And she did. She knew Tripp would always be there for them. "Could we talk, please?"

"Sure. I'll be right over."

"No. Not tonight. It's late and it's been a long evening. There's a meeting about renovating the gym tomorrow. Could we meet after that?"

"Yes. That's fine. You don't have to worry about the custody thing." He seemed to think that's what she wanted to talk about.

"I'm not. I want to talk about you and me."

"Oh."

"I'll see you tomorrow."

"Sure."

TRIPP HUNG UP AND STARED at the phone. What did that mean? No matter what Camila wanted to talk about, he would be there tomorrow, and he would fight to be a part of her life.

Chapter Nineteen

The next morning, Camila felt as if she'd just been released from prison and she kept smiling. Jilly was happy too—there would be no custody hearing.

Jilly made a face sitting at the table eating oatmeal. "I was like a total baby yesterday. I just wanted my mama." She took a swallow of milk. "I'm a total knucklehead, too. I'm twelve years old and I can speak for myself. I'm telling Mr. Daniels that I'm staying with you."

Camila sat down, knowing they had to talk about something else. "Jilly, why is Patrick's photo in your drawer?"

"I thought of putting it on my nightstand, but I didn't want to make you sad. It's in my drawer, in my secret place. When I want to see what he looks like, I just open it and there he is, but…"

"But what?"

"When I look at him, I feel, like, funny. I'm supposed to have feelings for him, but I don't. He's just someone I don't know. Is that really bad?"

"No, baby." Camila hugged her. "Benita gave me something I want to show you." She grabbed her purse and fished out Travis's picture. "This is my father and I feel a little strange when I look at him, too. So I think I'll put this in a secret place and look at it when I feel a need to."

"Like, totally cool, Mama."

"We're cool." Camila smiled.

Jilly gave the victory sign. "The Walker girls are cool."

"You bet."

The house was cheerful again, with Jilly there, laughing and talking. In the afternoon, Benita taught Jilly some new dances that Camila had never heard of. But she laughed and laughed. She kept looking at the clock though, eager to see Tripp. Her life had been full raising Jilly, but now the woman in her needed fulfillment, needed to be touched by a man— one special man—Tripp.

Later, the girls' basketball team had a special practice and Camila left early to watch some of it, hoping Tripp might come early, too.

Sitting in the stands, she watched her daughter sprint around the court. She was very competitive and Camila suspected that was partially Tripp's influence. Jilly was a combination of so many people, which was good. It made her who she was—a wonderful young girl.

Camila was lost in the action, the squeak of sneakers against the hardwood floor, the shouts of Coach Smythe, the grumble of the girls. When Lurleen plopped down beside Camila, she was taken aback and felt her space invaded. Lurleen never sought her out and she was wondering why she'd chosen to sit by her today.

Jilly made a basket and waved to Camila. She waved back.

"Do you know how much I hate you?" Lurleen asked, her words slurred slightly.

"On a scale of one to ten?" Camila asked with a lifted eyebrow.

Lurleen did not pick up on the humor. "All I hear from my kids is Jilly's mama does this and Jilly's mama does that and I'm getting sick of it. I'm sick of you, too. Ever since high school I've wanted to scratch your eyes out."

Camila drew back. "Why? You were the popular one, cheerleader, homecoming queen."

"You know why, don't you?" she whispered, and Camila could smell the liquor on her breath. Lurleen was drunk; Camila was glad when the girls finished practice and headed for the lockers. Coach Smythe went to his office and that left the two of them sitting on a bench with years of resentment between them.

"I was easy, not like you." Lurleen searched for something in her purse. "You shouldn't have been so cold, so stuck up, then maybe the boys wouldn't have been so set on having you. Every time Wallis looks at you, he drools and I hate you for that." She pulled a small flask out and twisted off the top.

"You shouldn't be drinking here around the kids," Camila told her, trying to digest what Lurleen was saying, but she wasn't making much sense.

"Don't tell me what to do," Lurleen spat, taking a swig from the flask. "Wallis is having an affair."

Camila frowned, thinking she should just get up and walk away. But she'd been doing that for years. She wasn't walking away anymore. This conversation was way overdue.

"If you're thinking it's me…"

Lurleen laughed, stopping her. "Oh, Camila, the pure maiden of Bramble, I know it's not you."

Lurleen had never called her that before and she was startled, to say the least. "Then why do you say such nasty things about me?"

"Because I can. Because it makes me feel good to see that look on your face."

Camila sat in complete stupefaction. Was that why people said hurtful, untrue things? She'd defended herself with silence and that silence had condemned her and fueled the rumors that much more. New strength surged through her.

She took the flask out of Lurleen's hands.

"Hey. What do you think you're doing?"

"Taking the liquor away from you." She paused purposely. "Because I can. Want to try and take it back from me?"

"You can have the damn thing. I got more in the car."

"You're drinking and driving with your kids in the car?"

"That's none of your damn business, Miss Goody Two-shoes, Miss Perfect. All the boys wanted you. That's why I hate you. You could have had any boy in high school, even my husband, but you didn't want any of them—not even poor Patrick."

Camila was aware that Tripp had walked in, along with several other people. If she got up and walked away, Lurleen would stop her insane tirade. But walking away was not a way out this time. This had to be settled.

"They got even, though, didn't they, Camila? Putting the drug in your drink turned you into the woman they wanted. Wallis and Vance planned to join Patrick. Big brother, Tripp, went upstairs and they chickened out. They knew he'd kick their ass if he found out what they were planning."

Anger shot through Camila followed by a terrifying fear. Camila could feel the train coming again and this time would be the last, this time she wouldn't survive. That was the old reaction and it was fresh within her. But not anymore. This time she was driving the train and if she was going to feel this pain, so were a lot of other people.

Before a scathing word left her mouth, Wallis walked up to Lurleen. "You're drunk. Go home."

"Here's my husband, a pillar of the community in his own mind."

"Shut up," Wallis hissed and jerked Lurleen to her feet, but she pulled away.

"What? You don't want Camila to hear your plans for her that night? You couldn't stand it that Patrick had her and not you. I was there and that's the way you treated me. You bastard. I know you're sleeping with the new waitress at the Hitchin' Post."

"Shut her up," Vance said to Wallis.

More people walked into the gym and Tripp moved to stand beside Camila. That made her feel better, stronger.

"Cousin Vance." Lurleen laughed. "Wallis's running partner, his partner in crime."

Wallis grabbed Lurleen's arm and tried to pull her away, but again she jerked back. "Do you think you're the only one who sleeps around? Do you think no one wants me? Well, you're wrong. Patrick wanted me."

The gym became so quiet that the tick of the clock on the wall could be heard.

Camila was the first to speak. "What are you talking about?"

"The next day Patrick was so hurt over what he'd done to you that he came looking for Wallis, wanting revenge. He found me instead and we figured the perfect way to get revenge. We bought a couple of six-packs and went to Lover's Point. We had sex with the radio blaring, then we went riding and Patrick let me drive. I wanted to see how fast the Corvette could go and Patrick kept saying, 'Faster, faster.' We were laughing, happy, then a deer came out of nowhere and I swerved to miss it. I…I lost control and…and I just remember an awful paralyzing fear and Patrick's screams. I still hear his screams."

The tick of the clock became louder.

"You bitch," Wallis said under his breath.

"How did you get out of the car?" Tripp asked in a faraway voice.

"When I came to, I saw Patrick was dead and I tried to get out, but my door wouldn't open. The glass on the window had been shattered and I crawled through it. I was trembling and close to hysteria, but I managed to climb over the fence and I sat in the woods for a long time not knowing what to do. I just started walking through the woods toward town. I came to Mill's Creek and washed the blood from my face and my arms. No one saw me as I came through the back way of our house. I went into my room and locked the door. I didn't want anyone to know I'd been driving." Tears ran down her face. "I killed Patrick and I can't live with it anymore." Loud sobs racked her body.

Wallis turned away.

Camila did the only thing she could. She put her arms around Lurleen and hugged her. "I'm sorry you had to live with that all these years."

Lurleen drew back, a shocked look on her face. "Don't be nice to me. Please don't be nice to me."

"That's all I can be," Camila told her. "I'm tired of all the backstabbing nasty rumors fueled by hurt egos." She looked at Wallis. "I'm sorry you felt you had to hurt me and Patrick because we were different."

Wallis's face turned a shallow white. "Let's just forget Lurleen got drunk and blabbed all this."

"That would be easy, wouldn't it?" Tripp said. "For you and for all the terrible things the Boggses have done—to Camila, to Patrick. You even attacked an old man who's not able to defend himself."

"I had nothing to do with that," Wallis denied. "Your dad tried to hit Otis and he shoved him and Grif fell down. We took him to the clinic."

"That was very big of you." Tripp clenched and unclenched his hands, trying to control his temper.

"I think we'll continue this conversation at the station," Horace said.

"Horace, Horace." A boy ran into the gym. "The Boggs boys are throwing rocks at Unie's house."

"Goddammit, what's the matter with this town?" Horace headed for the door.

Camila ran out of the gym, needing to get to Unie before anyone could hurt her. She hurried to Betty Sue standing at the door. "Please take Jilly to my mother and tell her to keep Jilly there until I come."

"Sure." Betty Sue seemed to be in shock and Camila knew she'd heard part of what had been said. "Are you okay?"

Camila gave her a quick hug. "I'll talk to you later. Please take care of my daughter."

She ran for her car, but someone caught her arm and she swung around. "I'll take you," Tripp said. "My truck is right here."

She jumped into his truck and they sped toward Unie's. "You okay?" Tripp asked the same question as Betty Sue.

"I don't know," she answered honestly. "I'm feeling so many things and I…" Her voice faded away as they spotted Cameron and Dillon running to their bikes at the curb.

Tripp screeched to a stop, reached for his rope in the back seat and got out. Within seconds, the rope twirled above his head and sailed through the air, landing in a perfect circle around Cameron and Dillon. Tripp jerked the lasso and it tightened, holding the boys together. They struggled, trying to get away, but Tripp kept tightening the rope.

"Let us go, you bastard," Cameron shouted.

Dillon was speechless.

Camila stood looking at Unie's house. Every window was broken out and she wanted to cry. Unie couldn't afford this. The roof was already leaking.

Horace drove up, followed by a stream of cars.

"What do you boys think you're doing?" Horace asked.

"Make him let us go," Cameron cried, his face red.

"You're not going anywhere until I find out how much damage you've done."

"My grandad'll fire you." Dillon spoke for the first time.

"That may be true, son, but at this moment I'm still chief and you stay tied."

Wallis and Vance came running up. "Let the boys go," Wallis yelled.

"My advice to you and Vance is to shut your mouth and get

your checkbooks out," Horace told them. "No one's leaving here until I found out what kind of damage has been done."

Bert came storming through the crowd. "Horace, you better let my grandson go this instant."

"If you don't stay out of this, I'll arrest you."

"Like hell. This eyesore should have been burned to the ground long ago. If people like Camila Walker hadn't kept helping the old bat, she'd be in an institution somewhere."

Camila barely heard what was being said as she hurried to Unie's door. She knocked. "Unie, it's Camila. Let me in. Please let me in."

Tripp heard the plea in her voice and he handed the rope to Slim. "Don't let up."

"Don't worry. These little demons aren't going anywhere."

Camila kept calling to her, but Unie wouldn't respond. "Unie's scared," she said. "I can't get her to come to the door."

"Maybe she's not home," Tripp suggested.

"She's always home by now."

Tripp pushed through the shrubs to get to a window. Shattered glass was everywhere, but he managed to pull back a dirty curtain and he could see her sitting by the fire. He turned to Camila.

"She's in there."

Camila knocked and kept shouting, but still got no response. "Something's wrong."

Tripp looked at Horace. "What do you think?"

"It's up to Camila."

"I'll kick the door in if you want me to," Tripp said.

Camila pulled her jacket around herself. She didn't want to scare Unie further, but she couldn't leave her here either with all the windows broken out. It was supposed to be freezing by morning.

"Okay, but let me go in first."

"Deal." With one kick, the door split into several pieces. Tripp and Horace pulled them away.

"It's okay, Unie. It's Camila. Don't be afraid." She kept talking while they worked, hoping Unie realized they weren't going to hurt her.

With the last board removed, Camila rushed in and stopped. The blood drained from her face and her heart stilled. "Oh my God! Oh my God!" Unie sat by the fire Camila had lit earlier, her head tilted to one side. She was dead. Camila didn't need to touch her to know that.

As she reached down to turn off the fire, she saw Lu Lu under the sofa. She squatted and picked her up, holding the cat in her arms. Tears filled her eyes at the cruelty of kids, the cruelty of teenagers and the cruelty of mankind in general.

"Camila." She heard Tripp's voice and she turned to him. He enfolded her in his arms. "I'm so sorry."

She took strength from his touch then faced the people edging into the room.

Wallis and Vance stood staring at the sight. Lurleen pushed into the room and stopped short. Slim and Joe Bob pulled Cameron and Dillon inside. Something in Camila gave way. Years of being quiet, years of trying to fit in, years of trying to prove her worth came down to this moment.

"Wallis, you said Unie should be put in an institution. She was a nuisance to the town. Your son learned how to hate and get even from you and he learned it well. Just as your son did, Vance." She spared Vance a glance. "So why the sad faces? Why isn't everyone happy? Unie is gone. Her house can be torn down and you can rejoice because a human life means nothing to you."

Wallis shuffled his feet. "I didn't want this."

"Bert." She turned to him. "You won't need to have Unie committed now. Why aren't you celebrating?"

Bert looked away.

Horace stepped forward. "An ambulance is on the way. I'll take these two ruffians to the station."

"Daddy," Cameron wailed. "You said she was a nuisance. You said—"

"You're not putting my son in jail, Horace. We don't know what happened here."

Melvin and Thelma Boggs hurried in. "Oh, God," Melvin said under his breath.

"Ma, do something," Bert pleaded.

Thelma looked at her great-grandsons. "Did you boys do all this damage?"

Cameron and Dillon hung their heads.

"What did you think you were doing?" Thelma asked.

Cameron raised his head. "Daddy, Grandpa and Uncle Bert said she was a nuisance and should be put away. We were just playing, trying to scare her and—"

Thelma held up a hand. "Not one more word. Take them away, Horace."

"Ma," Bert begged.

Thelma turned on her son and grandsons. "I'm ashamed of all of you." On those words, she walked out.

For once the Boggses had nothing to say. Horace took the boys by the arms and led them to his car.

"Camila," Lurleen appealed. "Do something. Horace will listen to you. Please do something."

Camila was numb. She brushed past Lurleen and stopped by Slim. "Please stay here until they pick up Unie's body and take care of Lu Lu for me." She handed him the cat.

"You can count on it."

Camila dashed outside, hardly aware of the stares. She started to run and she kept running, past the residential section to the railroad tracks, to nowhere. She was running to nowhere, to oblivion, to block out everything she'd learned today.

Her breath locked in her throat and tears stung her face as she sank onto the railroad tracks, staring down that long expanse of rail. This wasn't fictional. This was real.

Two strong arms lifted her to her feet. "Camila, what are you doing?" Tripp asked.

She wiped away tears with the back of her hand. "For years I've had this fictional train in my dreams. I can hear the whistle, but I can't move. I can't do anything—only wait for the pain. Then I wake up and realize it was just a dream. Tonight the train was real and I...I...how could they do that? How could...?"

"Shh." Tripp took her in his arms and held her for a second. "Come on, my truck is over here."

She walked with him to the truck and got in. "I have to go to Jilly."

"You need some time."

"Yeah." She tucked her hair behind her ears. "I'm a mess, but I need to call Jilly." She shrugged. "I have no idea where my purse or cell phone is."

"Millie said to tell you she had them. She found them in the gym after the scene with Lurleen." He handed her his phone. "You can use mine."

Staring at the phone, she took a deep breath and poked out Benita's number. She told Jilly she was going to be late and for her to stay with Benita, then she spoke with her mother telling her what had happened and asked her not to tell Jilly. Camila had to do that herself, when she was stronger.

She closed the phone. "I want to go somewhere I can be alone," she said, looking at him, "with you."

He nodded and started the truck. "I know the perfect spot."

She leaned back against the headrest and closed her eyes, trying not to think, trying not to hear Lurleen's words and trying not to see Unie's body.

It was dark now and she realized they were at Lady Luck. Tripp drove to the barn and corrals. He got out and she followed, watching in a numblike state as he whistled and a horse came galloping to the fence.

He saddled the horse and led the mare to her. "This is Cayenne, but she responds to Cay. How about a ride to a secluded area?"

"Sure," she answered, willing to go anywhere as long as he was with her.

It was a chilly moonlit night and she could see clearly as he swung into the saddle. Cay moved slightly and she heard the creak of leather. He held out his hand to her. "Put your left foot in the stirrup and swing up behind me."

She placed her hand in his and did as he instructed. Within seconds, she was on the back of the horse holding tight to Tripp.

"Okay?" he asked.

"Yes," she replied, resting her face against his back. Just touching him made her feel so much better.

With a nudge from Tripp, Cay set off at a trot through the woods. The easy rhythm of the horse lulled her into a better frame of mind. Cay slowed and Camila looked up to see trees all around them and a small pond glistened in the moonlight.

"Where are we?" she asked.

"This is the backwoods of Lady Luck. I mowed the weeds the other day and remembered all the times I came here to fish with Dad as a kid. I loved it and it's very peaceful." He helped her slide to the ground. "I brought a horse blanket." He removed it from the front of the saddle and she hadn't even realized it was there. "We can sit by the water and talk or just do nothing."

She walked to the edge of the water. The wind blew her hair across her face and she didn't bother to brush it away. Tripp spread the blanket out and she sank down. The night was all around them, deep blackness, just as it was around her heart. But the night couldn't hurt her—not like the people of Bramble had.

She started to cry—for Unie. She didn't care what they had done to her, but it broke her heart that Unie had to die frightened and alone. Tripp reached for her and she clung to him.

"I'm so sorry, Camila." He stroked her hair. "So sorry you've been hurt again."

"How could they do that? Be so careless with another person's life?"

"Like you said, they learned from Wallis and Vance. Kids imitate their parents. That's why Jilly is so wonderful. She takes after you."

"This will be hard on her."

"She has you and me to help her through it."

He'd said *you and me* like they were a couple, and to Camila that sounded good. It sounded right. For years she'd tried to be the perfect mom, the perfect citizen, the perfect everything, just hoping people would see her for the good person she was. But not anymore. She was going to be herself like she'd told Benita and she wasn't suppressing her emotions. She rested her head on Tripp's shoulder.

Tripp watched her, hoping to ease the turmoil in her. It worried him that she hadn't mentioned what Lurleen had said. He'd wanted answers, but the answers were nothing like he'd expected. He was trying very hard to keep his anger under control—for Camila.

"Do you want to talk about what Lurleen said?"

"You were right," she replied. "Someone else was driving the car."

"That's about the only instinct that was right. Everything else I could never have imagined. It makes me so angry."

"Me, too," she admitted. "But when we give in to the anger and hatred that's when bad things happen."

"Yeah, but it's still hard to control."

She reached for his hand. "For years I blamed myself for Patrick's death because I couldn't love him the way he wanted. But I'm not to blame. I realize that now. If he could have sex with Lurleen, that means he didn't love me all that much."

"I think Patrick wanted the girl that no one else could have."

She linked her fingers with his. "That's why he wanted to turn our friendship into something more."

"Yeah."

"You have no reason to feel guilty either," she told him.

"No. There were a lot of people blaming themselves for Patrick's death, but Patrick is the only one to blame."

The wind picked up and blew through the trees, rustling, whistling, and the guilt floated away without any hesitation. And they both let it go.

She turned to look at him in the darkness. "I'm so glad you were there that night. I don't even want to think about what…"

"Shh." He gently rocked her. "I will always be there for you—always."

"Kiss me," she begged.

His lips softly touched hers.

"The day of Jilly's party, you asked how that made me feel and I said it reminded me of that night. But it didn't. I lied because I was too afraid of all the emotions inside me, afraid to express them. Later I realized the fear came partly from my mother, but also from the fact that you believed the rumors."

"Cam—"

She placed a finger over his lips, stopping him. "In a way, I believed them myself because I felt I'd driven Patrick to do what he did, especially by coming on to his brother. Maybe that's what I had to prove to myself, to this town—that I was a good person."

He kissed her hand. "You are a good person, inside and out. And I will never believe anything else for the rest of my life."

"Kiss me," she begged again and he gladly obliged, kissing her over and over. Between kisses, she murmured, "That makes me feel young, happy and very much a woman. I never realized how much I needed to feel that way—not until you touched me."

"Camila," he breathed against her mouth and deepened the kiss. Neither held anything back. Their lips and hands roamed freely, exploring, discovering each other. He bore her down on the blanket and the kiss went on. Finally he rested his head in the hollow of her neck.

She gulped in air. "Benita says what I feel for you is chemistry between a man and woman. But it's so much more."

He raised his head, his hair falling across his forehead. "What is it?"

She brushed his hair back. "I've loved you since I was sixteen years old when Patrick introduced me to his rodeo brother."

"Oh, Camila. I…"

"I remember it vividly." She caressed his face. "Patrick took me out to Lady Luck and you were roping calves and Morris was timing you. You were the most handsome man I'd ever met and I felt weak in the knees and a little faint. I'd never experienced an attraction like that before."

"I remember it, too." He rained kisses in the V of her blouse and on her neck. "I was instantly attracted to a teenage girlfriend of my brother's. I thought you were the most beautiful sight I'd ever seen with your dark eyes and hair and I was jealous of Patrick."

"Through all the years, the pain, that feeling has never changed for me," she told him, finally unafraid to open up and expose her emotions. She trusted Tripp.

"Me, neither," he admitted. "I love you. I'm going to love you forever."

"I love you, too," she breathed a moment before his lips took hers. The night and the chemistry took over and Camila lost herself in his touch, his kiss and it was everything she'd ever dreamed it would be.

Tripp had dreamed of this more times than he cared to remember and this was nothing like his dreams. This was better. She was real and he felt himself exploding with incredible pleasure at her gentle caress, her scent, her softness. But there was a line he knew he wouldn't cross.

"Camila," he groaned, his voice hoarse. "We have to stop. I don't have any protection and I don't want our first time to be like this."

She ran her hands through his hair, holding on to him, not wanting to stop. But she knew he was right. There would be a tomorrow for them.

"You've been through so much tonight and…"

"Just hold me," she said, her voice shaky. "Just hold me."

He rolled to her side and pulled her against him. They lay silently staring at the stars, their heart rate subsiding.

Her hand rested on his chest and she could feel the steady beat of his heart. They lay holding onto each other.

"When things settle down, we'll plan a wedding and you'll wear a white dress…."

"I have a twelve-year-old daughter."

"Doesn't matter." He trailed his fingers through her long tresses. "I want everything perfect for you—the way it should it be."

"As long as I have you, everything will be perfect."

"Always. I promise from this day forward."

Soon they got to their feet.

"I better go to Jilly. I can tell her now."

He gave her a long kiss, then tore his mouth away. They mounted Cay and rode back to Lady Luck.

The night had been horrendous, but through the pain, she and Tripp had admitted their love. They'd also found a way to deal with the past. Now they had to handle the present and the people of Bramble. Camila felt no fear. She and Tripp would do it together.

Chapter Twenty

The days that followed weren't easy. Jilly was very upset about Unie's death and her main concern now was taking care of Lu Lu. Camila and Tripp were there to help her adjust. For the first time in her life, Camila had someone to help her with Jilly—someone to lean on. She 'd never realized how good that felt.

The medical examiner's report said Unie had died from a heart attack, probably between eight and nine o'clock that morning—that's why the fire was still burning. So she was dead when the boys had started throwing the rocks. That was such a relief for a lot of people, especially Camila. It gave her peace that Unie had not died frightened.

Camila went to Temple to make arrangements for Unie's funeral. She posted her death in the paper hoping a relative would come forward. Intending to pay for the funeral herself, she was surprised when people started coming in with donations. Almost every person in Bramble stopped by, including Thelma Boggs. She gave Camila a blank check, telling her to fill in the amount. Her first instinct was to tear it up, but she could see that Unie's death had had a profound effect on everyone in this small town. A woman they had shunned, they now embraced.

Camila, Benita, Millie, Tripp, Slim and Joe Bob went

through Unie's things. The men cleared out the old worn furniture and carried it to the dump. Camila saved a few pieces that she felt were salvageable in case a relative showed up. The ladies sorted through Unie's personal belongings. Millie and Benita were being civil to each other and that was wonderful to see.

In a drawer, they found a faded birth certificate for a baby boy who'd lived two days. Unie had had a son. With the certificate were love letters to a married man in Waco. The baby had been born in Waco, where Unie must have lived when she'd been young and pregnant. When the man wouldn't marry her, she'd come home to live with her parents.

The letters and birth certificate explained a lot about Unie. The loss of her child and her lover had done something to her and she'd become a recluse. Unie may have been a loner but Camila would make sure she had a proper burial.

A man wearing a suit, with a briefcase in his hand, entered the house. They all stared at the stranger.

"The lady at the diner said I could find Camila Walker here," he said.

Camila pushed to her feet from the floor, boxes strewn around her. "I'm Camila."

The man shook her hand. "I'm Joel Benson from the Nation Bank in Temple."

"Oh." Camila had no idea who the man was.

Tripp and Benita walked over to see what the man wanted.

"I took care of Eunice Gimble's account."

Camila frowned. "What account?"

"Her savings account—the money she was saving for her son."

Camila was dumbfounded. "She talked about saving money for her son, but I had no idea she'd set up a savings account."

"She had an account for many years." Mr. Benson laid his briefcase on the coffee table. "She wanted the money to go to her son, but I learned that he had died as a baby. The address she gave is her own." He pulled out some papers. "Miss Gimble added a stipulation that if her son was no longer living, the money was to go to Camila Walker."

"What?"

"Isn't that sweet," Millie said. "After all the times you helped Unie, she remembered."

"I don't want anything." Camila was in shock. She didn't want money for helping Unie.

"Come on, chick, you can take us all out to dinner," Benita said.

Mr. Benson handed Camila an envelope. "You can buy a lot of dinners with that."

She stared at the envelope. Tripp put his arm around her. "Take it. It's what Unie wanted."

Her hand trembled as she withdrew a check. She stared at the amount then glanced at Mr. Benson. "There must be some mistake."

"No, ma'am." Mr. Benson shook his head. "Four hundred sixty-seven thousand dollars and some odd cents."

Everyone gasped and looked over Camila's shoulder.

"Where…where did Unie get this kind of money?" was all she could say.

Mr. Benson shrugged. "She's had an account at the bank for sixty years and her small social security check was on direct deposit and the interest added up."

"But she had nothing," Camila said. "She lived in poverty. She needed this money to live on. For God's sake why didn't you do something?" Anger bolted through her. Unie had been eating cat food and the money had been just sitting there.

"I barely knew the woman," Mr. Benson said in his defense. "Mr. Cravey handled her account then he died about ten years ago. That's when I got the account. I only met with her a couple of times, and now I'm just carrying out her instructions. She said Camila would know what to do with the money." He closed his briefcase and walked out.

Tears rolled down Camila's cheeks and Tripp took her in his arms. "Don't," he said, stroking her hair.

"This isn't right," she sniffled into his shoulder. "She needed so many things and…" She stopped and wiped at her eyes, remembering what Mr. Benson had said. "Ten years ago I was twenty and struggling to make a living for Jilly and me."

"But I bet you had time for Unie."

Camila thought back to when she started helping Unie. When she'd been a teenager, she'd helped Unie unload the cans from her truck. When her grandmother had had leftovers, Camila would sneak out of the house and take them to Unie. "Yes. I always tried to help her because she had nothing and people were mean to her."

"Unie appreciated all the love you gave her and this is her way of showing it."

Camila gave him a quick kiss, an idea forming in her head. "Yes. Unie said I'd know what to do with the money and I do."

Tripp glanced at Benita and Benita glanced at Millie. They didn't know what she had in mind, but they knew it would be selfless.

THE NEWS OF THE MONEY soon spread through Bramble and Camila tried to return the donations for Unie's funeral, but no one would take their money back—not even Thelma Boggs. Camila postponed the funeral as long as she could, hoping a relative would come forward to claim Unie's body. But Unie belonged to the town of Bramble.

The day of the funeral, the whole town shut down and the schools closed. The hearing for the boys had been earlier in the week and they were put on probation for a year. The judge also ordered the boys to do community service. One of the jobs they had to do was pick up all the aluminum cans around

Bramble once a week. Wallis and Vance had to pay for the receptacle to store the cans then see that they were sold and the proceeds donated to the school gymnasium fund. Camila thought that was a great idea.

Unie's body had been brought from Temple and Camila and Tripp stood at the back of the church greeting people along with Jilly, Benita, the Danielses and Morris. The church was packed with the citizens of Bramble.

Camila hugged Betty Sue and Jolene, and they took their seats with their kids.

"Are we gonna stand here all day?" Grif grumbled.

"Be nice, Grandpa," Jilly warned.

"You're getting as bossy as your grandma."

Jilly grinned. "That's, like, real good, huh, Grandma?"

Leona hugged Jilly. "Yes. It takes more than one strong woman to keep Griffin in line."

"Hmmph," Grif replied. "I'm finding me a seat. Come on, Jilly, you can sit with me."

"Grif, Jilly…" Leona spluttered to a stop. "Let's go, Jilly. He's as stubborn as an ox."

"Guess I better go, too," Morris said. "Might need a referee and I left my whistle at home."

Camila leaned against Tripp. "Jilly's very diplomatic and handles her grandparents with class."

"Hmm. Just like her mama."

They stared into each other's eyes and for a moment they were lost in the wonderful feelings they'd discovered.

"Cowboy, when are you going to marry my daughter?" Benita asked bluntly.

Tripp didn't even pause. "Just as soon as I can."

"We'll have the biggest wedding this town has ever seen and all the Walker women will dance for you."

Tripp held a hand to his chest. "Aw shucks, Benita. Don't know if my heart can take that."

"Cowboy, it will be a prelude to the honeymoon."

Benita was back to her old self, laughing and joking, and it didn't embarrass Camila. Those shackles from the past were gone, and she and her mother now understood and accepted each other for whom they were. And they still loved each other. That's what true love was all about.

Earl, his wife and his mother walked in. Earl shook Tripp's hand.

"How you doing?" Tripp asked Earl.

"Not too good," Earl answered. "It's an eye-opener to see my grandson's behavior reflecting my own."

"But something good has come out of this," Thelma said. "The town is pulling together as a whole and I have great hopes for this community and my family."

"Me, too," Camila said.

"Thank you, Camila," Thelma replied, and walked into the church.

"See you around, rodeo man." Earl followed his mother.

Melvin, Bert and their wives were behind them. "I don't know what to say to you, Camila," Bert said. "I thought I had Bramble's best interest in mind, but I was pandering to my own selfish, biased ideas. When my grandson starts to mimic my bad attitude, it's time to take a hard look at my life."

"A lot of us are doing that," Camila replied.

Bert looked at Tripp. "You had every right to hit me. Surprised someone hadn't done it before then."

Tripp nodded and Bert and the others moved on.

Change wasn't so bad, Camila thought. Mrs. Boggs was right—something good had come out of Unie's death. It had brought all the hatred and bigotry to the surface and the people of Bramble had a good look at themselves. That brought change—in attitudes and behavior—something she'd thought she would never see.

She froze as Wallis, Lurleen, Vance, Debbie, Cameron and

Dillon walked in. She'd seen them, but she hadn't spoken to them since that awful day. Wyatt had questioned Lurleen about Patrick's wreck and it was ruled an accident like it had been years ago. Everyone accepted that decision without any guilt—even the Danielses.

Wallis, Vance, Cameron and Dillon had been ordered by the judge to be pallbearers, so they had to be here. Slim and Joe Bob shared that duty.

Wallis walked up to Camila. Tripp stiffened beside her and Benita stepped closer. She would never have to face anything alone again.

"Camila, I…I'm sorry for everything that's happened." Wallis shoved his hands into his trouser pockets. "Now and… you know."

She swallowed, not able to speak.

"Me, too," Vance added.

"Thank you, Camila," Cameron and Dillon chorused without prompting from their parents.

Before she could respond, Cameron said, "Daddy ordered some barrels and we're going to paint them red and Mama's going to write Unie's Cans on them. We'll place the barrels around town and people can throw their cans into them. Maybe soon we'll have enough money to build a new gym. Jilly'll be happy about that."

"Yes, she would," Camila said, hardly able to believe the change in these people.

The group moved into the church.

"If that don't beat all," Millie said, grinning at Camila as she followed them.

"Come on, chick," Benita said. "We can't start this without you."

"Be right there." She turned to look at Tripp and he smiled.

"You're wonderful," he whispered, giving her a long kiss.

"The next time we're in this church, we're getting married and it can't be soon enough for me."

"Me, neither." They had agreed to wait to make love until they were married and now Camila was wondering if that was a wise decision. The restraint was getting to both of them, but Tripp wanted her to have a perfect wedding, everything a girl dreamed about. The only thing she dreamed about these days was him. She didn't think it would be too hard to change his mind. Later, she would do just that. She took his hand and she and the cowboy walked into the church to pay their last respects to Unie.

And the future awaited them.

In Bramble, Texas.

Epilogue

One year later

"Jilly, you're gonna get us in trouble again and I'm keeping a list, I want you to know."

"Stop whining," Jilly Daniels shouted back to her friend, Kerri.

"We're not supposed to ride our bikes on the highway," Kerri reminded her.

"This is important." Jilly rolled to a stop, her sneakers sliding on the pavement by the Bramble population sign on the outskirts of town.

"Everything is so important to you."

Jilly adjusted the kickstand and reached for the can of red spray paint in her basket. Button barked. "Shh," Jilly told her.

Kerri saw the can in Jilly's hand. "Oh, no, you're going to write on the sign, aren't you?"

"Yep."

"That's defacing public property. We'll be, like, arrested."

"They're going to change the sign anyway so I don't see a problem. This is the first thing I want my mama to see when her and Tripp bring the baby home. The one-thousandth citizen of Bramble—Walker Griffin Daniels. You can go home if you want, but I'm writing on the sign."

Kerri got off her bike. "Horace is gonna put us in hand-cuffs. I just know it—that's the first thing your mama will see—us in jail."

"Kerri…" Jilly stopped as Bert drove up beside them.

"I told you," Kerri breathed, moving closer to Jilly.

Bert rolled down his window. "What are you girls doing? You know your parents don't allow you to ride on the highway."

Jilly held the can behind her back. "I was just going to surprise my mama."

Bert glanced at their guilty faces then at the sign. "Were you going to write on the sign, Jilly?"

Jilly bit her lip, not wanting to lie, but not wanting to get into trouble either.

"You know they're putting up a new sign tomorrow. It's all part of the big celebration."

"Oh." Jilly pondered this. "So is it okay if I write on this one so my mama and Tripp can see it?"

"Yeah. Go ahead. I just stopped to tell you that they're erecting the marker for the new gym, just like Camila wanted—the Eunice Gimble Gymnasium in memory of Unie. Tripp wanted it dedicated to Camila for donating Unie's money for the project. I hope Camila will be pleased."

"She will."

"Good." Bert nodded. "You kids did a wonderful job raising money, too. Now we have a new gym instead of a renovated one."

"Cameron and Dillon raised a lot of it."

Bert nodded. "I'm very proud of them, but you're the one who showed them the way. I'm proud of you, too."

"Thank you, Mr. Boggs."

"Everything is ready for the celebration. Thought you might want to tell Camila about the marker, but don't mention the dedication. Tripp wants to surprise her."

"That's totally cool. Thank you, Mr. Boggs."

"Earl, Vance and Wallis have a crew hanging the welcome-home banners across Main Street for the celebration."

"Wow."

"Stay on the shoulder when you pedal back," Bert called, before he took off toward Bramble.

"Was that Uncle Bert?" Kerri asked, frowning.

"Yep. Unless he has a clone."

Kerri giggled, putting a hand over her mouth. "Bramble's a nice place to live now—all because of your mama."

"My mama's great." They did a high five, bumped their butts together and did a happy dance.

Morris drove up in the black Cadillac and got out. "I've been looking all over town for you, young lady. Benita said you went bike riding with Kerri, but you're not supposed to be out on the highway."

"I know, Morris, but I have to change the sign so Mama and Tripp will see it when they come home from the hospital. Mr. Boggs said it was okay in case you're going to tell me I can't."

"Well, come on, let's get it done so I can get you to Leona and Grif. They're at the community center finalizing plans for tomorrow and they're not too pleased you spent the night with Benita."

"They're not good at sharing, but I'm working on them." Jilly had wanted a part of her father and she now had that, but deep down she thought of Tripp as her father. She couldn't explain it. She just did and when he'd adopted her, it had made it real. She now had a father.

Jilly stretched to reach the sign, but she wasn't tall enough. She glanced at Morris.

"Lordy, lordy, girl, you gonna drive me to drinking."

Jilly giggled and Morris held her high so she could reach the sign. She sprayed over the old number then wrote *1000* above it. She printed *Walker Griffin Daniels* in bold letters at the top, and Morris lowered her to the ground.

"What do you think?" she asked, staring at her handiwork.

"Totally cool, like, really good," Kerri replied.

"Sometimes I don't understand a word you girls say." Morris shook his head. "I'll tell you what it's like. That's about as good as it gets. Gooder than dewberry wine. Gooder than snuff. Gooder than springwater in the hill country on a hot summer day after working cattle in the heat and—"

"We get the picture," Jilly interrupted, giggling.

"Then get your cabooses in the car," Morris said without skipping a beat. "I'll put your bikes in the trunk. Your grandparents are waiting for you then we're going home to Lady Luck to await Master Walker's arrival."

"I love living at Lady Luck and you're a cotton-pickin' angel, Morris." Jilly hugged him.

"Yeah, yeah, yeah."

As they drove away, Jilly had a secret smile. Mama and Tripp were going to love it. There wasn't a doubt in her mind.

Mama was the greatest, and Tripp was, too.

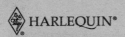

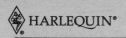

A good start to a new day…or a new life!

National bestselling author

ROZ *Denny* FOX

Coffee in the Morning

A heartwarming volume of two classic stories
with the miniseries characters you love! A
wagon train journey along the Santa Fe Trail
is a catalyst for romance as Emily Benton and
Sherry Campbell each find love.

On sale March.

The story continues in April 2006 with
Roz Denny Fox's brand-new story,
Hot Chocolate on a Cold Day.

SPECIAL EDITION™

Stronger Than Ever

THE IRRESISTIBLE BRAVO MEN ARE BACK
IN *USA TODAY* BESTSELLING AUTHOR

CHRISTINE RIMMER's

THE BRAVO
FAMILY WAY

March 2006

The last thing Cleo Bliss needed was
a brash CEO in her life. So when casino
owner Fletcher Bravo made her a business
proposition, Cleo knew it spelled trouble—
until seeing Fletcher's soft spot for his
adorable daughter melted Cleo's heart.

If you enjoyed what you just read,
then we've got an offer you can't resist!

Take 2 bestselling
love stories FREE!
Plus get a FREE surprise gift!

THE FORTUNES OF TEXAS: Reunion

**Coming in March...
a brand-new Fortunes story
by *USA TODAY* bestselling author**

Marie Ferrarella...

MILITARY MAN

A dangerous predator escapes from prison
near Red Rock, Texas—and Collin Jamison,
CIA Special Operations, is the only person who
can get inside the murderer's mind. Med student
Lucy Gatling thinks she has a lead. The police
aren't biting, but Collin is—even if it is only
to get closer to Lucy!

The Fortunes of Texas: Reunion
The price of privilege. The power of family.

Silhouette®
Where love comes alive™

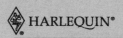
HARLEQUIN®

American ROMANCE®

Fatherhood

Fatherhood: what really defines a man.

It's the one thing all women admire in a man—a
willingness to be responsible for a child and to care
for that child with tenderness and love.

SUGARTOWN
by
Leandra Logan
March 2006

When Tina Mills learns that her biological mother
isn't the woman who raised her but someone her late
father had an affair with, she heads to her birthplace
of Sugartown, Connecticut, in search of some answers.
But after meeting police chief Colby Evans and his
young son, Tina realizes she might find more than her
mother in Sugartown. She might find her future....

Available wherever Harlequin books are sold.

www.eHarlequin.com HARLLMAR